# Brookstone

*Discoveries of the Present*

*Book 2*

Phillip Quinn

# Contents

# Dedication

To my family— and especially to my children, for your unwavering love, constant support, and boundless encouragement.

You've reminded me to believe in myself, to chase my dreams without hesitation, and to never stop creating. This book is as much yours as it is mine.

# Acknowledgments

Writing this book has been a journey filled with passion, vulnerability, and joy—and I couldn't have done it without so many people who believed in me along the way.

To the M/M romance community: thank you. The authors who came before me, whose stories lit a fire in my imagination and gave me the courage to add my voice to this genre—you continue to inspire me every single day. Your talent and bravery have carved out space for stories like mine, and I am deeply grateful.

To the readers and fans of M/M romance, you are the heartbeat of this genre. Your love for these stories, your enthusiasm for every trope and tender moment, and your unflinching support mean the world. Whether you picked up this book for the first time or you've been with me since the beginning—thank you for taking this journey with me.

To those of you who reached out with kind words, honest feedback, and genuine encouragement—you helped shape this book in ways you'll never fully know. Your insights gave me strength during self-doubt, and your messages reminded me why I write.

And to my incredible publishing team—thank you for believing in this story and in me. From edits to cover design to launch day nerves, your professionalism and heart kept everything on track. I'm beyond lucky to have you in my corner. This book is a labor of love, and it stands on the shoulders of the community. Thank you for being part of mine.

With love,

Phillip Quinn

# About the Author

Phillip Quinn is the author of m/m romance and mystery. He and his husband live in a small town in Alabama. With a passion for storytelling and a love of intricate mysteries, Quinn combines compelling characters and spicy, heartwarming romance in his debut book series, *Brookstone*. Set in the picturesque backdrop of a fictional Alabama small town, the series invites readers into a world where love and mystery collide in unexpected and thrilling ways.

When he's not writing, Phillip is an educator, dedicated to shaping young minds, a husband, and a proud parent of three. The same small-town values of loyalty, community, and love that inspire his writing also play a central role in his everyday life. As he embarks on this exciting new chapter as an author, Phillip hopes to bring readers a blend of heartfelt romance, thrilling intrigue, and a deep sense of place, making *Brookstone* a series that readers will return to time and again.

# Prologue

Brock Curry stepped out of his bedroom into the living room of his apartment wearing a pair of sleek, black designer boxer briefs that clung tightly to his thick, muscular thighs and sturdy waist. The fabric molded like a second skin, accentuating his full, plump ass and his impressive, well-endowed physique. With a confident stride, he led the two rugged muscle bears—fresh from an evening of playful passion—toward the door. Their rich, low laughter, lingering like a soft echo of their shared delight, mingled with the intoxicating scent of sex that still hung in the air.

As they reached the threshold, the playful energy lingered in the space between them. One of the men, with eyes that sparkled in the low light, casually traced a slow, appreciative line across Brock's broad, hairy chest. The caress, deliberate and lingering, spoke volumes as he leaned in closely, his breath warm on Brock's ear as he murmured, "We should do this again sometime," his voice soft yet loaded with unspoken promises.

Brock's deep blue eyes softened into a warm, easy smile that, while genuine, betrayed the guarded reserve within. "Yeah, we'll see," he replied, a gentle deflection that acknowledged the offer without committing to more than the transient thrill of the night.

The third man leaned against Brock's other biceps and reached behind him to knead Brock's firm muscular ass cheek with one hand while circling Brock's hairy stomach with his other palm. With a shared chuckle and a glint of knowing amusement, the man stepped out into the hallway in front of the elevator and watched Brock close the door behind them, the click echoing softly in the quiet of his downtown Atlanta condo.

Inside, the silence of his home offered a moment of solitude. Leaning casually against the door, Brock savored the stillness as it wrapped itself around him like a familiar blanket. His towering frame—6'6" of solid, rippling muscle and dependable heft—dominated the intimate space. There was an undeniable, earthy quality to him, an air of the woodsman ruggedness, underscored by the reddish-brown beard that framed his round face and hinted at his 41 years of seasoned life.

He glanced across the open-concept living space just to make sure his guests hadn't left anything behind. Not that they had spent more than 5 minutes in the living room before making their way back to the master suite. He walked into the kitchen to retrieve a beer before returning to the bedroom.

Methodically, he gathered the crumpled sheets and towels scattered from the night's abandon. The linens, still imbued with the faint musk of sweat and cologne, evoked memories of that heated intimacy. Running his calloused hands over the cool Egyptian cotton sent a shiver down his spine as the residual heat of passion mingled with the fabric's softness.

With purposeful efficiency, he tossed the soiled linens into the washer, the mechanical rumbling of the drum echoing the turbulence of his unsettled thoughts. Fresh, crisp sheets were then carefully smoothed over the bed with deliberate, almost ritualistic, motions before he made his way to the bathroom.

The glass-enclosed shower welcomed him like a private sanctuary. As the hot water cascaded over his body, Brock closed his eyes and tilted his head back, allowing the relentless spray to trickle down his broad shoulders, trace the muscular curvature of his spine, and slip sensuously along the crack of his robust rear. The steam swirled around him in thick, ephemeral tendrils, wrapping his skin in a moist embrace that felt almost like ghostly caresses.

Reaching for a washcloth, he poured an exuberant amount of his favorite mahogany body wash onto the cloth and began to work it into a rich, frothy lather, the scent mingling with the steamy humidity as it enveloped his broad chest, threaded its way over the coarse hair on his pecs, and smoothed over his solid abdomen.

Every inch of his body—from his sculpted neck and broad shoulders down to the intimate contours of his pits, cock, balls, and ass—was bathed meticulously. Despite the relaxing heat easing the tension in his muscles, his mind roiled with deeper, more somber reflections.

His fingers massaged away the residual tension from his neck and shoulders, yet inevitably, his thoughts drifted back to the last time he had craved not just physical warmth but an emotional connection. The memory of Jason Waters surfaced vividly: a man with a devil-may-care grin whose wandering eyes had once promised a tangible, real relationship. Brock had met the plumber on one of his construction sites and, against his better judgment, eventually caved to repeated invitations to dinner. The physical attraction was overwhelming, and the sex was incredible.

After a couple of months, Brock was imagining growing old together in wedded bliss. Instead, their time together had descended quickly into a painful montage of repeated betrayals—a dizzying carousel of other men's lingering, envious glances and furtive, late-night texts that Brock had tried, too often, to overlook.

Jason, who had relished playing out a sordid fantasy like a live porn scene by bedding numerous lovers—both gay and "straight"—had, in their final, explosive argument, offered tearful apologies that clashed brutally with the sting of his infidelities. "You're too good for me, Brock," he had sobbed, and though Brock had recognized the bitter truth in those words, the loss cut deeply.

Moving on from Jason had been beyond difficult. But he put himself out there trying to live out the old adage that the best way to get over one man is to get under another. And he had definitely succeeded in that. He found sex easily. And for an extended time, that's all he'd allowed himself to find. No need for names. Never a second encounter. Just sex, no emotional connection. Like the two guys he'd brought home tonight. Ron and Danny. Or was it Don and Randy?

Now, as Brock's hands glided sensuously over the contours of his own body, tracing the defined curve of his powerful thighs, he felt a deeper yearning—a craving that transcended mere physical release and sought a profound connection. The soap lathered richly over his skin, cascading down to the generous swell of his ass, each movement accentuating the solitude that clung to him like an invisible shroud.

His massive hand enveloped his half-erect cock, the shaft extending proudly beyond his grip, the exposed tip glistening with promise. "I'm not gonna find him in the bear bars," he murmured his voice a deep, resonant growl that reverberated softly against the cool, tiled walls, mingling with the steamy air.

Turning off the shower, he stepped out into the cooler air, each droplet on his skin catching the light as he reached for an oversized bath sheet. Wrapping the towel around his waist, the fabric barely meeting at his hip, he stepped off the bathmat onto the luxury heated floor. Droplets clung to his chest hair, catching the light as he moved through the steam-filled bathroom to the vanity. His reflection stared back at him, eyes tired but determined. He ran his fingers through his damp hair, slicking it back from his forehead.

In the mirror, he met his own gaze—a pair of deep blue eyes reflecting a mixture of weariness and quiet determination beneath the tousled, damp hair. As he adjusted the towel around his waist, its coarse texture brushing against his hips, his hand rested thoughtfully on the roundness of his firm furry belly, lost in contemplation of an uncertain future.

After drying off, he slipped into a pair of soft pajama pants and sank onto the bed with a creaking sigh of contentment. The mattress seemed to welcome his every curve as he reached for his laptop. With deliberate clicks and careful scrolling, he pulled up a bookmarked real estate listing that had captured his attention for months: four aged warehouses in a small Alabama town, tucked away yet conveniently positioned within a few hours' drive of Birmingham, Mobile, Atlanta, and even the sun-drenched beaches of the Florida panhandle. These buildings, unused for decades, loomed like silent sentinels—vast industrial spaces rising three to four stories, each with a rugged history waiting to be transformed.

His heart quickened at the vision of possibilities: luxurious lofts framed by floor-to-ceiling windows, the raw charm of exposed brick walls and soaring ceilings, all complemented below by enchanting storefronts destined to house art galleries, cozy cafés, and unique boutiques.

Even the thought of an open space for a bustling farmers' market sparked his imagination. He envisioned the aged brick walls polished to a warm glow, the reclaimed wooden beams restored to their original splendor—

a transformative rebirth of space and spirit. The renovations would be extensive and would take eight to ten months. But the potential was undeniable. This project sparked all of his creativity.

Yet, before he could fully indulge in this reverie, Brock switched tabs to explore more about Brookstone, Alabama. The digital images revealed a picturesque Southern town, seemingly suspended in time. Grand old houses with wide, welcoming porches sat beneath the generous shade of towering magnolias and draped crepe myrtles.

Quaint mom-and-pop shops lined the streets of the downtown square, hinting at close-knit communities where every neighbor likely knew each other's name and vibrant annual festivals celebrated local delights like fried pies and heritage crafts. This was a life far removed from the relentless clamor of nightlife and fleeting physical encounters—a life seemingly slower, gentler, and profoundly different from his current existence.

There was something quietly magnetic about the notion of moving and settling in Brookstone, a place where time appeared to slow and every day unfolded with a measured grace. "Could be just the change I need," he whispered under his breath, his fingers hesitating for just a moment before typing "Brookstone, AL – homes for sale" into the search bar. When a single result emerged, he clicked on it with an eager curiosity.

The listing that appeared was nothing short of breathtaking—a beautifully restored Craftsman-style house boasting a sprawling front porch and intricately preserved woodwork that spoke of generations past. Every detail of the house exuded history interwoven with modern comforts. Gleaming hardwood floors, imbued with a rich, golden warmth, flowed into a kitchen that promised both culinary delight and cheerful gatherings with an oversized island and high-end stainless steel appliances.

Upon viewing the expansive master bathroom, Brock couldn't help but chuckle softly. The shower, spacious and lined with classic subway tile and a generous glass surround, included two rain shower heads and multiple wall spray heads with a master keypad that selected temperature and which jets pulse jets of water. The shower seemed almost comically large—an ironic twist that would have comfortably accommodated a group of closely acquainted friends.

It was as if fate had laid out the possibility of an entirely new life before his eyes, teasing him with visions of transformation and renewal. "Alright," he resolved quietly, snapping his laptop shut with a firm yet hopeful finality, "Tomorrow, I'll make an offer on the warehouses—and the Craftsman."

On the same page as the listing was an ad for al.com, the state's online news site. What drew Brock's attention at first was the picture. It was of two women and a man. One of the women was dressed in a sharp navy suit with her dark hair pulled into a tight bun. The other woman and the man were dressed in deputy sheriff's uniforms. The headline read.

**BREAKING NEWS: FBI, Local Law Enforcement Solve Chilling 70-Year Serial Murder Case in Brookstone, AL**

*By Marianne Foster | for al.com*

Brock skimmed the article, primarily to see who the people in the photo were.

*BROOKSTONE, AL — After months of intense investigation, a special task force led by FBI Special Agent Joanne Stevens, alongside Brookstone Sheriff's Deputy Investigators Amanda Marks and Jim Williamson, has cracked a serial murder case that haunted the region for over seven decades.*

Brock skimmed the article, numbed to its contents by years of living in big cities riddled with crime and all manner of hate-driven violence. He did a quick search for Brookstone. It seemed to be that this was the one and only record of any kind of crime in the small community. His sheer size and experiences from his early years had given him an advantage in taking care of himself when he had to.

He reclined on his bed, gazing up at the ceiling as his mind buzzed with the vibrant prospects of what might be—a daring venture into a new hometown, a fresh start not just for an enterprise but for his life. For the first time in what felt like an eternity, the prospect of settling down in a radically different place didn't evoke a sense of loss or defeat. Instead, it glowed with the promise of beginnings he had long thought impossible—a real, heartfelt chance to build something lasting.

Small-town Alabama wouldn't have a thriving gay scene. He wondered if there were even any out gays in Brookstone. Statistically, there had to be a small population of LGBTQ people. But just how many were living out and proud as their authentic selves? Well, that is all about to change, he thought. I won't be waving rainbow flags or organizing the first-ever pride parade, but he would never hide who he was.

As his eyes drifted closed, he pictured it all vividly—a sanctuary where he could craft not merely a business but a home and ultimately, a life enriched with genuine connection.

# Chapter 1
## New Beginnings

The sun crept over Brookstone on a warm April morning, painting the quiet town in long, conflicted beams of golden light. Even as the cicadas droned a familiar tune and birds timidly broke the silence, there was an undercurrent in the air—a disquiet that hinted not every morning was as pristine as it appeared. Jim Williamson's patrol car rolled down Main Street, its engine sounding almost too familiar as if echoing memories, he wasn't completely ready to face.

Brookstone had long been a gentle Southern town, with its red-brick facades and modest storefronts that offered a semblance of unchanging comfort—a sanctuary in the slow passage of time. Yet that fragile peace had been shattered by the revelation of a decades-long dump of hatred and murder at the local junkyard.

Thanks to Jim and a few determined souls, the truth was unearthed, the weight of the past lifted, and for now, the town had returned to its quaint charm. Jim knew every twist and turn here—the crepe myrtle-lined streets, the relentless cadence of his patrol, and almost everyone by name—which usually steadied him in the chaos of life. But today, as he drove, he sensed a disturbance, a ripple of something unexpected within the familiar rhythm.

Nearing the edges of town, his eyes landed on the warehouse district—a somber collection of neglected buildings that stood like tired relics from an era long gone. Their faded bricks and shattered windows told stories of industrial vigor now replaced by decay. Four massive buildings arranged in an L-shape, two facing east and two south, enclosed a large, desolate courtyard overrun by weeds and age. Even in the cracked pavement and creaking, abandoned signs, a hint of lost splendor was there—but also a lingering sadness that made Jim's heart tremble with a strange mix of nostalgia and foreboding.

Today, however, these abandoned spaces thrummed with unusual activity. In a startling contrast to the town's sleepy character, architects, surveyors, engineers, and contractors buzzed around drafting tables set up on the sidewalk, their voices and the clatter of tools weaving an unfamiliar tapestry of ambition. Trucks parked in disarray opened to reveal tools and equipment as digital levels beeped and hammers struck with determined regularity. Jim slowed his patrol car to a crawl, his curiosity and a gnawing anxiety mingling.

He caught sight of Chandler Harris—his cousin's fiancé—engaged in animated conversation near one of the trucks with a tall, broad-shouldered man whose presence was impossible to ignore. There was an authority in the stranger's posture, a ruggedness that clashed uncomfortably with the town's laid-back façade. Jim's instinct screamed that something wasn't right; his mind wrestled with the allure of this new face and the discomfort of being drawn into something he wasn't sure he wanted to confront.

Parking by the cluster of construction vehicles, Jim stepped out, the crunch of gravel underfoot amplifying his inner unease. Adjusting his utility belt out of habit, he ambled toward the group, each boot heel echoing on the cobblestone path. His dark navy uniform, immaculate with crisp creases, did little to hide the inner turmoil he felt beneath— torn between the comfort of routine and the magnetic pull of something dangerously unpredictable. His dark, wavy brown hair, now a bit longer than usual, lent him an unintentional ruggedness, while his deep blue eyes flitted between duty and a hesitant, conflicted curiosity.

"Morning," Jim called out, his voice low and steady, masking the quiver of uncertainty within as he addressed Chandler and the intriguing stranger crouched over a set of blueprints magnetically attached to the hood of a truck. Jim knew Chandler as the lead electrical engineer on the multi-million dollar project that had everyone whispering since the warehouses were snapped up online in January. The project promised new business fronts and luxury apartments hidden behind the old brick, a transformative vision that both excited and unnerved him.

At Jim's greeting, the man straightened, his towering stature—at least four or five inches above Jim's own six-foot-one—drawing attention immediately. Clad in a crisp white button-up with sleeves casually rolled up and a loosened paisley tie that revealed curly russet chest hair beneath,

Brock Curry exuded confidence and a disconcerting raw charm. His meticulously groomed reddish-brown beard, tipped with just a whisper of silver, lent him a distinguished air, but as his soft blue eyes met Jim's, an unspoken intensity passed between them. Jim's pulse quickened, a reaction that both startled and troubled him—this was not just admiration; it was something deeper he wasn't sure he was willing to confront.

"How's it going?" Jim asked, his tone neutral though the conflict inside churned relentlessly. Chandler's warm smile offered a brief respite—a reminder of familiarity—while Jim's gaze roaming the blueprints betrayed more than professional interest. "Saw the activity from the road," he explained casually, though his voice bore hints of unspoken questions, "figured I'd come to see what's happening."

Brock, now fully facing Jim, stood a towering 6'6", his robust frame an embodiment of quiet power. His shirt strained over his muscular chest, revealing a subtle paunch that only added to his bear-like allure—a trait that stirred inexplicable emotions in Jim, blending professional respect with a disquieting personal attraction he couldn't admit to himself. Jim's mind raced as he extended his hand, forcing himself to focus on his duty. "Jim Williamson, Brookstone PD. Just making my rounds. Thought I'd see what all the buzz was about. Seems you're stirring quite the excitement," he said, struggling to steady a voice that trembled between casual interest and a forbidden intrigue.

Brock's handshake was firm, his eyes steady in a manner that both challenged and beckoned. "Brock Curry," he replied, his voice deep and velvety, smooth yet carrying an undercurrent of ambition. "Yeah, you could say that. Figured these warehouses needed a spark. Internet real estate is an amazing game, isn't it?"

Even as he spoke, Brock's gaze lingered a moment too long, sending an unwelcome thrill through Jim—a sensation that clashed violently with his training and self-image. Jim quickly averted his eyes, chastising himself internally for the distraction.

"Brock Curry," Jim echoed, arching an eyebrow in a mix of professional curiosity and personal disbelief. "The real estate developer from Atlanta?

I heard you've snapped up half the town already."

Brock chuckled, though the sound was tinged with a gravity that cut through the morning calm. "Not half, no—but I did secure the four warehouses and a house in town," he admitted, crossing his burly arms as if to steady himself against an internal storm. "Projects like this take time, and I need a base while I'm here." His voice hinted at both pride and vulnerability—a quiet admission that beneath the tough exterior, he was also laying the foundations for something more than just lucrative ventures.

Jim recalled the sprawling craftsman house Brock had bought—a gem filled with memories and an air of faded grandeur—and felt both admiration and creeping envy of Brock's bold reinvention. "Good call," Jim said, managing a casual tone even as his throat tightened. Yet beneath his words simmered an unspoken tension, a secret dialogue between his professional obligation and an irresistible pull toward Brock's enigmatic presence.

Chandler stepped in then, mentioning that Brock had been a quiet force behind the scenes until now and that his involvement was set to change everything. Jim's conflicted glance at Brock deepened as he absorbed the truth: there was more to Brock than just a business plan—there was passion, ambition, and perhaps an underlying search for something he was afraid to name.

Before Jim could press further, the discordant clang of metal sliced through the murmur of activity, followed by a tirade of curses from a worker. Brock's face tightened with irritation as he moved toward the disturbance, leaving Jim standing there with a mix of relief and disappointment. Even as Brock's broad back receded into the fading light, Jim's eyes lingered, torn between curiosity and an emerging desire that felt utterly foreign.

Left with Chandler, Jim sought to regain some sense of normalcy. Chandler, now at ease in his new freelance role, updated him on Brock's background—a net worth hovering just above $600 million, a self-made millionaire with a knack for reviving forgotten properties and transforming them into thriving ventures. The details, though impressive, only deepened Jim's inner conflict. On one level, he admired Brock's audacity and vision; on another, he resented the disruption of his quiet, methodical life.

Jim returned to his patrol car, unable to shake the memory of that charged encounter with Brock, the strange mix of admiration and discomfort stirring within him. Something about the man unsettled him, unbalancing a world he thought he had perfectly ordered.

Later that afternoon, as the sun began to sink, Jim pulled up to Spence's old house. Here, Brock was finalizing paperwork, and Spence—ever the familiar, comforting presence—was busy loading the last few boxes into his truck. The warm glow of dusk brushed the craftsman house's cedar shake siding and white-trimmed windows with a nostalgic light that made Jim's heartache with conflicted longing.

"Jim!" Spence called out, shattering the contemplative silence. "Come to help with these last few boxes?"

"Something like that," Jim replied with a half-hearted smile, clapping Spence on the shoulder before his gaze involuntarily shifted to Brock, busy at the front porch signing documents alongside Ken Kelton, the town lawyer. Their eyes met, and the earlier tension flared once more— a spark that ignited a battle inside Jim between his sense of responsibility and the lure of forbidden attraction.

"Just making sure everything's in order," Jim said, attempting light banter. "It looks like Brookstone's finest are keeping things running smoothly." His voice faltered briefly, betraying the inner dissonance he couldn't quite quash.

Brock, ever the picture of polished courtesy, replied with measured politeness as he returned a folder of papers to Ken. "I suppose I should thank you for making me feel welcome," he said quietly, his tone laced with a warmth that felt both inviting and painfully challenging to Jim. A blush crept over Jim's cheeks—a silent admission of a desire he wasn't ready to acknowledge openly.

"Just doing my job," Jim responded, striving for nonchalance even as every fiber of him rebelled against the growing attraction. "And if you ever need help with permits or have questions about the town, I'm here." He managed the words, though they hung between them as a cautious olive branch stretched across dangerous territory.

Brock's fleeting smile, reaching his eyes just for a heartbeat, stirred something deep in Jim—a feeling both exhilarating and unbearably risky. As Spence and Jim got back to loading boxes, Jim's mind churned over the day's events. His orderly, familiar world was shifting, and Brock's presence, his confident strength, and his unexpected vulnerability threatened to overturn everything. Was it just the excitement of a new project, or was there something more uncanny stirring in his heart?

After the boxes were tucked away, Spence handed Jim a key ring and a folder full of notes on the house's history. The three men exchanged cordial goodbyes. Brock's parting words lingered in the cool evening air: "Very nice to meet both of you, gentlemen. I look forward to being part of this beautiful community." As each went their separate ways—Jim to his apartment, Spence to the farmhouse, and Brock to his new home— the unspoken tension remained heavy and unresolved.

As the sound of Spence's truck faded and the quiet of the late afternoon enveloped Brookstone, Brock allowed himself a rare moment to breathe. The old Craftsman house, empty yet still resonant with warmth, felt like a blank canvas—an opportunity for new beginnings, both in business and in life. He wandered inside with a conflicted heart, each echoing step stirring a mix of hope and hesitation. Imagining his future furniture—a large leather sofa, a heavy wood coffee table, personal artwork adorning the walls—he felt both the thrill of possibility and the weight of expectations.

Climbing the creaking stairs to the master bedroom, Brock set down his suitcases and began to arrange his temporary bed with almost mechanical precision. As he gazed out of the large windows at the sprawling oak trees lining the street, a thousand thoughts cascaded through his mind. Brookstone held promise, yes, but it also reminded him of old secrets and the careful balance he was forced to maintain. Despite the genuine friendliness of Spence and Chandler, there remained an unspoken truth: a part of him still hesitated to reveal his true self in this close-knit community.

With the air mattress set and fresh linens spread out, Brock made his way to the expansive master bathroom. The oversized, tiled walk-in shower beckoned him, its rainfall showerhead promising both relief and a quiet escape. As he arranged his toiletries, a subtle conflict stirred within him—a battle between embracing the comfort of the present and the forbidden allure of fantasies he dared not admit.

Brock peeled off his shirt, the cool air of the AC contrasting sharply with the anticipated warmth of the steaming water. Standing under the rainfall, his dampened reddish-brown hair clung to his skin while the heat traced his muscular form. He ran his hands slowly across his chest, feeling the thick hair and the solid muscle beneath—a tactile reminder of his rugged nature, honed through relentless work and quiet contemplation. Deep within him, a forbidden thought began to surface as he remembered Jim Williamson—the handsome, authoritative cop whose every movement ignited a storm within him.

Brock's eyes closed as he scrubbed his beard, and his mind wandered into a realm of dangerous fantasies. He envisioned Jim—stripping off his uniform, revealing a perfectly proportioned physique and even a hint of vulnerability—and felt a surge of conflicted desire. The fantasy spiraled, blurring the line between admiration and lust, pulling him into thoughts that both thrilled and tormented him. He chastised himself silently; he had never been one to cross that boundary, especially not with someone so emblematic of law and order. Yet the image was too potent to ignore. With a shaking hand, he allowed the fantasy to linger just for a moment, a secret indulgence he knew he might soon regret.

The water poured over Brock, washing away the tension of the day—if only temporarily.

As he stepped out of the shower and wrapped a towel around his waist, he was keenly aware of the dualities in his soul: the hope of transforming not just warehouses but an entire community and the personal longing that threatened to upend the steady course of his carefully constructed life. There was so much to do, so many expectations, yet also more hidden desires than he was ready to confront.

In the dwindling light of Brookstone, as Brock unpacked his bags to open the door to new possibilities in his life and closed the door on a chapter of his past, he could not help but wonder whether the new beginning he sought might force him to confront parts of himself he'd long kept at bay. Amid the promise of progress and community, an internal battle raged—a turbulent mix of ambition, duty, and a forbidden yearning that could upend everything if left unchecked.

# Chapter 2
# Stirring Curiosity

Jim's apartment building sat on the edge of town, a modest two-story brick structure with a view of the creek that snaked behind it. He climbed the stairs to the second floor, fumbling with his keys before pushing open the door to apartment 2B. The familiar smell of his space—a mixture of leather furniture polish, old books, and the faint lingering scent of last night's pizza—greeted him.

He flicked on the lights, illuminating what his cousin Spence affectionately called his "nerd cave." The living room walls were adorned with framed vintage sci-fi movie posters—Star Wars, Blade Runner, and 2001: A Space Odyssey among them. His pride and joy, a glass display case, stood against the far wall, housing his collection of limited-edition action figures still in their original packaging. The shelves beside it overflowed with well-worn paperbacks and hardcover novels. The spines cracked from frequent reading.

Jim tossed his keys into the ceramic bowl on the entryway table—a handmade piece from last year's town craft fair—and unclipped his holster, placing his service weapon in the small safe mounted on his bookshelf. His fingers worked the combination lock with practiced ease before he shrugged out of his uniform shirt, leaving him in his white undershirt that clung to his muscular torso.

The kitchenette, separated from the living room by a breakfast bar, was compact but functional. His refrigerator was adorned with magnets from various sci-fi conventions he'd attended over the years. Jim pulled open the door, the cool air hitting his face as he reached for a bottle of local craft beer. The label featured the town's namesake creek illustrated in watercolor. He twisted off the cap and took a long swig, letting the bitter hops wash away the day's tension. The cold liquid slid down his throat, refreshing and familiar.

Jim sank into his well-worn leather couch, the cushions conforming to his body like an old friend. He grabbed the remote from the coffee table—a repurposed piece of industrial machinery with a glass top that Spence had helped him find at a salvage yard—and clicked on the television mounted on the wall opposite his sci-fi collection.

The screen flickered to life, illuminating the room with a blue glow. He flipped through channels before settling on a rerun of "The Expanse," one of his favorite shows. The space drama's complex characters and realistic physics had always appealed to his analytical mind. He kicked off his boots and propped his feet up on the coffee table, allowing himself to relax for the first time all day.

As the episode unfolded, Jim found himself only half-watching. The actor who played the gruff, bearded captain of a salvage vessel stepped into the frame, his commanding presence filling the screen. Something about the way he carried himself—broad-shouldered and confident, with a slightly weathered face framed by a well-groomed beard—triggered an unexpected connection in Jim's mind.

"Damn," he muttered, taking another swig of beer. The actor's eyes, intense and piercing even through the screen, reminded him unmistakably of Brock Curry.

Jim shifted uncomfortably on the couch. Suddenly, instead of following the plot, his mind wandered back to the warehouse district, replaying his encounter with Brookstone's newest resident. The way Brock's reddish-brown beard had caught the sunlight. How his rolled-up sleeves had revealed powerful forearms dusted with copper-colored hair. The rumble of his deep voice, warm and commanding all at once.

Jim's bottle paused halfway to his lips as his thoughts drifted further. He remembered the way Brock's eyes had lingered on him, just a beat too long to be casual. The slight curl at the corner of his mouth when he'd said goodbye. The undeniable presence he'd commanded filled any space he occupied with something that went beyond his impressive physical stature.

"What the hell," Jim whispered to himself, setting the beer down with more force than necessary. He ran a hand through his dark, wavy hair, slightly damp with sweat from the day's heat. This wasn't like him. He'd never found himself fixating on another man this way—analyzing every glance, replaying every word of their brief conversation.

Jim shifted on the couch, pressing the remote button to pause the show as the actor's bearded face froze on screen. He couldn't focus on the plot anymore—not when his mind kept superimposing Brock's features over the character's.

"Get it together, Williamson," he muttered, draining the last of his beer.

But his thoughts refused to obey. Instead, they wandered to places they'd never gone before. What would Brock look like without that crisp button-up shirt? Jim had caught glimpses of the chest hair peeking from his collar, and now his imagination filled in the blanks—a broad expanse of muscle covered in that same reddish-brown fur, perhaps trailing down his stomach in a tantalizing path.

Jim's breath caught in his throat. He'd seen plenty of men in various states of undress throughout his life—in locker rooms during his academy days, at the gym, and even during late-night shifts when his fellow officers changed into civilian clothes. He'd appreciated their physiques in an abstract way, noting who put in extra time at the weights or who could outrun him on the track. But that was different—clinical, competitive observations. This was something else entirely.

Heat spread through Jim's body, pooling low in his belly. He shifted again, suddenly aware of the growing tightness in his uniform pants. Looking down, he saw the unmistakable bulge pressing against his zipper. "Shit," he whispered, his voice strained even to his own ears.

He'd never had this reaction to another man before, not in the academy showers where he'd seen everything, not during the wrestling matches or physical training sessions where bodies pressed against each other in close combat. Sure, he'd stolen glances—who hadn't?—but they never affected him physically. Never made his heart race or his cock stiffen against his will.

Jim's mind was hard at work trying to make sense of these unfamiliar reactions. He'd always been attracted to women—their soft curves, delicate features, the way they smelled like flowers or vanilla. Men had just been... men. Colleagues. Friends. Nothing more.

Yet here he was, alone in his apartment with an erection straining against his zipper at the mere thought of Brock Curry's hairy chest. He closed his eyes, trying to will away the image, but it only intensified. His imagination conjured Brock's broad frame, those powerful shoulders tapering to a solid waist, that slight paunch that somehow only enhanced his masculinity. Jim could almost see the thick carpet of reddish-brown hair covering his pecs, perhaps with a dusting of silver that matched his temples.

Jim's hand unconsciously drifted down to press against his erection, trying to ease the ache. The gesture shocked him back to reality, and he jerked his hand away as if burned.

"Jesus Christ," he muttered, standing abruptly. The remote clattered to the floor as he paced across his living room, running both hands through his hair.

He'd never questioned his sexuality before. Not once. He'd dated women since high school—Sarah Jenkins, his high school sweetheart; Melissa from the academy; Kelly, the English teacher he'd seen on and off for almost two years before they drifted apart. Hell, he even hooked up with FBI Special Agent Joanne Stevens after working the junkyard case together. He'd enjoyed their company, their touch, their kisses. He'd never felt this... confusion.

Jim stopped at his bookshelf, eyes landing on a framed photo of him and Spence from last summer's fishing trip. They stood side by side, holding up their catches, grinning.

Jim's gaze lingered on the photograph, studying Spence's easy smile and confident posture. He remembered how his cousin had come out to him years ago, nervous but determined. Jim had hugged him fiercely and told him nothing would ever change between them. And nothing had.

Jim had never thought being gay was a choice. He'd seen firsthand through Spence how natural it was, how his cousin had always been the same person—before and after coming out. Jim had stood beside him through the town's initial whispers, had confronted the occasional bigot at the local bar, and had celebrated when Spence found love with Chandler. He'd been a proud ally, comfortable and secure in his own heterosexuality.

Until now, "This isn't happening," Jim muttered, pacing faster. His erection hadn't subsided; if anything, the mental image of Brock had only grown more vivid, more detailed. The tension in his body wasn't going away.

Jim stopped pacing, staring at his reflection in the darkened window. The truth was staring him in the face, but he'd never had to confront it before. He'd always been comfortable with who he was—a straight man who supported his gay cousin without question.

But this... this undeniable physical reaction to another man... it shook the foundations of everything he thought he knew about himself.

"Fuck," he whispered, rubbing his hand across his face. He'd spent his entire adult life defending Spence's right to be exactly who he was. He'd punched a deputy from the next county over when the man had made a slur at his cousin's expense. He'd given speeches at community meetings about acceptance and tolerance. He'd been the first to congratulate Spence and Chandler when they got engaged.

Jim's skin felt too tight, his uniform suddenly restrictive and suffocating. The persistent throb between his legs wouldn't subside no matter how much he tried to distract himself with other thoughts. He needed to cool down—literally and figuratively. He strode purposefully to the bathroom, flicking on the light.

His reflection in the mirror confronted him—flushed cheeks, dilated pupils, a thin sheen of sweat on his forehead. He barely recognized himself. "This isn't me," he muttered, though the evidence suggested otherwise. The tightness in his uniform pants hadn't subsided, his body stubbornly refusing to align with what his mind had always believed to be true.

With trembling fingers, he turned the shower knob all the way to cold, the pipes groaning in protest. He stripped quickly, tossing his uniform into the hamper with more force than necessary, his undershirt following, then his boxer briefs. His erection springing free and standing proudly.

The first blast of icy water made him gasp, his muscles tensing as goosebumps erupted across his skin. Jim stood beneath the frigid spray, letting it cascade over his heated flesh, willing it to wash away the unwanted arousal and confusion. His teeth chattered, but he remained under the chilly spray.

Jim backed up slightly so that the water stream was primarily focused on his crotch. He stared up at the ceiling and started counting backward from 100. By the time he reached 60, his racing hard-on had dwindled to only semi-erect. He turned the shower off, stepped out of the shower quickly, and wrapped himself in a towel in an attempt to bring the family jewels back to at least room temp.

Once he was sure his cock and balls were frostbitten, he slipped on fleece pajama bottoms and headed back to the kitchen for a double shot of bourbon. The dark liquid burned his throat and warmed his belly. But it also helped calm his nerves as well as his dick.

He brushed his teeth and climbed into bed. As the bourbon began to work its magic, he drifted off, contemplating just how he was going to handle this new desire growing in him and when or even if he should discuss this with Spence.

The next morning, sunlight filtered through the bouquet of vibrant crepe myrtle trees, casting intricate, lace-like shadows across the expansive, vintage front window of the Caffeine Kick. The scattered beams danced eagerly over the well-worn, checkered linoleum floor as if performing an ancient ritual.

In his regular booth, Jim sat quietly, cradling a cup of black coffee that had already cooled to a tepid temperature. He swirled it absentmindedly with a slow, rhythmic motion, his gaze fixed on the scarred tabletop. The rich aroma of freshly brewed espresso mingled with the delicate, sweet scent of cinnamon rolls that wafted from the bakery case, filling the air with an inviting warmth. Yet today, that comforting sweetness only deepened the contrast with the bitter taste in his mouth—and the uneasy heaviness that was slowly nestling in his chest.

He hadn't expected the peculiar stirrings from the night before—a mysterious, almost magnetic pull towards the enigmatic newcomer, Brock Curry. The man had arrived in Brookstone with an assurance reminiscent of high-rise sophistication, carrying with him the self-assured ease of someone who was accustomed to getting what he desired. His confident manner, his casual swagger in snug, form-fitting jeans, and even the flash of silver threading through his dark hair had left an indelible mark on Jim's thoughts, although none of these superficial details held his fascination for long.

What captivated him far more was something intangible—a subtle, alluring magnetism that defied mere physical charm. Brock's eyes were a potent stormy blue, as intense and foreboding as the sky that gathers dark clouds before a summer tempest. That look had seemed to peel back the layers of Jim's carefully held reservations, leaving him with a sensation as delicate and pervasive as the scent of honeysuckle drifting lightly on a spring breeze.

Jim took a deliberate sip of his coffee, wincing at the cold bitterness as it clashed with the sweet memories enveloped in the air. Why did the mere memory of Brock's penetrating stare leave him feeling so defenseless, so inexplicably drawn? Jim had initially thought, or rather hoped, that last night's surge of attraction would be a fleeting moment of self-discovery. Jim wasn't a man prone to dwelling on passing notions or nurturing desires that might unravel his carefully constructed solitude. Yet, try as he might to shun it, the impression clung to him like a soft but persistent whisper echoing in the corners of his mind.

As the morning passed and thoughts of Brock Curry continued to invade Jim's every thought, he made the decision to talk it through with Spence after work. But how to bring it up was one question. Just how to explain these thoughts, feelings, and physical reactions was another. Okay, there was no way in hell he would elaborate on the events of last night. He was just going to have to take it slow and let the conversation unfold as naturally as it possibly could.

Later that evening, Jim found solace on his cousin Spence's creaking wooden porch. The aged boards whispered underfoot as he and Spence settled onto a timeworn swing, its chains groaning gently with each slow, soothing sway. A warm, lazy breeze stirred the leaves of a towering oak nearby, carrying with it the fresh, earthy aroma of recently cut grass and the delicate perfume of blooming gardenias. From the sideyard,

Jennifer's melodious voice floated through the air as she swung playfully, serenading the beloved family pet, Tom, who basked in the cool, dappled shade.

The familiar setting, imbued with timeless charm, allowed Jim to lay down his burdens—a retreat where he could unburden his heart to Spence without fear of judgment. Tonight, after sharing a comforting supper invitation that had become a staple in his life, Jim recounted the day's perplexing events. Leaning back with arms folded, Spence's expression was a curious blend of concern and gentle amusement as he listened intently.

"So, you're telling me there's some new guy in town—the same fellow Chandler's working for on those warehouses—and you haven't been able to get him out of your head?" Spence's voice was laid-back but probing, his eyes twinkling with a mixture of mirth and astute observation.

Jim's brow furrowed as he rubbed the back of his neck, an unconscious effort to massage away the tension coiled like a tight spring there. "It's not like that," he protested softly, the words falling from his lips as hollow excuses. "There's just… something about him that feels out of place here. I mean, he's got plans to transform those dilapidated warehouses into swanky apartments and boutique shops. Why choose our little town for such a venture? Has Chandler shared much about him?"

Spence's gaze softened into a warm smile, touched by unspoken empathy. "Maybe he's just a man intent on making a fresh start," he replied, his tone mellow and understanding. "After all, all of us have taken leaps in one way or another." His words carried a quiet wisdom reminiscent of his own winding journey through hardships toward hard-won happiness. "Besides, when Zach Davies appeared on the scene and trailed me and, Chandler, you sure weren't this fascinated."

For a transient moment, the two cousins locked eyes, the weight of shared experiences drifting between them in the muggy air. Jim absorbed a deep, cathartic sigh that seemed to release some of the built-up tension from his shoulders. "I don't know," he admitted with quiet vulnerability.

"There's just so much about him I feel inexplicably curious about."

With a teasing arch of his eyebrows, Spence remarked, "Curious, huh? I haven't heard you use that word in ages. Seems like Mr. New Guy's got you more intrigued than you're letting on." A hearty chuckle escaped him, and Jim felt the warmth of a flush creeping up his neck as his face betrayed emotions he'd hoped to keep hidden.

Jim attempted to dispel the tension with a low rumble of laughter. "Alright, alright. I'm just trying to figure out what kind of guy he is—a puzzle I need to solve, that's all." Even as the familiar banter drifted into lighter subjects, Jim's thoughts lingered on Brock, as though his mind had already charted paths it was determined to explore.

At supper later that night, when Chandler joined the table, the conversation inevitably circled back to Brock. The soft clatter of silverware and the gentle murmur of Jennifer's playful chatter provided a backdrop of domestic intimacy, emboldening Jim to revisit the intriguing subject.

"So, any idea how many of these ambitious projects he's managed before?" Jim inquired casually while carefully studying Chandler's face for any flicker of candor.

Chandler relaxed into his chair, cradling a glass of sweet tea before responding. "From what I've gathered in our conversations, he's executed several major transformations similar to this one. But this—this is his first venture in a small town, not in one of the sprawling metropolitan centers. He's done warehouse conversions in cities like Atlanta, Huntsville, Savannah, Nashville… even Dallas."

Jim's furrow deepened with curiosity. "So why Brookstone? What exactly is he aiming to achieve here?"

Chandler's lips curved into a reflective smile, an intimate intrigue coloring his tone as he leaned in conspiratorially. "From the way he talks, it appears he's looking to invest in more than property. He wants to invest in the community—to build something that stands as a legacy rather than just a quick profit." He paused, his voice lowering almost to a whisper as if divulging a secret only the room could share. "And speaking of figures," Chandler added, "according to Forbes, he's worth 626 million dollars."

The staggering number hung suspended in the air, casting a spell of stunned silence over Jim and Spence as their eyes widened in shared disbelief.

"Well, that does explain how he wrote out a check covering the full asking price for my house," Spence mumbled, still processing the enormity of the figure.

Raising an eyebrow, Jim remarked, "That's one hefty investment for our small town." He hesitated a moment before abruptly shifting the focus. "So, how's the wedding planning coming along? Still on track for early June?"

As the conversation seamlessly shifted to color palettes, luxurious catering plans, and Jennifer's ever-growing excitement about her role as the flower girl, the evening slipped by. Yet, beneath the ease of domestic banter, Jim couldn't shake the inkling that there was more hidden beneath Brock's polished exterior—a depth of secrets awaiting discovery. That small, persistent spark of curiosity continued to smolder within him, a silent testament to his yearning to understand the enigmatic man behind the captivating smile.

The following day, Brookstone itself seemed to stir awake with a subtle hum of curiosity and unspoken apprehension as if the town were emerging from a lengthy slumber. The arrival of Brock Curry—with his articulate big-city visions and daring ambition—had ignited a gentle but palpable transformation. Main Street, flanked by quaint aging storefronts and timeworn, faded signs, exuded the air of a place that had remained untouched by modern frenzy.

As Brock ambled along its length, he couldn't help but feel the weight of cautious glances—glances that scrutinized a newcomer, measuring whether to extend a friendly handshake or withhold in silent reservation. The atmosphere was dense with a quiet defiance borne from generations steeped in tradition and a fierce loyalty to the familiar.

Brock's sturdy boots clomped authoritatively on the pavement as he crossed the street towards the local hardware store—a narrow, dimly lit haven that carried the rich, timeless scents of sawdust, machine oil, and weathered wood. Inside, the space was a delightful jumble: shelves lined with well-loved tools, paint cans, and curious miscellaneous parts, each bearing a coating of dust that told tales of decades past.

A solitary fan spun lazily in the corner, its soft whir a feeble counter to the warm, mustiness that enveloped the room. Behind the scarred, wooden counter stood Mr. Prescott—a silver-haired, rugged man with a grizzled beard and the sturdy build of one who'd devoted his life to honest labor. His steely blue eyes, reminiscent of a cold winter sky, locked onto Brock with an unwavering, measured gaze that dripped with both hard-earned experience and a dose of skepticism.

"You're the fella responsible for all that commotion at the old warehouses, ain't ya?" Mr. Prescott rumbled, his tone low and gravelly, edged with suspicion as he savored the sound of an unfamiliar name.

Brock offered a gentle nod, a charming smile gradually spreading across his face as he extended his hand in greeting. "That's right. I'm Brock Curry," he said, his tone relaxed and amicable, laced with an earnest hope. "I'm here to breathe new life into those aging buildings—to give Brookstone something fresh and invigorating to look forward to." His words carried a natural confidence, yet there was a subtle note of deference embedded within them, an acknowledgment that the town's traditions and the wisdom of its people might well outweigh the appeal of his modern checkbook.

Mr. Prescott did not immediately reciprocate the handshake. Instead, he idly rubbed his calloused palm along his jaw, his steady eyes never wavering from Brock's. "This town has its own rhythm," he said deliberately, each word measured. "Folks here don't take kindly to strangers marching in, presuming they know best."

Brock's hand slowly lowered, but his smile remained unshaken. "I completely understand," he replied softly. "I'm not here to bulldoze anyone's way of life. I want to work alongside the community. I've even been speaking with locals like Jim Williamson, who's been incredibly helpful. I'm starting to get a feel for what makes this place tick."

At the simple mention of Jim's name, something in Mr. Prescott's demeanor softened ever so slightly, though his cautious eyes retained their watchfulness. "Jim's a good man," he conceded with a gruff nod, his voice warmed by a grudging respect. "He knows these parts better than most."

Brock sensed a small victory in the old man's reluctant approval. Leaning in slightly, he pulled a neatly folded sheet of paper from the sanctuary of his back pocket and placed it on the counter. "I was hoping you might be able to help me out," he said, unfolding the list with a fluid, practiced motion. "I'm determined to source as many of the materials as possible from local suppliers. I want the work to be done by craftsmen and contractors who understand the nuances of this town."

Mr. Prescott picked up the list, his experienced eyes scanning its detailed inventory—a comprehensive catalog of lumber, hardware, and custom pieces, complete with the names of local contractors, each hailing from no more than a thirty-mile radius. "Well, I'll be," he murmured, a faint smile tugging at the corners of his weathered face. "You've clearly done your homework." Looking back at Brock with a glimmer of newfound respect, he added, "There's an abundance of lumber on here. We might need to order extra from the mill."

"That's perfectly fine," Brock answered with relaxed assurance. "I need as much as you can get to me by the first of next week. The remaining supplies can trickle in as they're ready. I'm also on the lookout for someone local who excels in crafting custom windows and doors."

Mr. Prescott nodded thoughtfully, setting the list aside with deliberate care. "I do know a few fellas who would be more than up to the task," he replied, his voice gradually warming. "Old Will Harcourt, for one—he's known for the finest custom carpentry this side of the Mississippi. I'll fetch his contact details and help sort out these supplies right away."

A genuine smile broke over Brock's features, the first tangible sign of being embraced by the community. "Thank you, Mr. Prescott," he said earnestly. "I truly appreciate your help, and I'm eager to collaborate on this project."

As they continued discussing project specifics, Brock listened intently to the cadence of Mr. Prescott's voice and the rugged pride with which he spoke about the town and its people. Every suggestion and every caution felt like a stepping stone, guiding Brock gently into the heart and soul of Brookstone—a place where his ambitious plans would be measured not merely in dollars but in trust and authenticity. The conversation was less a business transaction than an invitation to immerse himself in the local way of life.

When their discussion drew to a natural close, Mr. Prescott swept his hand across the counter and gave Brock's hand a firm, deliberate shake. "Keep your word," he warned, his tone a compelling mix of friendly counsel and subtle caution, "and you just might win over the people of this town."

Brock met the seasoned man's gaze with steadfast assurance. "I intend to," he promised softly, nodding gratefully. "And I'll make sure this project becomes something Brookstone can take pride in."

Stepping out of the hardware store, Brock found himself once again on Main Street, where the late morning sun cast elongated shadows that crisscrossed the sidewalk like intricate calligraphy. He felt the palpable weight of the journey ahead—not merely in the physical challenges of construction but in winning hearts and proving himself to a town guarded yet hopeful, a town where veterans like Mr. Prescott cherished the persistence of tradition.

Two days later, Jim pushed open the heavy glass door of *The Magnolia Diner* and was embraced by a symphony of enticing aromas: sizzling strips of bacon, freshly baked biscuits, and the undercurrent of robust brewing coffee. The diner's warmth enveloped him like a cherished, well-worn jacket—familiar, comforting, and unassuming. The low murmur of hushed conversations, punctuated by the soft clink of silverware on ceramic plates and the gentle shuffle of waitresses in pastel aprons, established a rhythm of everyday life. Sunlight streamed generously through the front windows, bathing the checkered tile floor in a golden, honeyed glow.

Jim's eyes roved over this picture of small-town charm until they rested upon Brock, who was seated at the counter with quiet confidence. Beside a half-empty cup of coffee and a neatly folded newspaper, Brock exuded an aura of calm assurance. Steam curled lazily upward from his cup, echoing the gentle tendrils of thought that seemed to surround him. Jim hesitated for a moment, feeling a flicker of something indefinable—a spark of curiosity and a stirring awareness pulsing steadily in his chest. It wasn't merely professional interest; it was as if destiny had nudged him before he could fully comprehend the emotion taking shape.

"Didn't expect to see you here," Jim noted, his tone casual yet laced with a trace of pleasant surprise as he slid onto the adjacent stool at the counter. With a quick nod to a passing waitress—prompting the immediate notation of his usual ham and cheese omelet paired with a side of grits—Jim settled into the familiar ambiance.

Brock turned toward him, his face transforming with a dawning recognition and a small, genuine smile that softened the lines etched by time. "Figured I'd sample some local flavor," he replied smoothly, his voice warm and inviting with a playful twinkle. "You can't truly know a place until you've savored its food." Lifting his cup with an effortless grace, he took a sip as though each taste was a new story unfolding.

Jim smirked ever so slightly, his fingers drumming lightly against the well-worn countertop. "The Magnolia's one of the best choices around— especially those biscuits, they're practically legendary," he confided in a lowered tone, as though bestowing a cherished secret. "Here, you won't find any pretense. It's all heart over lavish presentation."

"Fancy doesn't really entice me," Brock responded, his deep voice carrying a slight mischief. There was an unspoken intensity in the way he regarded Jim—almost as if he were gently peeling away layers, searching for the essence of the man beyond the surface. This unexpected directness stirred within Jim a quiet thrill, awakening a long-dormant sense of intrigue.

Jim leaned back slightly, crossing his arms as he studied Brock's composed demeanor. "So what draws you to a town like Brookstone?" he ventured, letting the question hover in the perfumed air between them. "It's a world away from the bustling energy of the big city, isn't it?"

Brock paused, his intense gaze wandering to the sun-dappled window where light spilled over the street. His eyes seemed to search for the right words as if unwrapping a delicate truth. "I suppose I've been looking for a place where I can build something enduring, something that outlasts fleeting trends," he said quietly, in a voice both low and reflective. "I'm tired of projects that flicker in and out of existence. Brookstone feels like it has the potential for genuine revival—and, in some way, maybe I need that reinvention as much as the city does." In his softly spoken confession, vulnerability surfaced—a glimpse of a weary soul who had experienced both promising beginnings and inevitable endings.

A surge of recognition rippled through Jim, mirroring his own restlessness and the profound notion that had woven him inseparably to Brookstone long after the allure of metropolitan glamor had dimmed. "Well," he said, a gradual smile unfurling on his face, "Brookstone might be headstrong, but it's brimming with heart. Folks here want to know you're in it for the long haul. We've seen too many promises vanish like a summer storm."

Brock's eyes locked with Jim's in a charged moment when the bustling din of the diner seemed to recede into a soft, indistinct hush. "I'm not going anywhere," Brock declared in a measured, steady tone. "At least, not until the job is truly done."

Jim felt his pulse quicken as a cascade of questions and uncertain wonder washed over him. Beyond Brock's pragmatic venture lay layers of complexity—a story buried beneath charm and ambition. Was this pull merely professional intrigue, or did it hint at a connection far deeper, one that beckoned him to explore uncharted realms within his own heart?

As Jim finished his breakfast, the familiar symphony of the diner—its clatter, chatter, and warm ambiance—slowly reclaimed his full attention. Yet, the lingering, subtle enigma of Brock's presence left Jim pondering the depth of his secrets—a narrative that had brought him, momentarily, to the very seat beside the intriguing outsider, leaving him to wonder just how deep that story might run.

# Chapter 3
# Crossing Paths

That Monday had arrived with an electric surge. The redevelopment buzz was in full swing as heavy trucks rolled down Main Street, their engines roaring and metal clanging in a symphony of change. Dumpsters were delivered like armored sentinels, and the incessant thud of construction equipment set hearts pounding. Curious onlookers paused in mid-stride while a few grumbled, disturbed by the intrusion into their tranquil routine. Even though Jim dismissed much of it as background noise, he couldn't ignore the low murmur of discontent swirling among the townspeople.

"Chief, relax," Jim assured the police chief on the phone as he spoke with calm determination. "I'll have a chat with Brock. He's got every permit in order and is entirely within his rights. But if it helps, I'll serve as the bridge between him and the city council so we can quiet these concerns."

With that settled, Jim strode down to the site, where dumpsters stood in rigid formation, burdened with accumulated rubble. Hard-hatted workers moved with purposeful urgency, their voices rising over the clatter and buzz of machinery. He soon found Brock near one of the imposing warehouses. Engaged in conversation with the crew foreman, Brock—sporting a faded blue T-shirt and rugged work boots—exuded natural authority. His deep, resonant voice carried effortlessly over the din as he discussed the day's progress.

"Hey there, Jim," Brock called out with a wink and a nod, his tone laced with gentle humor. "Did you come to check up on me, or are you just cruising by?"

"A bit of both," Jim replied with a playful grin, his eyes dancing with amusement. "I've heard some folks griping about the noise and the traffic. I told the chief you've got everything buttoned up on paper, but folks can be ornery. Maybe I can help temper things a bit."

Brock wiped the sweat from his brow with the back of his hand, his features shadowed by the relentless heat that made the air thick and oppressive. "Yeah, I've caught wind of a few complaints," he admitted, the hint of frustration evident in the set of his jaw. "I always knew small-town change would ruffle feathers, no matter how promising the future might be."

Jim nodded thoughtfully. "On that note, Mr. Prescott's been singing your praises to the council. He made sure they know you're hiring local contractors, and most of your materials are coming from his own store. That kind of local backing goes a long way here."

A warm smile spread across Brock's face as if a burden had been lifted. "That means a lot, Jim. I'm trying to do right by this town." He glanced at a worker hauling a stack of boards onto a trailer, adding quietly, "Brookstone deserves more than just being a sleepy stop on the highway."

Admiring Brock's unwavering conviction, Jim said sincerely, "You have a grand vision. This town just needs a little time to catch on. If you don't mind, I can arrange a meeting with the council to nip these complaints in the bud and give everyone a clear picture of what's coming."

"That might just be the ticket," Brock replied, gratitude shining in his eyes. "I'd love the chance to show them I'm not just a transient looking to pocket quick profits."

True to his word, the following week, Jim set up a town council meeting for a Tuesday evening in Brookstone's modest city hall—a building worn by time with scuffed wooden floors and rows of folding chairs facing an elevated council table. A few tired ceiling fans spun lazily overhead, barely stirring the stifling summer air that clung like a heavy cloak to everyone present.

Jim arrived early, the sound of his footsteps echoing softly across the worn floor. His eyes roamed across the room, taking in the familiar faces of Brookstone's hardy citizens—a blend of skepticism and cautious hope painted across their features. Before long, nearly every chair was filled by older residents whose lifelong connection to the town was written in the lines on their faces.

Soon enough, Brock walked in. Despite the buzz of anticipation, he remained calm and composed, his broad shoulders and confident stride instantly commanding the room. Tonight, he had traded his work boots and faded T-shirt for a crisp button-down and neatly pressed khakis, yet his presence was unmistakable—the same man who had been wrestling debris under the scorching sun now stood with quiet dignity.

As Jim approached him, he murmured, "You ready for this?" Brock let out a low, rumbling chuckle, massaging the back of his neck. "As ready as I'll ever be. It's a strange feeling standing before a room full of people who aren't sure if they want me here."

"Just be honest, Brock," Jim encouraged, clapping him on the shoulder. "They'll eventually see the heart behind your vision."

The meeting began when Marjorie Daniels, the council's formidable yet fair chairwoman, fixed her steely eyes on the assembly and brought the room to order with a commanding tap of her gavel. Her stern demeanor softened just enough for a brief pause as she adjusted her glasses and addressed the crowd.

"Ladies and gentlemen, thank you for coming tonight," she intoned evenly, her voice measured and authoritative. "We're here to discuss the redevelopment of the old warehouse district and to address any concerns about this transformation."

Turning to Brock, Marjorie gestured politely as he rose and made his way to the front. Clearing his throat, he cast a momentary glance at Jim before beginning, "Thank you, Ms. Daniels, and thank you to the council for allowing me to speak." His deep voice resonated with authentic emotion as he continued, "I know there are worries about noise, traffic, and what this project could mean for our beloved town. Allow me to explain not only what we are doing but also why it matters."

His gaze swept the room, resting on the faces of those who had been the most vocal critics—Mrs. Haverford, a town staple for over sixty years, and Mr. Anders, the local barber whose discontent with the traffic was well-known. "I grew up in a town much like Brookstone," Brock went on, softening his tone, "and I understand the fear that change can bring, especially when it feels like outsiders are intruding. But I'm not here to obliterate what makes Brookstone special. I'm here to enhance it—to build a future that honors the roots of the community."

He paused, his eyes flickering over carefully laid blueprints showing new businesses, communal spaces, and the delicate restoration of historic facades. "These warehouses have long stood empty. I see the potential to breathe new life into them. We're dedicated to preserving the soul of Brookstone. We're using local contractors and suppliers—nearly every resource comes from here; even our meals are sourced locally. This project is as much about keeping our money in town as it is about opening new opportunities."

Jim observed the gradual shift in the room's atmosphere; arms that had been crossed were now slowly uncrossed as nods of tentative approval replaced frowns. Even Mr. Anders leaned forward, his earlier resistance seemingly replaced by intrigue.

Brock continued with earnest conviction, "I know change is daunting, but I'm not here to bulldoze your history. I want to preserve it while inviting in the businesses that will ensure Brookstone not only survives but thrives."

A concerned voice broke in as Marjorie Daniels interjected, leaning forward. "Mr. Curry, while your intentions are noble, many are worried about the duration of this disruption—the noise, the traffic. Our town thrives on its peace and quiet."

Brock nodded thoughtfully. "I understand completely. We've adjusted our work hours to avoid peak times and have coordinated deliveries to ease traffic. I'm open to meeting anyone who has specific worries and discussing them one-on-one."

Mrs. Haverford timidly raised her hand, her voice shaking as she asked, "And when it's all done? You're not planning on attracting those giant chains, are you? We don't want our town swallowed by corporations."

Brock's smile was gentle as he replied, "No, ma'am, no chains. I'm focused on drawing in small, independent businesses—ones that enrich our community rather than overpower it."

A ripple of approval coursed through the crowd. At that exact moment,

Mr. Prescott—a quiet yet influential figure seated near the back—stood and declared, "Let me add that Mr. Curry has been dedicated to this town from the start. He hires local, buys local, and is committed to keeping Brookstone strong. We'd be unwise not to support him."

Nods and murmurs of agreement filled the room, and even the council members exchanged reassured smiles. Jim caught Brock's eye and offered him a subtle thumbs-up. The tension seemed to melt as both men acknowledged, without words, the significance of the moment.

Marjorie Daniels then softened her tone, "It appears we're largely united on the direction of this project. We'll monitor everything closely, but it's clear this redevelopment serves Brookstone well."

As the meeting wound down and the skeptical crowd began to disperse, Brock lingered by the door, shaking hands and exchanging a few hopeful words with former critics. Jim stayed back, watching Brock navigate the exit with the same understated dignity that had first drawn him in.

Once the room had emptied, Brock sidled over to Jim, his smile tired yet satisfied. "Thanks for your help tonight, Jim. I couldn't have done this without you."

Jim chuckled warmly, feeling the gratitude settle over him like a comforting embrace. "Honestly, you did all the legwork. I just helped smooth over a few bumps."

For a lingering moment, Brock's eyes held Jim's gaze—a silent promise of gratitude and an unspoken debt. "Still," Brock said softly, almost in a whisper, "I owe you one." Jim shrugged with a heartfelt smile. "Just doing my job."

Outside, the night air was cool and inviting as they leaned against the hood of Jim's SUV, watching the soft glow of streetlights stretch long shadows across the cracked parking lot. The recent council meeting's tension had given way to a calm understanding between them. The soft hum of the night mingled with the lingering warmth of their conversation, hinting at possibilities beyond business.

Jim broke the silence, his voice gentle as he asked, "You mentioned you're from a small town. How did you end up in the big city, renovating buildings for a living?"

Brock hesitated, his eyes darkening with memories. After a moment, he shifted his weight against the SUV and offered, "Yeah, small town. It's not too different from here, really. It just wasn't a great place to grow up. My dad was a mean drunk—always angry when he came home—and my mom… she was timid, terrified of him but too scared to leave. She had resigned to the idea that that was all life could be." He brushed his hand across his neck as if trying to wipe away the memory.

Jim listened intently, the warm glow from the streetlights illuminating Brock's pensive profile. "We were dirt poor," Brock continued, his voice rough with recollection. "My dad couldn't keep a job, and mom scraped by working as a waitress. By the time I was fifteen, I'd grown tall and strong enough to stand up to him. One night, after another bout of his anger, I finally fought back."

A heavy silence fell between them before Brock continued, "That same night, I came out to them. I thought if I was ready to stand up, I might as well be true to who I am. My dad hurled every insult about having a queer son that he could muster and kicked me out. My mom just sat in the corner, crying." His voice softened into regret and shame at the sound of his own words.

Jim's brow furrowed in understanding as he asked quietly, "And that was the last time you saw them?"

"Yeah," Brock replied in a low rasp as if exhaling a lifetime of pain. "That was it. After that, I bounced around—crashing on friends' couches, anyone who'd take me in. Eventually, a kind contractor, who was my best friend's dad, took pity on me. I learned carpentry, roofing, plumbing—anything I could get my hands on. I worked every odd job, saving every penny."

Jim's mind spun with admiration and a growing respect for Brock's resilience and new knowledge confirming Brock's sexual orientation. An unexpected thrill buzzed through him. "That must have taken incredible grit," he said softly. "Building yourself back up from nothing."

A faint smile tugged at Brock's lips. "It wasn't easy," he admitted, "but by twenty-four, I managed to get a grant and bought my first property. I poured everything I had into renovating it. That was fifteen years ago. When it sold, I reinvested almost every penny to buy another place. After my third property, I obtained my real estate license and officially started my company." He paused, his eyes distant as if reliving the early struggles. "I never stopped working. I always kept my hands on deck— I didn't want to be the guy just barking orders."

Jim could see the pride shining in Brock's eyes and added, "You've come such a long way. I can see that you put your heart and soul into it."

"Yeah, well," Brock said ruefully, "it kept me busy and kept my mind off other things." His voice trailed off as he glanced at Jim, inviting him to probe further.

"Other things, like…?" Jim asked with gentle curiosity.

Brock sighed, running a hand through his hair. "Relationships, mostly. I was with a guy in Atlanta for a couple of years—Jason. He was a plumber, and we had our moments. But it ended about three years ago, not so amicably. Since then, I've poured myself into the business."

"Three years is a long time to be alone," Jim observed thoughtfully. "Have you ever thought about jumping back in? Getting back out there?"

Brock raised an eyebrow and grinned crookedly. "Oh, I've dabbled in the dating apps. Plenty of guys just out for a hookup." He chuckled, his deep tone playful as he added, "And, well—I'm pretty handy."

Jim laughed, though his smile waned as he considered the complex layers behind Brock's words. "Still, loneliness can be rough," he murmured softly.

"Tell me about it," Brock agreed, his gaze softening as he surveyed Jim. "What about you? You grew up here, right? Spence's mom is your aunt?"

Jim nodded, a faint smile on his face. "That's right. My mom and Spence's mom were sisters. After my parents retired to Pensacola, I moved back. Let's just say my luck with love hasn't been great. I've had my ups and downs, but nothing serious—maybe I haven't met the right woman yet."

A fleeting moment of disappointment crossed Brock's eyes at the mention of "the right woman," though it was quickly masked by tempered optimism. "Well," Brock said, pushing off from the SUV and turning to Jim with a thoughtful expression, "you never know. Sometimes the right person shows up when you least expect it."

Jim's gaze lingered on Brock for several charged seconds before he nodded with a quiet smile. "Yeah...I guess you're right." He was intrigued by Brock's use of the word person instead of woman.

The night air seemed to thicken with unspoken understanding, a delicate energy that danced between them. As they parted ways, both men carried a renewed sense of anticipation—a feeling that this connection might lead to treasures beyond routine business or friendship.

Later, as Jim drove away, his mind still replayed Brock's coming-out confession—a matter-of-fact revelation shadowed by pain and regret that stirred something deep within him. He'd always assumed he was straight, never contemplating otherwise. Yet Brock's easy smile and commanding presence had begun to upend all those long-held notions, leaving Jim both bewildered and exhilarated.

Over the next ten days, their connection deepened almost imperceptibly into a quiet routine. Mornings began over steaming cups of coffee, their conversation drifting from redevelopment logistics into surprisingly personal territories. Jim made a point to pass by the job site during his long shifts. Each visit was a small window into the evolving vision Brock was shaping.

One late afternoon, as the sun dipped low and bathed the almost-cleared lot in golden light, Jim returned to the warehouses. A text from Brock had announced that the demolition phase was finally over, and Jim's curiosity urged him to see the transformation firsthand. The site was unusually still—the day's clamor replaced by a serene silence, as though the very ground were exhaling after weeks of relentless labor.

Brock stood near an open bay, clipboard clutched in hand, the last rays of sunlight igniting a warm glow on his skin. His shirt, soaked with sweat and dust, clung to his muscular frame. Every contour—from his broad chest sprinkled with dark, sweat-matted hair to the gentle roundness of his belly—told a story of relentless hard work.

Jim cleared his throat as he approached, a crooked smile tugging at his lips. "Long day, huh?" he asked, his voice soft yet resonant in the warm, still air.

Brock looked up, his eyes bright with mischief, and grinned in return. "You could say that." He carefully set his clipboard on a nearby workbench before heading toward his truck. Rummaging in the backseat, he pulled out a fresh shirt with casual ease. "Feels like I've been out here for a month," he joked in a low, rumbling timbre. Without a second thought, he began peeling off his drenched shirt, revealing a sweat-slicked body that shimmered in the fading light. Grabbing a towel, he methodically wiped beads of sweat from his thick neck and broad, defined shoulders, his movements both deliberate and unhurried.

Jim's eyes involuntarily lingered on the raw display of physicality—the glistening skin, the way the shirt clung and revealed hints of hardened muscles, even the subtle outline of his nipples peeking through tufts of hair. A rush of heat blurred Jim's vision, and he quickly pretended to examine the scattered debris, though part of him was magnetically drawn back to Brock.

Catching Jim's lingering gaze, Brock's expression turned knowingly ambiguous as he applied deodorant before fanning himself with the clean shirt. His voice dropped a notch, "So… you never did tell me why you stopped by today."

Jim attempted to steady his voice, feeling the evidence of his arousal hidden beneath the tight fabric of his uniform pants. "I guess I just wanted to see how things were shaping up. You mentioned the demo was finished and framing nearly wrapped up, so I had to check it out." He rubbed the back of his neck, adding in a husky tone, "And, I was curious—why Brookstone? Most folks would pass over a place like this without a second thought."

Brock shrugged, slipping into the fresh shirt with practiced ease. His gaze met Jim's steadily, every inch of him exuding earnest sincerity. "Brookstone's different," he said softly. "This isn't just another city project where someone slaps up condos and calls it a day. There's history here, in these old buildings, and in the people who call it home. When I first saw these warehouses online, I couldn't let them go. I was searching for something real—something that wouldn't vanish like the latest trend."

Jim's heart tightened at the raw passion in Brock's quiet confession. "I get that," he whispered, his voice laden with unspoken truths. He buried his hands deeper in his pockets, trying to hide the unmistakable reaction stirring within him. "Sometimes you just want to be part of something that feels enduring…it has to mean something."

A charged silence stretched between them as the sun's last rays bled away into twilight. Jim's eyes drifted from Brock's captivating lips back to those deep, probing eyes, each second heavy with possibility. His mind raced with thoughts of crossing an invisible line, even as he wrestled with the propriety of it all.

With a gentle clearing of his throat, Jim finally stepped back. "I should… probably get going," he stammered unsteadily. "But let me know if you need anything else."

Brock's gaze remained steady and warm, a subtle smile curving his lips as he replied, "I will. And hey, how about you let me cook dinner for you one night? Consider it a thank-you for all your help on this project."

Jim's heart leaped in his chest as he met Brock's inviting eyes. For a long, suspended moment, the weight of that simple proposition filled the air between them—a promise of something more intimate than either had dared imagine. "Yeah," Jim managed, his smile quiet but genuine. "I'd like that."

Brock's smile widened, his eyes twinkling with the certainty of shared secrets. "Good," he said, as if fate had already sealed the deal.

As Jim turned back toward his SUV, his pulse pounded in his ears, and his mind swirled with thoughts of unexplored paths. The pull of an unknown future, charged with both risk and the thrill of possibility, made him wonder if perhaps this was exactly where he was meant to be. The soft warmth of Brock's gaze lingered, and as Jim drove away under the starry canopy of night, he found himself eagerly anticipating that dinner—more than he'd ever intended to admit.

# Chapter 4
# Dinner Date

The Saturday sun was slowly dipping toward the horizon as Brock moved through his meticulously arranged kitchen, the inviting aroma of rosemary and garlic swirling in the warm air. Every moment of his day had been dedicated to tonight—countless hours spent marinating perfect steaks, handpicking and arranging vibrant, fresh-cut flowers, and adjusting every detail of his table setting with painstaking care. It wasn't simply about impressing Jim; it was about unveiling a side of himself that had long remained hidden from the world.

Brock paused to survey his home, ensuring that every item was exactly in place. After weeks of reworking the old Spence decor into a fusion of rustic charm and contemporary style, every room now told its own story. In the living room, the exposed brick fireplace merged with rich stained wood trim, complementing plush leather chairs and exposed beams that echoed warm memories. In the dining area, a salvaged, vintage chandelier bathed the polished oak table in a soft, golden glow. Every detail had been thoughtfully chosen, creating a space that was both nostalgic and modern.

Taking a slow, steadying breath, Brock ran a hand through his hair and checked his appearance one last time in the mirror along the hallway. His faded jeans and casual button-down shirt might have suggested a laid-back persona, but underneath, a current of nervous energy buzzed, a reminder that it had been far too long since he'd put in this sort of effort for someone.

Then came the doorbell. Brock's heart skipped a beat. He wiped his hands on a dish towel and stepped to the door, opening it to reveal Jim standing there. Jim looked effortlessly appealing in his dark, well-fitted jeans and a crisp polo shirt. His hair was charmingly tousled, and the ease in his smile was disarming. "I hope I'm not too early," Jim said, his voice a blend of excitement and a hint of nervousness as he offered a six-pack of his favorite IPA with a playful grin.

"Just in time," Brock responded warmly as he stepped aside to invite him in. "Please, come on in and make yourself comfortable."

Jim's gaze wandered appreciatively over the spacious, well-designed interior—the open floor plan, the inviting furniture, and every carefully selected accent piece. "Wow," he breathed, his voice laced with genuine admiration. "This place is incredible. I remember visiting Spence so many times over the years, and now it feels like a completely new world. You've really transformed it."

A swell of pride filled Brock. "Thank you," he said modestly. "I poured my heart into it. I thought you'd appreciate a little tour. Let me show you everything I've done."

Room by room, with increasing detail and animated dialogue, Brock guided Jim along. He explained the story behind the reclaimed wood floors and pointed out vintage fixtures that had been touched up with modern styling. "Look at the wall art," Brock remarked, his hand gesturing toward carefully placed pieces. "I wanted a palette that was deep and resonant—rich dark blues, warm cream tones, with occasional contrasts that really pop unexpectedly."

The tour reached the study, where Jim paused before a worn leather chair set next to a tall bookshelf filled with an unexpected mix of construction manuals and classic literature. His voice softened as he spoke, "I love this look—it's like the house is telling its own history, each piece a chapter. It even seems like something straight out of an interior design magazine."

Brock met his gaze and smiled. "That was exactly my plan. I wanted it to feel distinctly like home."

As they returned to the dining room, the gentle hum of anticipation increased. The meal was spread out with deliberate care: steaks perfectly seared to a tantalizing brown, roasted vegetables glistening with caramelized edges, and a salad drizzled with a viscous balsamic glaze. A bottle of wine, already allowed to breathe, rested beside two exquisitely set glasses.

"Wine, or should we start with the beer you brought?" Brock inquired, his eyes dancing with warmth.

Jim's response was thoughtful, "I think the wine will perfectly compliment your incredible cooking. Let's begin with that and save the IPA for later."

They settled into their seats, and as they began their meal, every bite of food was matched by an exchange of increasingly intimate dialogue. Between forkfuls, Brock opened up about his childhood, the odd jobs that built his practical nature, and his fateful decision to leave the relentless pace of city life behind for a dream of lasting change in Brookstone. "In the city, everything felt too rushed," Brock admitted quietly, eyes intent. "The projects were built just to sell quickly. Here, I can invest time—create something enduring."

Jim nodded with understanding, leaning forward as he said, "I can see that passion in every corner of this house. What you've built—it's truly impressive."

Brock's gaze softened as he looked across the table, almost hesitating as he added, "Hearing that from you means a lot, Jim." His tone carried a vulnerability that belied his confident words.

Before long, the food was finished, and the wine glasses were nearly empty. Brock suggested, "Why don't we take our drinks out on the back porch? The crispness in the evening air is a relief after such a warm meal."

Outside, the cool air mingled with the lingering aroma of dinner and freshly cut grass, and the sky deepened into twilight, dotted with the first hints of emerging stars. Brock eased into one of the cushioned patio chairs, beer in hand, and pointed toward the wide, open yard. "I was actually thinking of adding a pool here someday… and perhaps a hot tub by the pergola."

Jim laughed softly as he took a thoughtful sip of his beer. "You're not planning to turn this place into a full-blown resort, are you?"

Brock grinned, his eyes twinkling in the dim light. "Nah, nothing that extravagant. I just want it to be a space where both guests and I can really unwind."

Their dialogue continued to flow easily, with laughter and playful teasing underscoring the unspoken energy between them. Amid their easy banter, each accidental brush of a hand and lingering glance kindled a deeper connection. Jim's senses were on high alert—he noted the subtle scent of cologne on Brock's skin and found himself increasingly drawn to the warmth in Brock's steady, confident laugh.

When Brock's shirt shifted to reveal a sliver of tanned skin above his jeans' waistband, Jim's heart raced. He took a longer swig of his beer, trying to mask the sudden heat flooding his face. Brock, noticing the effect, teased kindly, "Looks like you might have had a bit more than your usual share tonight. I can't imagine you driving like this."

Jim chuckled, his tone self-deprecating. "Yeah, probably not my best idea. Thanks for looking out."

A pause fell between them before Brock offered, "I have a guest room set up with fresh linens and everything. You're welcome to stay if you're not feeling up for a drive."

Jim's eyes flickered with relief and a hint of something tender. "Really? That sounds amazing. I'd like that."

They exchanged a lingering look that spoke volumes, neither fully willing to articulate the cocktail of emotions swirling between them. Rising from their seats, Jim felt the comforting and confiding presence of Brock beside him as they retreated back into the house.

Inside, Brock led Jim upstairs to a charming guest room, its cozy aura enhanced by a queen bed draped in a soft, inviting quilt. "I hope this feels as comfortable as it should," Brock murmured in a quiet, reassuring tone.

Jim stepped into the room, his eyes roaming appreciatively before finally meeting Brock's steady gaze. "It's perfect, truly," he replied, his voice almost a whisper, heavy with gratitude.

There was a pregnant pause, a silence replete with unspoken wishes before Brock broke it with a soft, "Well then, good night."

As he turned toward the hallway, Jim's quiet call halted him.

"Brock?"

Brock paused, turning back slightly with a raised eyebrow in gentle inquiry. "Yes?"

Jim's voice wavered slightly as he responded, "Thank you… for dinner. For everything tonight."

Brock's expression softened into a smile, his eyes filled with a sincere warmth. "Anytime, Jim. Anytime." With that, he continued down the corridor, leaving Jim watching him with an intensity that lingered long after the door closed behind him.

Jim slumped onto the guest room bed, his mind buzzing with unspent energy and emotion, the taste of the evening still vibrant on his lips. He wondered if perhaps tonight had hinted at something far deeper than a simple dinner—a connection that yearned for more.

A short while later, Brock found himself pausing outside the guest room once more. His hand rested against the door, slightly ajar, and he could hear the soft rustling of fabric within. Gently, he knocked and stepped closer. The door inched open an extra bit, revealing Jim standing in the soft lamplight, gazing at a collection of framed Star Wars movie posters that adorned the wall above an antique dresser. Each poster, complete with signatures from George Lucas and the original cast, made up a prized collection that spoke of Jim's lifelong love for the saga.

Yet Brock's attention was drawn away from the artwork. His eyes roamed slowly over Jim's form. There, standing in nothing but a pair of thin, almost translucent white boxer briefs, Jim's toned and well-defined physique was illuminated by the room's subtle lighting. Every muscle along his broad back, chiseled shoulders, and tapering torso was revealed in arresting clarity.

A soft dusting of dark hair traced a path from his chest to the waistband of his briefs that barely concealed a delectable bulge outlining his dick and balls. His skin glowed with a natural, healthy sheen. Brock's heart pounded, a heat rising unmistakably along his chest and cheeks as he found himself almost entranced by the sight. His own cock coming to full attention at the sight of nearly naked Jim.

For a full minute Jim stared at Brock as his gaze consumed every inch of him. Jim's head jerked slightly as he realized he'd been caught staring. His cheeks burned crimson as he offered an awkward, self-conscious laugh while reaching for the plush robe draped at the foot of the bed. "Uh, sorry about that," he mumbled, voice thick with embarrassment as he wrapped the robe around his shoulders and cinched it tightly at the waist. "I didn't expect you back so soon."

Instantly snapping out of his reverie, Brock cleared his throat and fumbled to shift the focus away from Jim's exposed allure. "No, it's…it's fine," he stammered, taking a tentative step into the room. Holding out a stack of plush white towels and a washcloth, he added, "I just came to leave these for you. I run a full-service establishment here." he chuckled. Their fingers briefly brushed an electric contact that neither could fully ignore amidst the charged silence.

Jim accepted the towels with a warm, appreciative smile. "Thanks, Brock. You've really thought of every little detail. This guest room feels more like a luxury suite," he remarked, a teasing lilt in his voice.

Brock leaned casually against the doorframe, his arms folded as he continued, "I want you to feel right at home. And I thought you might appreciate the Star Wars collection, too. I've always had a feeling you're a sci-fi enthusiast."

The transformation in Jim's expression was instantaneous. His eyes lit up with genuine excitement as he stepped closer to the posters. "Oh, absolutely," he exclaimed with delight, his voice bubbling with enthusiasm. "I've been a fan for as long as I can remember. These pieces… the signatures, the original artwork—they're like treasures from another world. How on earth did you manage to put together such an amazing collection?"

Brock chuckled softly, a mixture of pride and humility in his tone as he replied, "Let's just say it took persistence, a bit of luck, and more money than I'd care to admit. I spent years tracking down those elusive posters. The one from A New Hope, in particular, almost broke the bank—it took nearly five years to secure it and cost more than everything else combined."

Jim's gaze softened further as he said, "That's really something. I'm a lifelong fan, but I've never seen a collection this impressive outside of the occasional convention."

A playful smile danced on Brock's lips. "Then I guess we're both a bit nerdy, aren't we? I never imagined you'd be as into sci-fi as I am."

"Are you kidding?" Jim laughed warmly. "Sci-fi is in my blood. My dad used to take me to every opening night. I still vividly remember going to see The Phantom Menace as a kid—it was magical."

Brock's smile widened, his heart warming at the nostalgia that mingled with their shared interests. "Those sound like beautiful memories."

They fell into a rhythm of gentle, flirtatious conversation, the charge between them palpable. Brock felt an irresistible tug, a desire to step closer and close the widening gap. His pulse quickened as he noticed the clock on the bedside table—a silent reminder of the delicate balance they teetered on. Reluctantly, he pulled back. "Anyway," he said, voice returning to a more casual tone, "the guest bath is stocked with everything you might need—soap, shampoo, lotion, even hair products."

Jim, though a trace of disappointment flickering in his eyes, managed a grateful smile. "Thanks, Brock. You really have outdone yourself."

I just want you to be completely at ease here," Brock replied, his hand grasping the door frame as if tethering himself back to reality. "I'll let you get some rest now. Good night, Jim."

"Good night," Jim whispered, his tone heavy with lingering warmth as he watched Brock retreat down the hall, feeling the weight of the moment settle over him.

As Brock walked back down the hall to his bedroom, he was engulfed by conflicting emotions—relief at having kept some control, yet regret that the magnetic pull between him and Jim was so dangerously potent. His cock still throbbed in his tight jeans. Leaning heavily against his own door, he exhaled slowly, trying to quell the persistent images of Jim's body and that easy, charged smile.

Yet, no matter how much he tried, Brock couldn't dismiss the thought that tonight had shifted something between them. The subtle, electric current in the air was not a fleeting moment—it was the beginning of something deeper, something real. Brock was pretty sure Jim had been checking out his package while he was checking out Jim's beautifully sinful body. And for the first time in a long while, he found himself suspended between the urge to move closer and the fear of overstepping unspoken boundaries.

Brock returned to the master suite with his mind awash in vivid, almost inescapable images. The memory of Jim standing there, clad in nothing but those near-transparent white boxer briefs, was seared into his consciousness. Jim's toned, sculpted body, that pert bubble butt and more than ample bulge—each muscle defined under the soft glow of the bedside lamps—evoked both admiration and desire.

As Brock closed his bedroom door behind him, a heavy sigh burst from his lips. He ran his fingers through his hair, warming the back of his neck, and for a moment, his hand drifted to adjust the evidence of his arousal— a signal from a part of him long left dormant.

Crossing his spacious bedroom, Brock opened the door to his walk-in closet. Methodically, he began to undress, tossing his clothes into the wicker hamper with deliberate care. Standing before a tall mirror that lined the inside of the door, he studied his own naked reflection for a long moment. He knew he was handsome in his own rugged way—a bear with a body that carried its own quiet strength. He smoothed his hand over the firm, the rounded softness of his fuzzy belly, then savored the sight of the well-muscled, perky curves of his own ass. A fleeting, irreverent thought crossed his mind: "Jim has a beautiful ass, too—I bet it's as solid as mine." The memory made his cock throb. Chuckling softly to himself, he quickly shoved the thought aside as he slipped into a pair of silk sleep shorts.

Brock sank down onto the edge of his bed, the fresh linens cool beneath his fingers as he gripped the edge of the mattress. He could still see it in his mind's eye—Jim's smile, that teasing little smirk as he turned to head to his room. His skin tingled at the thought of reaching out, letting his hands run over that smooth, warm flesh. As the image played out in his mind, his breath deepened, his pulse quickening with the growing tension in his body. His cock was now standing at full attention, aching for release.

He leaned back against the headboard, closing his eyes as his hand moved to his hairy chest, flicking the hard nub of his nipple before fingertips tracing a path down to his stomach, then even lower. It wasn't just Jim's body that stirred him; it was the energy between them, the unspoken pull. He could imagine Jim's voice, low and teasing.

*"What's the matter, Brock? Can't take your eyes off me?"* It wasn't just the words, but the way Jim might say them, playful but with an edge as if daring Brock to do something about the desire building between them. And Brock began to stroke his throbbing erection. Sliding languidly up and down his substantial length.

In his mind, the scenario unfolded. Jim was closer now, just inches away. Brock could almost feel the warmth of his breath, see the slight rise and fall of his chest. *"You've been looking at me like that all night,"* Jim's voice murmured in his fantasy, the words sending a shiver down Brock's spine. He could imagine Jim reaching down, untying the robe and letting it fall to the floor in a heap at his feet. *"Why don't you do something about it?"*

Brock's hand picked up the pace as he leaned over to the nightstand and retrieved a bottle of lube, and squeezed out a small amount on the tip of his already leaking cock. He circled his hand over the slick top and then returned to stroking with the new smooth gliding sensation afforded by the liquid. His breath hitched as he imagined reaching out to Jim, drawing him close, the feel of that firm, youthful body pressing against his. There was a vulnerability and a strength in the idea, a moment where boundaries blurred and needed to be taken over.

He could almost hear Jim's quiet gasp as he pulled him close, their bodies colliding with a mix of restraint and urgency. The thought alone made Brock's heart race and his cock throb. His senses heightened as he let himself indulge in the fantasy of what it might feel like to finally act on the tension simmering between them.

His fingers tightened around the girth of his dick, the sensation intensifying with each passing second. His imagination took him further, Jim's voice echoing in his ears, now a breathless whisper. *"I've wanted this, too,"* he might confess as if admitting a secret kept for far too long.

The fantasy wrapped around him, enveloping Brock in a rush of heat and longing. It wasn't just about satisfying a need; it was about the connection, the possibility of something real, something more. With that thought, the fantasy seemed to shimmer, blurring the line between what he desired and what he feared wanting too much.

He opened his eyes, breath heavy, and allowed himself a moment to bask in the sensations, the remnants of that imagined encounter as he shot thick ropes of cum up onto his hairy stomach as his climax overtook him. There was a thrill in the longing, an excitement in the potential for what might happen if he dared to push the boundaries between him and Jim. But for now, it was just a fantasy, one that left him both fulfilled and craving more—a reminder of the feelings he thought he'd buried long ago, but that was now reawakening in unexpected and enticing ways.

# Chapter 5
# Denial and Discomfort

Jim woke late that Sunday, a dull ache in his head reminding him of the extra beers he'd had last night. As he lay there, staring at the ceiling, flashes of the previous evening came back—Brock's easy laughter, the gleam in his eyes when he'd talked about his plans for the backyard, the way he'd looked at Jim when he'd stood there half-naked in the guest room. Jim groaned, burying his face in the pillow. He tried to push the memory away, tried to shake off the heat that crept into his cheeks whenever he thought about it.

It was admiration, he told himself. That's all it was. Brock had a self-assuredness that Jim envied—a confidence in who he was and what he wanted that Jim had never found in himself. He admired that about Brock. It wasn't anything else.

But then why had his gaze lingered, tracing the lines of Brock's shoulders, the curve of his jaw? Why had he felt that restless urge in his gut to step closer, to reach out and touch him?

Jim's phone buzzed on the nightstand, pulling him from his thoughts. It was a text from Brock, casual and friendly, thanking him for a great evening and saying he'd left a thermos of coffee on the kitchen counter. Jim's fingers hovered over the keyboard, struggling to think of a reply. He was grateful for Brock's hospitality, of course, but something in him balked at the idea of keeping up the friendly banter. It felt too… intimate, too dangerous now. He texted a quick thanks back and tossed the phone aside, letting out a heavy sigh.

As he got up and made his way to the kitchen, Jim's thoughts drifted to Joanne Stevens, the FBI agent he'd hooked up with a few months ago. She'd been confident, assertive, and a little wild—the kind of woman who knew what she wanted and wasn't afraid to go after it. The chemistry had been there, sure, but it had always felt more like a game, a temporary distraction, than something real. He hadn't felt any deeper connection, hadn't wanted more from her than what she'd offered. That night had been fun but not memorable. Nothing stuck with him the way his moments with Brock seemed to be lingering now.

He tried to convince himself that his mind was just playing tricks on him, that he was reading into things too much. But the pull he felt toward Brock wasn't just admiration. It wasn't the same kind of friendship he'd felt for other men in his life. There was something undeniably different about it, a magnetic draw that made his stomach clench in a way he wasn't used to. He glanced at the thermos Brock had left for him and felt an unexpected pang of longing, which unsettled him even more.

After he finished the coffee, he headed back to his apartment. He settled into the driver's seat of his SUV, and that's when he noticed more than one neighbor out and about on this lazy Sunday morning. So people would know that he'd spent the night at the house of the newcomer to the town. The gay newcomer. It was completely innocent. He'd had too much to drink and just crashed there. No big deal. Easily explained. He tried to clear his head on the drive home. But, the ride proved unsuccessful.

He walked into his somewhat messy living room and flopped down on the couch. In a bid to clear his head, Jim turned on the TV, flipping through channels without really seeing what was in front of him. His mind kept drifting back to Brock, to the way he felt when Brock's gaze had lingered on him just a little too long. Almost against his own will, Jim found himself on his laptop, searching for videos that might help him make sense of what he was feeling. His fingers trembled slightly as he typed "gay porn" into the search bar.

The variety of results that appeared on the screen was overwhelming. There were so many different kinds—so many labels, subgenres, variations. He felt a flush of embarrassment as though someone could see what he was doing. His eyes darted over the thumbnails, his mouth dry, his fingers hovering over the touchpad. He wasn't sure what he was looking for or even why he was doing this, except that he needed to know. He needed to understand why his mind kept circling back to Brock and what that might mean.

He clicked on a video that seemed relatively tame and watched, his emotions a chaotic mix of curiosity and discomfort. Two guys that looked like swimsuit models sat on a small sofa, chatting about how their girlfriends weren't putting out and how horny they were. The scene progressed to jerking off. Jim thought, I'm pretty sure tons of guys have jerked off together, although he never indulged with a buddy. Some of it intrigued him, while other parts left him feeling even more confused. The two men undressed completely and reached across, jerking each other. Then tentatively, one leaned over and started sucking the cock of his friend. Taking the thick length down his throat to the base. This was nothing like his experiences with women—there was a different kind of intensity, a roughness and a tenderness combined that stirred something in him. The guy that had been sucking cock withdrew from the pulsing cock of his buddy and moved in for a kiss. It was tentative at first but quickly deepened, and the men explored each other's bodies with their hands and mouths with their tongues. Jim's heart raced. Suddenly, he realized he was hard, and he slapped the laptop shut. He tried to shake off the feeling, to push it down as just another meaningless impulse. Time for a shower. A cold shower.

Later that afternoon, Jim called Spence. They hadn't talked in a while, but he needed to speak to someone who might understand—someone who might have some insight. After the usual small talk, Jim found himself hesitating, unsure of how to broach the subject.

"Hey, uh, I've got a bit of a… strange question," Jim said, his voice faltering. "You know Brock, right?"

Spence chuckled on the other end. "Sure do. I went by the warehouses a couple of times to see Chandler or drop off something and had the chance to meet him. Really nice guy. What's going on? Did he invite you to one of his backyard parties yet?"

"Not yet," Jim replied, forcing a laugh. "I'm just… I don't know. Trying to figure something out. He mentioned he's, uh… a bear?" The term felt foreign on his tongue. "What did he mean by that?"

"Yeah, that's kind of his thing," Spence said. "In the gay community, 'bear' usually refers to a bigger, hairy guy who's masculine. It's kind of a subculture. Why? What did he say to you?"

Jim shifted in his seat, his cheeks heating up again. "No, no. He didn't. I just—" He broke off, trying to find the right words. "It's nothing, really. Just… curious. Never heard that word used that way."

Spence's voice softened. "Jim, is there something you want to talk about? I mean, if you're questioning anything, it's okay, you know. It's not uncommon to feel confused."

Jim clenched his jaw, swallowing hard. "No, I'm fine. It's nothing like that. Just… never mind. I'll see you guys Wednesday night for supper."

But as he hung up the phone, the sense of unease didn't go away. If anything, it intensified. He felt like a rope being pulled in opposite directions. On one hand, he wanted to retreat into the familiar and the safe. On the other, there was this undeniable curiosity that kept nudging him closer to something he wasn't sure he was ready to face.

He returned to his laptop and, almost impulsively, searched for "gay bear porn." He wasn't entirely sure what to expect, but when the first video started, he found himself drawn to the ruggedness and masculinity on display.

One of the men had a build very similar to Brock and had a bushy dirty brown beard and chest hair. His mind flashed back to Brock, shirtless, mopping the sweat from his hairy muscular chest the other day at the construction site. His breath quickened as he imagined Brock in those roles—the body hair, the broad shoulders, the gruffness of the men—everything about it seemed to resonate with a part of him he hadn't fully acknowledged. His body reacted before his mind could catch up, and his cock throbbed uncomfortably in the tight confines of his jeans.

Out of sheer necessity, he unbuttoned and unzipped his Levi's to release his straining erection. He let out a low groan that mirrored the sounds from his computer. Jim gently kneaded and stroked his dick as he focused on putting Brock's face on the burly men in the video. Intrigued, he watched the entire 17-minute scene.

By the time he finished watching, he was left feeling both aroused and ashamed. But the urgency of his aching balls drove him to continue stroking. As he picked up the pace, he couldn't help picturing Brock. The vision he'd compiled from Brock and the porn stars from the video. Then he imagined Brock pulling him into a strong embrace and claiming his mouth in a passionate kiss. This pushed him over the edge, painting his black *Stranger Things* t-shirt with the evidence of his climax.

After the release, Jim sat frozen for a moment, staring at the mess on his shirt. What had just happened? He'd never gotten off to images of men before. The realization made his stomach churn with anxiety. Quickly, he wiped himself clean, slammed the laptop shut, and tried to push the experience from his mind.

Monday morning found Jim at Caffeine Kick, nursing a large black coffee and trying to forget the confusion of the weekend. He'd barely slept, his mind a battleground of conflicting thoughts. Each time he closed his eyes, Brock's face appeared, sending a jolt through his system that kept him wide awake until dawn.

The coffee shop was bustling with its usual morning crowd—locals grabbing their fix before work, a few tourists passing through, and the regular group of retirees who gathered at the corner table. Jim had chosen a spot near the window.

Jim's attention was drawn to the booth behind him as two elderly women settled in with their coffee cups. He recognized them immediately - Ms. Emma Caldwell and Ms. Ruth Bennett, fixtures at First Baptist for as long as he could remember.

"I simply cannot believe Spence would even ask Pastor Walters such a thing," Ms. Emma said, her voice carrying clearly despite her attempt at a whisper. "To officiate a ceremony that goes against everything the Bible teaches us!"

Jim tensed, realizing they were discussing his cousin. He pretended to focus on his phone while straining to hear their conversation.

"The pastor could have been kinder about it," Ms. Ruth replied, stirring her coffee slowly. "Telling Spence and Chandler they weren't welcome anymore was uncalled for. Spence has been a member of that church his whole life."

Ms. Emma's pearl necklace clicked against her saucer as she tapped it firmly against the table. "The Bible is quite clear on this matter, Ruth. Leviticus 18:22 states that a man shall not lie with another man as with a woman. It's an abomination."

Ms. Ruth sighed, shaking her head. Her curly gray hair bounced slightly with the movement. "Emma, you can't just cherry-pick verses. What about 'love thy neighbor as thyself'? What about John 13:34, where Jesus commands us to love one another?"

Jim found himself unable to look away from his phone now, his coffee cooling as he remained perfectly still, listening.

"Love the sinner, hate the sin," Ms. Emma replied primly, taking a delicate sip of her coffee. "Pastor Miller is right to uphold biblical principles. A church wedding for two men? It's simply unthinkable."

"It's simply not Christian," Ms. Emma continued, her voice rising slightly. "First, the school board makes him principal, putting him in charge of impressionable children, and now he wants the church to validate his... lifestyle? There are boundaries that shouldn't be crossed."

"The children adore Principal Harlow," Ms. Ruth countered, her gentle voice firm with conviction. "He's transformed that school with his kindness and dedication. The test scores are up, bullying is down, and the teachers have never been happier."

Jim shifted in his seat, torn between walking away and staying to defend his cousin's honor.

"That's beside the point," Ms. Emma sniffed. "Romans 1:27 speaks of men committing shameful acts with other men and receiving the due penalty for their error. We cannot ignore God's word."

"And Galatians tells us the fruit of the Spirit is love, joy, peace, patience, kindness, goodness, faithfulness, gentleness, and self-control," Ms. Ruth replied, her voice warming with passion. "Where is the kindness in turning away two people who only want to celebrate their love? Where is the gentleness in making them feel unwelcome in their spiritual home?"

Jim's fingers tightened around his coffee cup. His cousin Spence had been like a brother to him growing up. The thought of him being rejected by the community that had raised him made Jim's blood simmer.

"It's not about kindness, Ruth. It's about moral standards," Ms. Emma insisted. "If we start accepting everything in the name of love, where do we draw the line? Next thing you know, we'll be blessing all sorts of arrangements."

"Arrangements?" Ms. Ruth's voice took on an edge Jim had rarely heard from the usually gentle woman. "Spence and Chandler are not an 'arrangement,' Emma. They're two people who have committed their lives to each other. Two people who have shown more Christian love and charity than half the congregation combined."

Ms. Emma's face flushed with indignation. "I will not sit here and be lectured about Christian values by someone who clearly has lost her way. The Bible—"

"The Bible also says judge not lest ye be judged," Ms. Ruth interrupted, setting her coffee cup down with a decisive clink. She gathered her worn leather purse and rose from her seat, smoothing her floral print dress with dignified movements. "I believe I've heard quite enough. After sixty-seven years, I think it's time I found a church that actually practices what Jesus preached."

She buttoned her cardigan and looked down at Ms. Emma, whose mouth had fallen open in shock.

"Now, if you'll excuse me, Emma," Ms. Ruth concluded, her voice trembling slightly with emotion rather than age.

Jim watched as the elderly woman made her way toward the door, her shoulders squared with quiet dignity despite the slight tremble in her hands. Without thinking, he rose from his seat, abandoning his half-finished coffee. The conversation he'd overheard had struck a nerve too raw to ignore.

"Ms. Ruth," he called, catching up to her just outside the café door. The morning sunlight caught in her silver curls, giving her an almost ethereal glow.

She turned, surprise softening into recognition. "Jim Williamson! My goodness, I didn't know you were there."

"I didn't mean to eavesdrop," he admitted, suddenly feeling awkward. "But I couldn't help overhearing about Spence and Chandler."

Ms. Ruth's eyes filled with emotion. She reached out and hugged Jim. "You are a good man. Your cousin and Chandler are good men. Know that not everyone holds those bigoted and outdated views."

The warm smile Jim had always associated with Ms. Ruth returned. She patted him on the shoulder. "Have a good day, and don't you think another think about that old bitty, Emma. I know I won't." She turned and walked away leaving Jim with a renewed smile as well.

The next few days were uncomfortable. Jim found himself withdrawing from Brock, who undoubtedly noticed the shift. He missed Monday morning coffee at the diner. For the rest of the week, he was more reserved, his easy laughter stifled, his responses short and distracted. And Jim hadn't been by the construction site since their dinner.

Brock, in turn, began keeping things professional, refraining from any friendly touches or invitations. There was a glint of disappointment in Brock's eyes whenever their paths crossed, but he kept his distance as if sensing that Jim needed space.

Meanwhile, the town had started to notice how much time Jim and Brock had been spending together. A few nosy neighbors had made casual remarks—offhand comments about "the bachelor club" or how nice it was that Brock had found a new friend. Even rumors of the night Jim's SUV was parked in Brock's driveway overnight last Saturday. But there was an underlying curiosity, an edge of judgment in some of their words, that made Jim bristle with defensiveness. He wasn't sure why, but he felt like he had to explain himself, to reassure them that he and Brock were just friends. Just neighbors.

The more he pushed back against the town's curiosity, the more he realized it wasn't just them he was trying to convince—it was himself. And that revelation left him more unsettled than ever.

Brock found himself lingering in his truck just a little longer each morning, staring at the dashboard and trying to summon the right excuse to swing by the police station, which was also city hall. There was always some paperwork to follow up on, some minor permit issue he could use as a reason for dropping in. But each time he imagined himself standing awkwardly at Jim's desk, pretending to care about zoning regulations, he felt like a fool.

He hadn't expected to feel this way. Not again, and certainly not about someone like Jim Williamson—a man who, from everything Brock had gathered, had always dated women and probably had a straightforward idea about where his interests lay. But the way Jim had looked at him that night, half-naked and blushing, had sparked something in Brock. It wasn't just lust, although there was plenty of that. It was hope, a yearning for the kind of connection he hadn't had in a long time, if ever.

He couldn't get the image out of his head: Jim standing in the guest room, that slight pink flush creeping up his neck as he reached for the robe, trying to cover himself while still stealing glances at Brock. It was the way Jim's expression had flickered—caught somewhere between embarrassment and curiosity as if he'd been exposed and intrigued at the same time. Brock's stomach tightened every time he thought about it, the tension coiling inside him and refusing to let go.

But since that night, things had changed. Jim had withdrawn as though putting up some invisible wall between them. He still greeted Brock with the same polite smile and still nodded when they passed each other in town, but there was a distance now. The easy camaraderie they'd started to build seemed to have vanished almost overnight. It was as if Jim had pulled back into a shell, and Brock wasn't sure whether he'd pushed too hard or whether he'd just imagined something that wasn't there.

It left Brock feeling lost, doubting his instincts. Maybe he'd misread everything. Maybe Jim had just been freaked out by Brock catching him in his underwear, and that was all it was. Maybe he wasn't interested in men at all, and Brock's open, appreciative stare had just made him uncomfortable. God knows that had happened before, with other men who hadn't been able to reconcile their friendliness with his attraction.

His thoughts drifted back to that moment in the guest room. He remembered how his pulse had quickened when he'd first seen Jim standing there, the soft light filtering in from the window and casting shadows across his strong, well-defined chest. There had been something raw and honest about the sight of him—a vulnerability Brock hadn't expected to see in someone who always seemed so self-assured. And Brock had felt a pull then, something he hadn't allowed himself to feel in a long time. But now, he questioned whether it had been real or just wishful thinking.

He found himself making excuses to drive through town more often than necessary, circling around the station just in case Jim happened to be outside or taking a break. He wandered by during lunch hours, hoping for a chance encounter, telling himself he was only looking for a friendly face to share a meal with. But when he spotted Jim leaving the diner one afternoon, talking to another officer, the young, attractive woman he'd met a couple of times, Amanda. They laughed at some shared joke, and Brock felt a bitter pang of jealousy that he had no right to feel. He had no claim on Jim—didn't even know if he'd want that kind of claim. But it hurt all the same, this growing sense that he was developing feelings for someone who might never be able to return them.

Later that day, he found himself in the hardware store, pretending to browse the aisles even though he wasn't in need of anything. His thoughts kept drifting back to Jim and the way his heart seemed to pick up whenever he caught sight of him. Brock's fingers absently traced the edge of a paint can, the cool metal grounding him as he took a deep breath. What was he doing? It wasn't like him to pine over someone, to loiter like a teenager with a crush. He was a grown man—he'd had relationships before and had felt heartbreak before. But this was different. It wasn't just physical desire; it was the ache for something deeper, for someone to see him and accept him for all that he was.

That was when Brock heard the familiar low timbre of Jim's voice at the front of the store. His pulse leaped, a mixture of anticipation and dread swelling in his chest. He wasn't sure what he'd say if Jim saw him here, lurking in the aisles. It was ridiculous, really. He was a grown man, not some lovesick kid, and yet here he was, hoping for just a moment of Jim's attention. He took a steadying breath and made his way toward the front, keeping his movements casual.

Jim stood at the counter, chatting with the cashier about some repair project he had coming up. He was in uniform, his sleeves rolled up to his elbows, and there was a relaxed smile on his face that made Brock's breath hitch. He looked different when he smiled like that—softer, younger, with a hint of mischief in his eyes. For a moment, Brock just watched him, his heart doing a slow, painful somersault in his chest.

He was about to turn and head out the door when Jim glanced his way, and their eyes met. Jim's smile faded slightly, replaced by something more guarded, but there was a flicker of recognition there, too—a momentary flash of the old familiarity that had once been growing between them. Brock forced a smile, raising a hand in greeting.

"Hey, Jim," he said, trying to keep his voice even. "Didn't expect to see you here."

Jim's nod was polite, but his posture was stiff. "Yeah, just picking up a few things." His tone was friendly enough, but there was a formality to it that hadn't been there before. It was like a wall had gone up between them—a wall Brock wasn't sure how to climb.

"Got a project going?" Brock asked, his hands finding their way into his pockets as if they could somehow ground him in the midst of his uncertainty.

Jim shrugged, avoiding Brock's gaze as he picked up the bag the cashier handed him. "Just some work around the house," he said, his voice trailing off. There was an awkward pause, and Brock could feel the tension in the air, thick and palpable.

The silence stretched on, and just when Brock thought about cutting his losses and heading out, Jim's eyes flicked back up to meet his. There was a question there, something unspoken but searching. Brock could see it—the hesitation, the conflict. It was there for just a moment, but it was enough to make his chest tighten.

"Listen," Jim said, almost reluctantly, "about the other night…" His voice was low, a hint of embarrassment coloring his cheeks. "I'm sorry if I—if things were… awkward."

Brock swallowed, a bitter smile tugging at the corner of his lips. "No need to apologize," he replied, keeping his tone light even as his heart sank. "I'm the one who walked in on you, after all."

Jim gave a small, uncomfortable chuckle, scratching the back of his neck. "Yeah, I guess." He hesitated, glancing down at the floor. "I just… I don't want you to think I'm, you know, weirded out or anything."

Brock's heart leaped at the words. He took a half-step closer, his voice softening. "Jim, you don't have to explain yourself. If you ever want to talk—or just hang out again—you know where to find me."

Jim's gaze met his once more, the guardedness still there but tempered with something else. Curiosity, maybe. Or perhaps it was hope, just like the kind that had been growing in Brock. But whatever it was, it faded quickly as Jim offered a tight-lipped smile. "I appreciate it, Brock," he said, his tone steady and polite. "I'll… keep that in mind."

And with that, Jim turned and left the store, leaving Brock standing there with a hollow feeling in his chest. He wasn't sure if it had been a step forward or just another reminder of the distance between them. All he knew was that he was falling for Jim, and it was a slow, torturous kind of falling. One that felt like it would either end in a soft landing or a hard crash and Brock wasn't sure which one he feared more.

# Chapter 6
# Back on Track

Jim found himself perched on Brock's weathered back porch as the final rays of summer sunlight slipped behind ancient trees, bathing the yard in soft, intermingling hues of gold and blue. He rested on one of the timeworn wooden steps, a cold bottle of beer in hand with beads of condensation trickling down his fingers.

The humid air carried the delicate scent of pine mixed with freshly cut grass while the evening chorus of cicadas began their gentle serenade. It was a simple pleasure—being outside, surrounded by the familiar warmth of Brock's laughter, the sound weaving its way into his heart.

It had taken another week to reach this moment—a careful climb past the uncertainty that had sprouted like wild vines between them since that awkward night at Brock's house. The compelling need to have Brock back in his life had ultimately triumphed over the distance that once separated them.

Now, as they shared a relaxed conversation over beers, Jim sensed a glimmer of normalcy returning. The tight knot of tension in his stomach gradually softened, unwinding under the gentle power of reminiscence and resolve.

With quiet determination, he decided that he could manage the unspoken attraction, even bury it if needed because the depth of their friendship was far too precious to let slip away over emotions that still swirled with confusion.

"Come on, man," Brock called out from a deck chair just a few feet away, his voice laced with teasing mischief. "You can't seriously believe that the Millennium Falcon would fall to a Star Destroyer in a real fight. It's all about speed, agility—"

Jim shook his head, chuckling as he took a hearty swig of his beer. "Sure, if you ignore the fact that a Star Destroyer packs enough firepower to carve a hole the size of Texas in any ship, fool enough to get in its way."

Brock scoffed, leaning back comfortably in his chair and casually crossing one ankle over the other knee. His snug T-shirt clung to his broad shoulders and defined chest, the fabric emphasizing his every movement. Jim quickly averted his gaze, unable to ignore the sudden warmth in his cheeks—a flush that had nothing to do with the cool evening air.

"I'm just saying," Brock continued, a playful glint in his eye, "Han Solo has never lost a fight that he couldn't talk his way out of."

Jim's laughter mingled seamlessly with the ambient hum of the night, evoking memories of countless shared afternoons filled with light-hearted banter. In that moment, he realized just how much he had missed the effortless camaraderie they once enjoyed. He had worked hard to push aside his doubts and remind himself that Brock was still the same loyal, spirited friend—and that whatever flickered between them did not need to unmoor their bond.

Even if that subtle spark of attraction flared up every now and then, Jim reassured himself it was nothing more than deep admiration, much like the appreciation one might have for another's confidence or witty charm. Brock was undeniably attractive, and anyone observing him would agree—but for Jim, it was simply part of the essence of his best friend.

"Alright, alright," Brock said, lifting his bottle in a mock gesture of surrender as his eyes met Jim's over the small distance between them. "You win. I suppose the Star Destroyer does trump the Falcon. But just wait until I tell the guys at the bar—you'll be public enemy number one."

Jim's smirk was full of good-natured defiance as he met Brock's gaze. "Let 'em try," he replied, his voice carrying a challenge. "I'm ready for whatever they throw my way."

A brief silence ensued, punctuated only by the soft murmur of cicadas and the distant hum of cars on a faraway highway. In that quiet moment, Jim caught a look in Brock's eyes—a blend of affection and something deeper, an unspoken longing that Jim recognized all too well and had learned to sidestep. Clearing his throat, he set his empty bottle on the step beside him.

"You ready to head inside?" Jim asked softly, a gentle invitation threading his tone. "That sci-fi marathon isn't going to watch itself."

Brock blinked, a spark of mischief in his crooked smile as the moment flashed by, and he nodded, murmuring, "Yeah, sure." Rising from the chair with a fluid, almost predatory ease that sent an unexpected thrill through Jim, Brock led him inside. The living room's cool air embraced them, a soothing caress on Jim's skin that heightened every sensation. As Brock walked ahead, Jim couldn't help but steal a lingering glance at the powerful curve of Brock's muscular thighs clad in scandalously short shorts, drawing attention to the inviting swell of his round ass. Flustered, Jim shifted his gaze to the television, collapsing onto the leather couch, his pulse quickening.

The room was bathed in dim, intimate light, with Brock already having arranged their customary movie night setup. A bowl of buttery popcorn sat temptingly on the coffee table, its rich aroma mingling with the tantalizing scent of Brock's cologne—a woodsy, clean fragrance that seemed to whisper promises as Jim breathed it in with a little too much longing.

As the movie began, the simmering tension between them transformed into a charged, comfortable silence. The familiar flicker of the screen, combined with the inviting warmth of the room, wrapped around them like an unspoken promise. Jim nestled on one end of the couch while Brock stretched out regally opposite, legs extended, ankles crossed, and an arm casually draped over the back cushion. Jim's throat tightened as his eyes traced the undeniable allure of Brock's physique.

Though he tried earnestly to focus on the movie, Jim found himself repeatedly sneaking glances at Brock. His well-defined chest and arms, his tree trunk-like thighs, and the more than impressive bulge lifting the crotch of his shorts each took a turn of focus. The way the TV's light danced over Brock's face—highlighting the shadowed lines of his beard and glinting in his auburn hair—lent him an effortlessly rugged allure that made Jim's heart race. He knew he should avert his gaze, that his wandering eyes invited dangerous thoughts that impacted his own bulge as he hardened, yet each stolen look only deepened the magnetic pull between them.

Just as Jim wrestled with his growing desire, Brock turned and caught him in the act. Their eyes locked, a charged stillness hanging between them as if time itself hesitated. In Brock's gaze was a silent question, a yearning inquiry: What are we doing? Where could this lead? Jim's pulse hammered in response, and before the moment could spiral into something undeniable, he tore his eyes away, refocusing on the flickering screen.

"Hey," Brock intoned softly, his voice low, carrying a hint of vulnerability beneath its usual confident timbre. "You alright?"

Jim offered a quick, too-hasty nod. "Yeah, yeah. I'm fine…just got lost in the movie. I mean, aliens never have beards as impressively full as yours," he added with a playful edge that belied the intensity simmering beneath his words.

"Right," Brock replied with a teasing uncertainty, effortlessly tossing a handful of popcorn into his mouth, his gaze never fully leaving Jim's. "You know," he continued, his tone dipping into a more intimate cadence, "I'm really glad we're doing this again. Just hanging out. I missed it."

"Me too," Jim responded genuinely, as if admitting the truth made him feel bolder. He hadn't realized how much he ached for this—simply being in Brock's presence, surrounded by an unspoken intimacy that needed no definitions. "Honestly, you're probably the best friend I've ever had," he added softly, almost embarrassed by the admission and the lingering warmth of desire it brought.

Brock's expression softened, confidence melting into a tender vulnerability. "Same here," he said, his voice dropping to a near-whisper. "I haven't really felt this way with anyone else." After a brief, nervous pause, he chuckled lightly, "And trust me, I don't say that to everyone."

Jim grinned, the tension lingering now mingling with an unmistakable charge of attraction. "So I should feel pretty lucky, then?"

"Damn right," Brock replied, his grin glowing with a mix of mischief and something deeper, a promise of more unsaid possibilities.

Their conversation drifted seamlessly to lighter topics—work, the latest town gossip, and Brock's ever-evolving renovation projects—yet every shared laugh and every fleeting glance carried an undercurrent of desire. By the end of the movie, the bowl of popcorn was nearly empty, and Jim felt lighter as if the air itself between them had shifted with an erotic energy he hadn't known he was craving.

As they rose to stretch, Brock turned to Jim, his eyes sparkling with a mischievous allure. "Alright, I've got a surprise for you," he said, his tone teasing yet laced with something more. "Be back here Friday night. I'll order pizza, and I've got something extra special planned."

Jim's expression transformed into a mix of intrigue and anticipation. "You're on. See you Friday. I get off at six, so…seven?"

"Perfect," Brock replied, the promise lingering in his voice, leaving no doubt that their connection was evolving into something far more intoxicating than friendship ever had been.

When Friday evening finally arrived, Jim pulled up to Brock's house just as the pizza delivery guy arrived, their timing almost theatrically synchronized. Jim stepped into the warm, inviting foyer carrying the heavy pizza boxes and called out in a playful tone, "I'm here, big guy. Ready for my surprise?" His words echoed off the walls, laced with anticipation.

In the kitchen, Brock emerged like a conductor, ready to set the evening's mood—a towering, oversized picnic basket cradled in his arms. The basket overflowed with neatly arranged paper plates, crisp napkins, assorted cutlery, and, notably, a six-pack of beer resting in a small, ice-filled bucket that clinked pleasantly as he set it down.

"Perfect timing," Brock remarked, his voice rich with a mix of humor and pride. He eased himself onto the couch, remote clutched in hand, and it wasn't long before the television erupted into a riot of brilliant pinks, blues, and yellows. The sound system boomed, filling the room with an immersive symphony of audio that perfectly synchronized with the vivid display.

Jim's gaze shifted to the screen as the opening sequence of a show familiar from Spence's enthusiastic mentions began to play. His brows knitted in curious surprise.

"Is that… RuPaul's Drag Race?" he asked, his voice mingling incredulity with a spark of delight.

"Damn straight—or, you know, maybe not so straight," Brock joked, his laughter warm and rich. "But yes. I think it's time you got a little culture in your life."

Jim's eyes danced with a mix of amusement and intrigue as he turned toward Brock. "Are you seriously telling me you watch this?" he inquired, a half-smile tugging at his lips.

"Religiously," Brock replied, settling deeper into the plush embrace of the couch and patting the empty space beside him. "Come on, you'll love it. Trust me."

With a resigned sigh that bore the weight of a thousand friendly challenges, Jim joined him on the couch. As the show began in earnest, Jim found himself irresistibly drawn in—not only by the lavish extravagance and razor-sharp humor of the performers but also by the unfiltered confidence and raw authenticity they exuded. A tangible freedom radiated from their every move, a joyful defiance that struck a chord deep within him.

"I just love Angeria! She's just gotta make it to the top four!" Brock's voice was animated with excitement and anticipation, and his eyes sparkled as he took in every detail on the screen. With each laugh that Brock shared at a clever quip and every gasp he emitted at a dazzling reveal, Jim couldn't help but steal glances at his friend, warm sensations unfurling slowly through his chest.

Brock, meanwhile, lounged back into the sofa, his eyes occasionally drifting toward Jim, who remained fixated on the screen with a captivating blend of amusement and curiosity. Brock's gaze softened as he recalled seeing that same inquisitive look on Jim's face before—the slight furrowing of his brows, the hint of a crooked, lopsided grin that seemed to say he was momentarily lost in thought. Yet tonight, something was subtly different.

As the television cast its vibrant glow across Jim's features, his blue eyes sparkled with a secret, simmering interest that sent a shiver of recognition through Brock's body. It was as if a delicate, electric energy pulsed between them, reminiscent of static building up before a sudden storm.

Brock felt it creeping along his spine, pooling in his stomach as he stole another glance at Jim. He tried desperately to force his focus back to the riot of glittering costumes and theatrical performances on screen, hoping that the spectacle might anchor his thoughts elsewhere. But nothing could distract him—not even the scathing, fiery critiques from Michelle on the other end of the conversation. He could still sense Jim's presence close enough to catch the steady rise and fall of his chest, and the faint, alluring aroma of his cologne—a clean, woodsy fragrance that had become intertwined with Jim's very essence—drifted between them. This heady scent was more intoxicating than any beer or whiskey they had ever shared, leaving Brock's mouth unusually dry and his pulse racing as an inexplicable desire nudged him closer.

He stopped short, caught in that familiar battle between yearning and self-restraint. What was he doing? This was Jim—his best friend with whom he had shared countless evenings filled with beer, sci-fi movies, and deep, dividing conversations about life. It shouldn't feel this way. It shouldn't provoke his body into a chaotic awakening full of latent needs every time Jim was near. And yet, it did—and it was becoming increasingly impossible to conceal. The struggle was not just within his mind; his body, too, fought against the surging tide of affection, trembling in urgent anticipation.

Taking another sip of his beer, the smooth, cool liquid slid down his throat but did little to ease the burgeoning heat within him. As the show progressed, Brock allowed his gaze to wander again to Jim. This time, he lingered a moment longer, taking in every line and curve—the graceful drape of Jim's arm over the back of the couch, the subtle flex of his forearm muscles as he shifted his weight.

The soft, loose fabric of his Yoda T-shirt hugged his form in just the right way, hinting at defined muscles and the gentle contour of curves that stole Brock's attention—over the confident swell of his biceps, the delicate dip at the base of his throat, and the way his collarbones peeked out beneath sun-kissed skin. Each simple detail magnified Jim's attractiveness, deeply ensnaring Brock in a web of forbidden admiration.

And the proximity between them seemed to conspire against him. Jim continued to shift his position, inching ever closer to the couch without a word of noticing. At one point, his knee gently grazed Brock's leg—a light, almost imperceptible touch—but for Brock, it was as if a jolt of electricity had surged straight to his very core. The soft tickle of their leg hair brushing against each other only heightened the sensation, sending a shockwave of heat and desire that he swallowed down hard, desperately trying to maintain a facade of calm and rationality.

"You alright?" Jim's voice cut through the haze of his distraction, grounding Brock back to the present.

Startled, Brock blinked rapidly as his heart danced erratically in his chest. "Yeah, I'm good," he replied too hastily, a crooked grin surfacing to mask his inner turmoil. "Just—can't wait to see your reaction when they lip sync for their life," he added, playfully imitating RuPaul's iconic cadence.

Jim chuckled, his eyes alight with amused delight.

"Told you," Brock continued, tossing a piece of popcorn casually into his mouth. "But you gotta admit, these queens have guts. To put themselves out there like that? It takes balls."

Jim erupted into laughter. "Their balls are 'tucked' away!" he quipped, causing both to share a moment of light-hearted banter.

Brock's smirk belied the torrent of thoughts suddenly flooding his mind—images of other kinds of daring displays bubbled beneath his skin. He admired Jim's effortless confidence, the joyful way he laughed and joked about virtually everything, qualities that Brock cherished deeply even though he rarely admitted it.

In truth, Brock was in awe of Jim—not merely as a cherished friend, but as someone who seemed to fully embrace his own identity without reservation. Brock couldn't help but wonder if he would ever summon that same fearless certainty within himself. The unanswered question gnawed quietly inside him, a mix of envy and longing that spiraled beyond his control.

As the show continued, Brock sank deeper into the soft cushions, the heat building low in his belly and pooling in a subtle but insistent ache that radiated outward. His eyes, almost involuntarily, drifted back to Jim. He took in every detail—the strong, defined line of his jaw, the shadow of a scruff along his cheeks, the natural curve of his lips as Jim laughed heartily at a particularly witty remark from one of the queens.

In that moment, Brock's mind flirted with an impossible fantasy: what would it be like to kiss those lips? His fingers twitched with an impulsive yearning as though begging to reach over and trace the rugged texture of Jim's stubble, to caress the soft contour of his mouth, if only for a fleeting second.

A sudden internal battle surged within Brock. What was wrong with him? Every inch of his body betrayed him, craving something forbidden with a powerful intensity, yearning for a man who might never return the sentiment.

Sure, Jim was tolerant and open-minded—never having hesitated in the face of Brock's playful flirtations or cheeky innuendos—but does that truly signal romantic interest, or was it simply the gentle affection of a good friend indulging in light-hearted banter?

Brock's mind raced as he tried to decipher the subtleties between friendly glances and something deeper, a covert intimacy hidden in the accidental touches and lingering looks. Perhaps those shared glances were insignificant, and those casual touches nothing more than friendly affection.

Perhaps even that night a few weeks ago, when Jim's eyes had lingered a little too long over Brock's bare chest, was nothing more than an innocent anomaly. And yet, tonight, an undeniable tension crackled in the air between them—a palpable energy like static before a summer storm, woven through every lingering glance and every accidental brush of knees as they shifted positions. The once spacious living room now felt confined, charged with an unspoken desire that Brock struggled to deny.

Finally, Brock tore his gaze away from Jim's entrancing features and leaned forward, grasping his beer bottle to distract his trembling hands. He took a long, contemplative drink—the cool liquid doing little to temper the fervor ignited within him—and set the bottle down. In that moment, his hand brushed against Jim's on the table, a fleeting, electrifying touch where fingertips grazed over knuckles. The contact sent a rush of warmth sweeping through him, and when he looked up, he met Jim's steady, dark gaze that was both unreadable and deeply compelling.

"Brock…" Jim began softly, his voice laden with hesitation as though he were on the verge of confessing something significant.

Brock's heart pounded furiously. "Yeah?" he managed in a hushed tone, the single word heavy with anticipation.

Jim seemed to waver, his eyes flitting momentarily to the flickering TV screen before returning to Brock's face. He opened his mouth as if to speak, then paused, shaking his head slowly with a half-apologetic, rueful smile. "You're right," he finally said, his voice gradually gaining confidence. "This show is wild. I don't know how I've gone so long without seeing it. We have to watch Snatch Game next week."

A long-held breath escaped Brock, mingling relief with quiet disappointment as the fleeting, charged moment between them dissolved, swallowed up by the comforting chatter of the television and their shared laughter. Yet, hidden beneath this veneer of camaraderie, that spark persisted—a subtle, electric hum that resonated like a live wire, waiting for the day when one of them might dare to bridge the unspoken gap.

Leaning back against the couch, Brock's thoughts swirled as his pulse continued its erratic dance. He wondered—quietly, desperately—if he would ever muster the courage to be as brave as he needed to be or if he'd remain condemned to a dream of something fervently desired, yet always seemingly just out of reach.

# Chapter 7
# The Wedding

As the day slipped gracefully into the evening, the sun bathed the farmhouse in a warm, golden light, its rays painting the sky in soft hues of amber and rose. The sprawling backyard, set against vast, lush fields, overflowed with guests whose laughter and whispered greetings mingled with the gentle rustle of the breeze.

Rows of pristine white chairs stood in careful alignment, all facing a magnificent archway extravagantly adorned with a cascade of marigold and ivory blooms. Each delicate petal shimmered in the early light, interwoven with twinkling fairy lights that began their slow, enchanting dance as dusk drew near.

Long, flowing navy-blue ribbons trailed down the aisle, their rich hue providing an elegant counterpoint to the farmhouse's rustic charm as if draping the scene in a subtle promise of timeless grace. Near the weathered back door of the farmhouse, Jim stood quietly, meticulously adjusting his marigold bowtie for what felt like the tenth time. He felt a gentle cascade of emotions—excitement, pride, and a deep, rekindled sense of belonging that had long eluded him. His glance swept over the gathering of dear friends, cherished family members, and familiar townsfolk, each clad in their finest. He noticed Ms. Ruth with her newfound friends from the Holy Redeemer Episcipal Church and smiled brightly at her as she waved at him. Then his eyes met Brock's. Seated near the back in a cream-colored summer suit, Brock returned Jim's gaze, and in that fleeting moment, it was as though the entire community of Brookstone had gathered to share in this luminous chapter of his life.

Soft, melodious strains from a nearby string quartet filled the air, their gentle music wrapping around the guests like a tender embrace. Jim drew a deep, steady breath, absorbing the fragrance of wildflowers, the fresh aroma of newly cut grass, and the sweet, nostalgic hint of Ms. Claudean's cakes wafting delicately from the dessert table. His eyes then found Jennifer poised at the threshold of her role as flower girl.

Attired in a flowing, airy white dress topped with a delicate crown of tiny daisies, she resembled a woodland sprite come to life. Her braids, intricately tied with matching marigold and navy ribbons, bounced playfully as she held her basket brimming with soft petals.

The gathered crowd fell silent with anticipation as Jennifer stepped gracefully down the aisle, her face glowing with innocent pride and joy. With every step, she scattered petals into the air, creating a vivid, ever-changing mosaic of color that transformed the aisle into a pathway of hope and promise.

Following her, Cheryl—Chandler's devoted best woman—took Jim's arm, and together they strolled down the aisle. Dressed in an exquisite navy pantsuit accented with shades of cream and marigold that perfectly mirrored the bouquet she carried, Cheryl radiated a refined elegance.

At the far end of the aisle, Chandler emerged, arm in arm with Spence. Both men looked dashing in matching navy suits, their marigold bowties hinting at the warmth of their hearts. A collective exhale of admiration and wonder rippled through the assembled crowd as Chandler's serene yet commanding demeanor captured every onlooker's gaze. His hazel eyes, filled with gentle determination, locked onto Spence's, and in that silent exchange, a world of shared understanding and love was revealed.

Spence's face, lit with a mix of nervous exhilaration and pure, unbridled joy, conveyed that he truly belonged in this moment more than anywhere else in the world. A quiet, peaceful aura enveloped him, a stark contrast to the often tumultuous rhythm of life, making his presence all the more enchanting.

As Chandler's tender smile deepened, Spence's features softened, and it was clear to every witness that, in that single suspended moment, they were the only two souls inhabiting a universe filled with their own private magic.

Under the flowering archway, their hands reached out instinctively, fingers intertwining as if they were meant to be that way from the very beginning. Jim's eyes flickered to Chandler, whose expression overflowed with both awe and deep love, and in that shared glance, Jim felt his heart swell with quiet contentment. Standing beside his cousin and dear friend, he reveled in witnessing a union as sacred and profound as the first blush of dawn.

The officiant, Mother Merrily Dorset's voice, then rose in gentle authority, seamlessly blending strength with tenderness as she spoke of love's transformative power and of the intimate journey that had brought Spence and Chandler to this day. As the sun dipped lower, casting the gathering in a mesmerizing glow of amber, the fairy lights overhead seemed to shine with greater brilliance, their sparkles echoing the magic of the moment. It was as if the evening had been woven from the fabric of a dream, every detail harmonizing perfectly. Jim found his gaze drifting back to Brock, sharing a fleeting look brimming with quiet, shared secrets, each glance intensifying the fluttering butterflies in his stomach.

When the time came for vows, Spence stepped forward, his steady voice filled with heartfelt emotion. "Chandler," he began, his words tender and true as he squeezed Chandler's hand, "I never imagined that I'd find myself here under a starlit sky, surrounded by those dear to us, pledging to share my life with someone who sees and cherishes every part of me. Yet, you entered my life and showed me that love can be so wonderfully simple, so deeply fulfilling, and so fiercely beautiful—worthy of every battle we might face together."

A warm murmur of approval rippled through the assembly as Spence continued, emotion shining in his eyes. "You are not only my best friend but the heart of my world, my sanctuary of joy and peace. I promise, with every beat of my heart, to stand beside you, to laugh with you, and to embrace every twist and turn of life as one. I am profoundly grateful to be intertwined with you."

Chandler's eyes glistened with unshed tears as he slowly blinked them away, each word from his heart heavy with the weight of their shared dreams.

"Spence, you are everything I never knew I so desperately needed," he murmured, his voice thick with moving sincerity. "You infuse my life with light, warmth, and the purest joy. With you, I feel I can breathe completely and live fully. I vow to cherish you, protect you, and build a future as vibrant and beautiful as this very moment."

Jim watched with tender admiration as he noticed a single glittering tear shimmer in Spence's eye before he quickly blinked it away. In a crescendo of emotion, the officiant pronounced them married, and the pair leaned into each other, sharing a kiss both gentle and profound. In that kiss lay the promise of every whispered dream and every unspoken hope, leaving the onlookers awestruck and breathless. The garden erupted in joyful applause, the cheers echoing like the harmonious chorus of a fairytale, as the newly united couple turned to face their loved ones, hands locked together in a timeless embrace.

The reception began as dusk draped its velvety cloak over the farmhouse, casting the yard in a bath of soft, ambient light that seemed to whisper secrets of the coming night. Long tables, elegantly draped in deep navy cloths and tastefully adorned with vases brimming with marigold and ivory blooms, were arranged beneath the sprawling canopy of ancient trees. Overhead, delicate strands of fairy lights twinkled like scattered stars, bathing the joyful gathering in a warm, mesmerizing glow. The air buzzed with the sounds of laughter and the melodic clink of glasses as guests gracefully took their seats.

Jim found himself seated beside Brock, whose playful teasing about his meticulous attention to detail with the bowties added a layer of light-hearted camaraderie to the evening. "You're such a good best man, Jim," she quipped with a mischievous wink, "and looking absolutely sharp." Jim chuckled, his gaze wandering over to Spence and Chandler, who drifted elegantly between tables. They exchanged heartfelt hugs and infectious laughs, their closeness so natural it appeared as if this union had been woven into the fabric of time.

Dinner unfolded as a sumptuous feast—a glorious spread of Southern delights that coaxed even the most reserved appetites into reaching eagerly for seconds. KoKo and Jennifer flitted between the tables, their laughter mingling with the soft murmurs of admiration as they proudly displayed the delicate petals still nestled in their hair, each giggle punctuated by collective "oohs" and "ahhs" from the mesmerized crowd.

As the evening deepened, the couple claimed their moment under a beautifully arched gateway to share their first dance. The music shifted seamlessly into a soulful melody that seemed to encapsulate the air itself as Chandler swept Spence across the dew-kissed grass. Their movements were graceful, almost otherworldly, their private smiles and tender glances creating a bubble of intimacy amid the revelry. It was as though the rest of the world had faded into nothingness, leaving only the soft rhythm of their synchronized steps and the poetry of their connection.

By the time Jim joined the dance floor with Amanda, the night had crystallized into that rare, timeless moment where the clamor of the outside world melted away. He twirled KoKo in dizzying circles, her delighted squeals harmonizing with the night's joyous symphony, and later, he shared an exuberant dance with Mary Dean, whose laughter and breathless excitement punctuated every spin and step. The night overflowed with bursts of laughter, shared stories, and the resounding promise of memories yet to be made. When Jim returned to his place at the table, Brock leaned in with a playful glimmer in his eye and asked, "Do I get a dance with the best man?" His tone straddled the line between jest and a gentle inquiry about their space in the night's unfolding drama.

Jim chucked, but a deep crimson blush washed over his face. Brock laughed. "I did want to ask you a serious question. I have a couple of VIP weekend passes to the Atlanta comic-con next weekend."

"That's not a question," Jim joked.

Brock smirked and continued. "Well, I was wondering if you'd like to go with me? It's going to be a blast!"

"Well, Mr. Curry, I think that sounds like a lot of fun. I'd love to go. Thanks for inviting me."

They shared a warm smile before they excused themselves to speak to other guests.

Later, as Jim lingered near the dessert table, savoring a rich, decadent piece of Ms. Claudean's signature chocolate groom's cake, a gentle hand rested on his shoulder. Turning, he found Spence looking at him with eyes filled with profound gratitude. "Thank you, Jim," Spence murmured softly, his voice layered with sincerity and warmth. "For everything. For being here. For being my friend."

Jim's throat tightened with emotion as he replied, "It has been an honor, Spence. You and Chandler deserve every bit of happiness this world can offer." In that moment, as they embraced, time seemed to slow—a quiet interlude of deep friendship and pure love that resonated amidst the swelling music and the luminous glow of the evening. The world, touched by that shared warmth, appeared a little brighter, a little more hopeful.

As the night wore on and the stars began to glitter overhead, Brock felt a serene peace settle over him like a soft, familiar blanket. In the midst of Spence, Chandler, and the throng of cherished friends, he recognized that he, too, was finding his place in this welcoming small town—a community bound together by love, laughter, and memories that would forever sparkle in the heart.

# Chapter 8
# Comic-Con

The early morning sky was a washed-out, grayish-blue as Brock and Jim busied themselves, loading the car with an assortment of snacks, a sturdy cooler, and their overnight bags. A subtle electric thrill danced in the air—a mirror of the excitement brimming in Brock's heart. He stole a glance at Jim, who was casually tossing the last of their gear into the backseat, his easy grin lighting up his face. Jim's relaxed demeanor, accentuated by his well-worn faded jeans and a beloved Star Wars T-shirt, sent a ripple of warmth through Brock's core, stirring feelings that he tried desperately to keep under control as he climbed behind the wheel.

Their three-hour drive to the convention just outside Atlanta became a canvas for shared passions. The car pulsed with the sounds of classic rock interwoven with their playful banter as they debated passionately about which sci-fi franchise truly reigned supreme.

With every mile, Brock's nervous excitement mounted, each peal of Jim's laughter and even the briefest accidental brush of Jim's shoulder igniting sparks of a deepening, unspoken attraction. In those fleeting moments, as Jim leaned closer to show something on his phone, an unexpected warmth bloomed between them, making Brock's heart quicken with both anticipation and a hint of longing.

By the time they arrived at the buzzing convention center, the sun was high and generous, drenching the scene in a golden glow that made the vibrant crowds seem almost magical. Enthusiastic cosplayers, dressed in intricate costumes, mingled freely with fans of every age, their animated conversations and spontaneous laughter adding to the infectious energy swirling in the air. As Brock and Jim stepped into the main exhibit hall, Brock's pulse raced—not just from the sensory overload of voices, life-sized robot displays, and the tantalizing aroma of buttered popcorn drifting from nearby concession stands, but also from the magnetic excitement he felt every time his eyes met Jim's.

"Man, this place is incredible," Jim breathed, his eyes wide with awe as he took in the meticulous rows of booths and the extravagance of the set pieces around them. Brock watched intently as Jim's gaze flitted from a near-perfect, life-sized replica of the Millennium Falcon cockpit to a vibrant group of fans dressing up as different iterations of Spider-Man. Observing Jim's restless, joyful exploration, Brock felt the growing pull between them intensify, a magnetic thread weaving steadily through his heart.

"Right?" Brock replied with a grin, his voice carrying the warmth of his inner affection. "I could easily see us spending all day just wandering around here." His words hung in the air, laden with an unspoken invitation as his eyes met Jim's, both of them laced with a spark of something tender and forbidden.

A soft, lingering smile danced on Jim's lips—a smile that sent an unmistakable twinge of longing shooting through Brock's veins. Yet, he quickly masked the depth of his feelings, reminding himself that the weekend was meant for fun and camaraderie, not the messy terrain of emotions he wasn't quite ready to explore openly.

They began their tour at the vendor tables, where comic book artists and writers eagerly showcased their creations and animatedly recounted the stories behind their latest issues. Brock lost himself in the vivid illustrations and glossy pages as he carefully thumbed through a stack of comic books, his eyes occasionally drifting to Jim. Jim, meanwhile, moved fluidly from one table to the next, engaging animatedly with a vendor costumed as Captain Kirk.

In those moments, Brock could only watch from a distance, marveling at how effortlessly Jim fit into this world of vibrant energy and shared passions, his presence making Brock's heart lurch with a growing, unspoken attraction that layered every glance and every smile with a deeper, more personal meaning.

As the day progressed, their senses were nearly overwhelmed with enthusiasm and excitement. They attended two panels—one exploring the intricate intersection of science and science fiction that had left Jim practically glowing with intense fascination and another led by a celebrity Q&A where cast members from Battlestar Galactica mingled effortlessly with the audience. By this point, Brock's feet throbbed in protest, and his stomach gnawed at him with hunger—a hunger that danced in rhythmic, enticing echoes with the ache in his chest. Yet his enjoyment was palpable, far surpassing anything he'd felt in what seemed like ages.

"Dude, that panel was awesome," Jim declared with a vibrancy that made his eyes sparkle as they sauntered toward the theater next door for the marathon screening of The Matrix franchise. "I can't believe how into it some of those actors still are. Like, that guy who played Apollo—you could tell he absolutely lives for this stuff."

"Yeah, it's pretty cool," Brock replied, forcing his attention away from lingering too long on Jim's expressive face. His voice had an edge of anticipation; his focus split between the verbal banter and the undercurrent of something much more charged simmering beneath the surface. "And I still can't believe we got him to sign your DVD set. I thought for sure we'd be stuck at the back of the line forever."

A chuckle burst from Jim as he sidled into Brock with a playful shoulder bump. "Guess we got lucky. Good thing you know how to charm people." The word "charm" sent an unexpected jolt through Brock. For a fleeting second, uncertainty and desire tumbled through his mind—was Jim teasing him, or did the comment carry a secret meaning? But as they neared the theater doors, the moment evaporated, their thoughts swept away by the pressing excitement of the night.

Inside the dimly lit theater, they nestled into their seats, a sea of fellow devotees adorned in Neo and Trinity costumes enveloping them. When the lights finally dimmed, and the opening scenes of The Matrix burst into life on the screen, Brock felt a new kind of anticipation stirring within him—dense, intoxicating, heavy with a promise like the beguiling charge in the air before a storm erupts.

Throughout the films, as the narrative of rebellion and destiny unfolded, their bodies inched closer with each passing moment. Even as they were both absorbed by the electrifying on-screen action, neither could ignore the magnetic pull drawing their physical presence into intimate proximity. During the third movie, when Neo and Trinity shared a rare, quiet moment of vulnerability, Brock's fingers brushed against Jim's along the shared armrest. That brief collision of skin sent a shockwave through him—a spark so innocent yet fiercely incendiary that his entire body seemed to ignite. Jim's hand flexed imperceptibly as if tempted to linger longer, to dare the connection to deepen.

They remained like that, with their hands hovering tantalizingly close, neither willing to risk crossing that invisible boundary. Brock felt as if he was standing on the very edge of an abyss—an abyss filled with desire and fear in equal measure. The terror of plunging into unknown depths clashed with the heady allure of possibility.

When the marathon finally concluded, they emerged from the theater well past midnight. The sultry night air wrapped around them like a whisper of secrets, with the sky a glossy expanse of inky black punctuated by a scatter of hesitant stars. As they made their way back to the hotel, their conversation flowed effortlessly, animated with film critiques and teasing remarks—but that energy dimmed when they reached the check-in counter.

"Um, we've got a bit of an issue," the clerk announced while tapping at the keyboard with unwelcome efficiency. "There was a mix-up. Instead of two queen beds, there's only a king available. We don't have any other rooms open at the moment. The convention's got us completely booked."

A tightening in Brock's stomach signaled the arrival of an unforeseen tension as he exchanged a sharp look with Jim, who had grown uncharacteristically still beside him. "Uh, well... I guess we can make it work," Brock managed, his casual shrug belying the flurry of anxious thoughts. "It's just for one night."

Jim nodded slowly, his expression guarded yet hinting at a secret vulnerability—an ember of something unspoken in his eyes. "Yeah, no problem," he said, his voice even while carrying an undercurrent of hesitant longing. "We've crashed in worse places, right?"

The elevator ride was steeped in a charged silence, each floor reminder of the increasing proximity that sparked daring fantasies. When they stepped into the room, the expansive king-sized bed dominated the space—crisp white sheets and an inviting, plush comforter spoke of warmth and intimacy. But all Brock could focus on was the undeniable truth: they'd be lying side by side, their bodies separated by nothing more than a whisper of fabric and a breath of air.

"Guess I'll take the left side," Jim joked with a weak laugh as he tossed his bag onto the bed, pulling out a pair of gym shorts in an almost ceremonial manner. "Unless you've got a preference."

"Nah, left side's fine," Brock replied, his voice betraying a tremor of nervous anticipation. As he retreated to the bathroom, the cold splash of water on his face did little to cool the fire, warming his flushed cheeks. His reflection in the mirror revealed much more than physical fatigue— his eyes shimmered with a mixture of desire and trepidation. It was just a bed, he reminded himself, just two grown men sharing a room, yet the situation vibrated with unspoken intensity.

Upon emerging, he found Jim already nestled beneath the covers, idly flipping through the channels. The faint illumination exposed Jim's torso—firm, sculpted pecs dusted lightly with dark hair. Brock's eyes flickered, trying to convince himself that it was nothing more than a passing glance, though his heartbeat was drumming a sexy, insistent rhythm.

"Nothing but infomercials," Jim murmured, flicking the TV off and casting the room into a deliberate darkness punctuated only by a soft glow from the city outside.

Slipping into the bed beside him, Brock's muscles tensed with each inch he consciously surrendered into the shared space. He could feel the heat radiating from Jim's body, tantalizing proximity that made his throat parched and his chest tightened with desire. Lying there, listening to the steady, hypnotic rhythm of Jim's breathing added fuel to the intimate tension fanning the silence between them.

"Hey, Brock?" Jim's voice was a low murmur as if testing the waters in the near-total quiet.

"Yeah?" Brock whispered back, his words nearly lost in the pounding cadence of his heart.

For a moment, the darkness seemed to pulse with the weight of what lay unsaid. Jim hesitated, and in that suspended pause, Brock felt as if he could almost decipher the longing in Jim's gaze—a silent confession teetering on the brink of vulnerability. Finally, Jim exhaled softly. "Thanks for today. I really needed this. I truly had a great time."

"Me too," Brock replied, voice heavy with sincerity and something more—a confession of budding desire. Lying side by side in the dark, the closeness was almost overwhelming, leaving him to hope for more even while trembling at the implications.

The rest of the night dissolved into a haze of fragmented dreams and daring, furtive glances. Each moment was drenched with sexual tension, a delicious, lingering promise. In that intimate cocoon of shadows and near-touching skin, both men drifted on the cusp of an undefined, tantalizing revelation—a shared secret waiting just beyond the shy barrier of their restraint.

When morning arrived, the first rays of sunlight filtered through the curtains, casting a gentle glow across the room. Brock awoke to the realization that during the night, they had unconsciously drifted closer, with Jim's hand lying tantalizingly just millimeters from Brock's throbbing erection.

The proximity sent a shiver down Brock's spine, and he took a quick, shaky breath before carefully rolling over and slipping out of the bed. His heart pounded as he rushed to the bathroom, hoping against hope that Jim wouldn't notice his morning wood. Brock desperately needed to jerk off, but the risk of Jim hearing him was too great. Instead, he opted for a quick, cold shower, letting the water cascade over his heated skin, calming his racing thoughts.

Once dressed, he emerged from the bathroom and stole a glance at the bed. Jim was sitting up; the sheets tented around his hands where they cupped his own arousal, a deep blush across his face. Brock's mind raced with forbidden fantasies of pulling the sheet away, revealing what he had so often imagined. But he restrained himself, turning instead to the door.

"I'll head down and grab us some coffee and pastries while you jump in the shower," he said, his voice steady despite the turmoil within.

Jim sighed heavily as the door clicked shut behind Brock. Relieved, he allowed himself a moment to slowly stroke his erection, grateful not to have to parade across the room with his tented gym shorts betraying his need. He hurried to the bathroom, heart pounding, praying that Brock didn't change his mind and return unexpectedly. Unlike Brock, Jim took the opportunity to relieve the built-up pressure in his balls during his shower.

The ride back was a delicate dance between awkward silences and the kind of easy conversation that felt like pieces of a puzzle, almost fitting together. Brock's mind was a whirl of uncertainty, unable to shake the memory of the spark he'd felt the night before—the unspoken longing that seemed to linger in the air. Yet, as Jim laughed and joked about the convention, it was almost enough to convince Brock that whatever had flickered between them had vanished with the dawn.

Almost. Because in those fleeting moments when Jim's eyes lingered on him a second too long, and in the subtle brush of their shoulders as they walked to the car, there was an undeniable tension, a promise unspoken. It shimmered just beneath the surface, an electric current waiting for one of them to reach out and embrace it.

# Chapter 9
# Things Heat Up

The acrid smell of charred wood and scorched plastic still clung to Jim's nostrils as he navigated the streets across town, a stark reminder of the chaos that had erupted just hours earlier. He and Amanda had been called out to a fire investigation. When he heard the address, his heart stopped for a minute. His apartment building remained standing, but the fire had wreaked havoc on the east wing, leaving behind singed walls, soaked carpets, and a maze of damaged electrical and plumbing systems that would require a complete overhaul.

The fire had originated in a vacant apartment on the bottom floor at the far east end of the building. This unit was under repair and renovation for the next occupant, with potential wiring issues being a likely cause. However, there were a few peculiarities about the blaze. The fire had been most intense in that particular apartment, reducing almost everything to ashes.

Fire Chief Rogers had pulled Jim aside just before he'd left the scene, his weathered face grave as he gestured toward the gutted apartment.

"Williamson, we found evidence someone was living in that vacant unit," Rogers said, keeping his voice low. "Empty food containers, makeshift bedding in the corner furthest from the windows. But that's not what's got me concerned."

Jim frowned. "What is it?"

"We detected traces of gasoline in multiple locations. Not just near the electrical panel where it supposedly started." Rogers ran a hand through his salt-and-pepper hair. "And the burn patterns... they're inconsistent with an accidental electrical fire. This has all the markers of being deliberately set."

A chill ran down Jim's spine despite the lingering heat from the blaze. "You're saying someone torched the place?"

"Can't confirm it officially yet, but between us? Yeah," Rogers nodded grimly. "The patterns are textbook arson. Multiple points of origin, accelerant trails leading between them. We found a partially melted gas can in the bathroom—someone tried to hide it in the tub, but fire's a funny thing. Sometimes, it preserves evidence even while destroying everything else."

Jim's mind raced with the implications. "Any idea who the squatter might've been?"

"Not yet. We found some clothing remnants that survived the worst of it. Men's clothes looks like. Large size." Rogers pulled out his phone and showed Jim a photo of a charred but recognizable work boot. "Size thirteen. And this was interesting—" He swiped to another image showing the blackened remains of what appeared to be construction tools.

"Someone with a connection to construction or trades," Jim murmured, studying the image.

"That's my thinking." Rogers put the phone back in his pocket and lowered his voice. "There's more. The accelerant wasn't just gasoline. We found traces of industrial-grade chemicals—the kind used in construction demolition. Not something your average person would have access to."

Jim's police instincts kicked into high gear. "Any specific leads?"

"Not yet, but I've got my best people analyzing the residue." Rogers glanced back at the building. "Whoever did this knew what they were doing. They wanted that unit completely destroyed. The question is why."

Jim nodded, his mind already cataloging possibilities. "I'll coordinate with your team. We need to identify that squatter and figure out if they were the target or the perpetrator."

"Or both," Rogers added grimly.

Jim tried to start putting the clues together but he was distracted by his own personal dilemma. He faced at least a month, maybe longer, away from his home. He'd packed a bag of essentials and dropped off all of his uniforms by the drycleaners before heading out to the farmhouse. He was luckier than some of the other residents. He had family in town. Now he just had to go and ask if he could crash with Spence and Chandler for a while. As he pulled into the driveway of Chandler's farmhouse, the weight of uncertainty pressed heavily against his chest. He hadn't yet had the time to contemplate what his next steps would be.

Drawing a deep breath, Jim knocked on the door, the familiar creak of the porch steps beneath his feet anchoring him in the present. The late afternoon sun bathed the white clapboard siding in a warm, golden light, casting long shadows that lent an air of tranquility and reassurance. For a fleeting moment, he almost managed to convince himself that this was just another ordinary visit, with nothing out of the ordinary to concern him.

The door swung open to reveal Spence, his blond hair slightly disheveled, as if he'd been running his fingers through it in thought or frustration. "Jim!" Spence exclaimed, his initial surprise quickly giving way to concern. "Are you okay? You look… frazzled."

Jim nodded, attempting a smile that didn't quite reach his eyes, a thin veneer over his exhaustion. "Yeah, I'm fine. There was a fire at my apartment complex. My place didn't burn, but the entire building needs to be evacuated for repairs—electrical, plumbing, you name it."

"God, Jim, I'm so sorry," Spence said, stepping aside to allow him entry. His hand brushed lightly against Jim's arm—a brief, intimate touch that sent a shiver racing down Jim's spine, more from the electric connection with Spence than any chill in the air.

Inside, Jim's eyes fell on Brock and Chandler, seated at the dining table, which was strewn with blueprints, sketches, and piles of papers. Chandler looked up, his hazel eyes widening with concern. "Jim, hey. You okay, man? We just heard about the fire."

"I'm alright," Jim replied, though the weariness in his voice betrayed him. "But I'm out of a place for a while. They're saying it'll take at least four to six weeks to fix all the damage."

Chandler shot a quick, knowing glance toward Brock, who sank back into his chair with a tight-set jaw as if the weight of the news was slowly sinking in. With a measured clearing of his throat, Chandler spread his hand toward the array of meticulously detailed blueprints strewn across the table. "Jim, since you're here, take a look at these," he said with quiet enthusiasm. "Brock and I have just been finalizing the modifications for the warehouse renovation."

Jim stepped forward, his eyes alighting on the intricate plans that mapped out every twist of electrical wiring and curve of new plumbing systems.

"Looks solid," he murmured, leaning in to trace the delicate lines with his fingertip. In that close proximity, he could sense Brock's presence—a reassuring warmth emanating from him as they huddled together, their arms nearly colliding in the shared space.

"Are you guys considering adding solar panels as well?" Jim inquired, raising his gaze to meet Chandler's steady nod.

"Yeah, we're going all out," Chandler replied, his voice brimming with pride. "By the time we're finished, it's going to be the most energy-efficient building in town."

A mischievous grin played on Brock's lips as his eyes briefly flicked toward Jim. "Maybe you should move in when it's done," he suggested lightly, his tone playful yet layered with promise. "Could be just the fresh start you need."

Jim chuckled softly and shook his head, a wry smile on his face. "Not quite ready to be a warehouse squatter yet." Yet, beneath his laugh, Jim detected a subtle, unspoken note in Brock's words—a hint that what was said might be more than just banter. As they bent over the blueprints together, the tension between them seemed to vibrate in the air, as if the carefully drawn lines were not merely ink on paper but invisible borders that both were delicately defying.

At that moment, Spence emerged from the kitchen bearing four glasses of sweet tea, the clinking of ice cubes in each glass punctuating his approach. "I figured you all could use a drink," he said, offering Jim a glass with a warm smile. "A little sugar boost, just in case."

"Thanks, Spence," Jim murmured, accepting the chilled beverage. The tea's sweetness coated his tongue while its coolness sent a pleasant shiver down his spine. His gaze drifted involuntarily to Brock, who was watching him from over the rim of his own glass. The look in Brock's eyes was enigmatic—his usual carefree manner replaced by something far more intense, as though a storm was simmering just beneath the surface.

Jim's fingers tightened around his glass, reluctant to break the hypnotic stare that connected them. The room around them seemed to recede, leaving only the charged space between the two, thick with unspoken words and hidden desires. Even as he felt Spence's observant eyes and Chandler's quiet curiosity, the moment teetered on the brink of becoming too intimate to ignore.

While the conversation gradually shifted back to the renovation details, the air remained heavy with that unexplained tension. Jim couldn't help but notice how close Brock had positioned himself—a proximity that allowed him to almost feel the heat radiating from Brock's skin and catch faint hints of his cologne. There were fleeting moments when Brock's knee brushed against Jim's under the table or when a stray hand momentarily grazed Jim's as they shuffled papers, and each accidental touch sent a jolt of electricity through him.

Eventually, as the discussion wound down, Brock and Chandler folded the blueprints with careful precision, stacking the documents into orderly piles. "Well, I should get going," Brock said, his eyes lingering on Jim for just a moment as he thoughtfully gathered his belongings. "Got a few errands to run before it gets too late."

Jim lingered in the transitional space between the dining room and living room, his breath still short from the residual tension of the day. He cast his eyes around the cozy living room—its antique lamps casting a soft, inviting glow, the eclectic tapestry of throw blankets and well-worn books a testament to the uniqueness of the men who inhabited it. The atmosphere exuded warmth and comfort that his own smoke-scented apartment, with all its familiarity, simply couldn't offer at that moment.

"Listen," he began hesitantly, rubbing the back of his neck as if to steady his nerves. His voice was gravelly, heavy with the remnants of the day's lingering stress. "I've been thinking... I could really use a place to stay for a while, at least until the repairs are done. Would it be alright if I crashed here? Just for about four to six weeks until everything's sorted out?"

Spence's eyes met Chandler's in a fleeting glance, his warm brown gaze mellowing as if softened by an inner light. He sank back into the welcoming curve of the couch, where the amber glow of the late afternoon sun caught the dancing sparkles of dust motes in the room.

"Of course, Jim," he said with heartfelt sincerity, his voice carrying a gentle assurance. "You're always welcome here." After a brief pause, his smile faded into a more thoughtful expression. "But… there's just one twist. Your parents will be in town in a few weeks, staying for four days. Space will be tight, though we'll figure out how to make it work during those few days."

A tiny crease appeared on Spence's forehead—a soft worry line that Jim rarely saw, hinting at the inner concern behind his calm words. It wasn't that Spence didn't want him around; Jim could sense the genuine care woven into every syllable. It was simply a matter of practical logistics, a sudden shift that demanded all of them balance their schedules more carefully than before.

In that moment, Brock's low, resonant voice cut through the conversation like a comforting baritone melody, drawing Jim's attention. "You could stay with me for those few days," Brock suggested warmly. His relaxed posture belied a quiet intensity in his eyes as though his mind was already sculpting a plan. "I've got a guest room and plenty of space. There's no need for you to be shuffling around while everything else feels so unsettled."

At Brock's invitation, a comforting warmth bloomed in Jim's chest. The thought of burdening Spence and Chandler—or disrupting his parents' plans during their visit—had weighed heavily on him, but Brock's offer presented a welcome escape from that worry. "I really appreciate it, Brock," Jim admitted, relief softening his voice. "That would make things a lot easier."

Brock responded with a slight nod and a small, reassuring smile. "No problem," he said, his tone easy yet earnest. "And if you need to swing by your apartment tonight for a few things, I can pick you up. We'll grab your essentials and then catch some dinner—something warm and satisfying, not just takeout or a quick bite from the vending machine at the fire station. Sound good?"

Jim's eyes darted back toward Chandler and Spence, who both offered gentle, encouraging nods. The plan felt right, and the promise of a proper meal was undeniably appealing. "Alright," he agreed, his voice firming with newfound resolve. "Let's do it."

As they drove through town, the orange and purple hues of twilight bathed the streets in a dreamy glow, casting an intimate shadow over the interior of Brock's Yukon. The vehicle rumbled along the road, its low growl the only sound between them, a charged silence that hung thick in the air. Jim kept his gaze fixed on the scenery outside, yet he couldn't help but feel Brock's presence beside him, an electric awareness simmering beneath the surface. As the landscape shifted from neighborhood houses to the charred remains of his apartment building, silhouetted against the deepening dusk, Jim's pulse quickened, a subtle unease mingled with anticipation tightening his chest.

"Are you okay?" Brock's voice broke the quiet, soft yet laced with an undercurrent of concern that made Jim's heart skip.

Jim swallowed, the sensation of dry heat lingering in his throat, more than just the smoke. "Yeah, just… it's weird seeing it like this." His voice dropped to a near whisper, the vulnerability palpable. "Even if it wasn't a perfect place, it was still home."

Brock nodded, his gaze lingering on the darkened building, but his attention seemed to shift back to Jim, the weight of it almost tangible. "It's always a shock, losing something familiar like that. Even temporarily." His hand flexed on the steering wheel, knuckles paling slightly as if he were restraining himself from reaching out. "But you're not alone in this. You've got people who've got your back."

There was a sincerity in Brock's words that tugged at Jim, a raw honesty that made him feel seen in a way he hadn't expected. It was more than just the words; it was the timbre of Brock's voice, the faint rasp at the edges that hinted at untold experiences, at depths Jim longed to explore.

Gratitude mingled with something warmer spread through Jim, chasing away some of the lingering chill.

They spent a few minutes in Jim's apartment, gathering clothes, toiletries, and a few keepsakes. The air inside was stifling, heavy with the scent of dampness and smoke, but there was also a tension, a closeness that made each movement feel significant. As Jim packed a bag, he was acutely aware of Brock moving through the apartment, his quiet efficiency captivating, his broad shoulders and tall frame seemingly too large for the small, dim space, yet fitting in a way that felt undeniably right.

When they were done, Brock closed the back of the Yukon with a solid thud, a sound that reverberated like a promise. "There," he said, his voice a comforting rumble that sent a shiver down Jim's spine. "You're all set. Now, let's get some food."

The restaurant Brock had chosen was an inviting, snug bistro tucked away just a few blocks from the bustling main road. Its dim lighting and charming decor created an ambiance that transported Jim far from the earlier chaos, wrapping him in a peaceful cocoon. The air was rich with the tantalizing aroma of garlic and freshly picked herbs, while a soft murmur of conversation mingled with the delicate clinking of glassware, infusing the space with warmth and intimacy. They settled into a cozy booth near the back, where a gentle overhead light cast a mellow glow upon their table, softening the edges of the evening.

As they nestled into their seats, Jim felt a profound calm slowly wash over him, the familiar ritual of dining out grounding his senses and restoring a fragile sense of normalcy. Brock reclined into his chair, his dark eyes locking with Jim's with an intensity that was both candid and disarming. "You know," he began in a tone that blended casual ease with earnest kindness, "you don't have to worry about imposing on Spence and Chandler. If you want, you could just stay with me for the entire time."

Jim's brow furrowed in mild surprise, the unexpected offer sending his heart into a brief, accelerated rhythm. In that suspended moment, his mind drifted back to memories of their Comic-Con trip – the way they had shared that vast king-sized bed, lying close yet not quite touching, like two magnets held at bay by some invisible force. There was an undeniable electric undercurrent that night, a shimmering pulse of possibility that still hummed softly between them in the ambiance of Brock's calm demeanor. "I wouldn't want to put you out," Jim replied slowly, his voice carrying both hesitation and genuine care. "I mean, six weeks is a long time, and I know you've got your own life. I don't want to be a burden."

Brock shook his head with unwavering conviction, his steady gaze soothing any lingering doubts. "You wouldn't be," he assured, his voice imbued with a quiet sincerity that resonated deep within Jim. "Honestly, I'd be glad to have the company. And besides, it would take some of the extra worry off Spence and Chandler—they're already juggling so much."

Jim studied Brock intently, looking for any flicker of hesitation or discomfort on his face, but all he saw was a soft openness that melted away some of the earlier tension. The idea of sharing a living space with Brock for such an extended period was both daunting and electrifying; their interactions always carried a subtle, unspoken tension that left Jim perpetually teetering on the edge of expectation. Yet, concurrently, there was a profound comfort in Brock's presence—a reassurance that he was the sort of man who kept his promises without fail.

"I... okay," Jim agreed almost before the thought had fully formed, his voice soft and tentative as a small smile began to play on his lips. "I appreciate it, Brock. Thank you."

Brock's own smile broadened, his eyes sparkling with a mischievous glint as he leaned forward slightly. "Guess I'll have to warn you, though. I'm a terrible morning person. And I've got a habit of cranking the AC way down at night so I can cocoon myself under all the covers without getting too hot."

A warm chuckle escaped Jim, and he felt the weight he had been carrying lift ever so slightly. "I'll keep that in mind," he said, raising his glass in a quiet toast. "To temporary roommates."

"To temporary roommates," Brock echoed with a gentle clink of their glasses—a soft, unspoken promise shared between two kindred spirits.

As the meal unfolded, their conversation blossomed effortlessly, meandering from the passionate crackle of a blazing fire to more light-hearted topics—nostalgic reminiscences of old movies, the latest quirky renovations at the warehouse, and even a few animated anecdotes from their Comic-Con escapade that sparked shared laughter. Jim began to notice the minutiae that made Brock uniquely captivating: the way his smile gently curved at the edges when amusement danced in his eyes, the rich timbre of his laughter resonating like a low melody, and the idiosyncratic habit of his fingers idly tracing the rim of his glass when he listened with rapt attention.

And so it was that every now and then, their eyes would meet across the table—a fleeting yet potent spark of connection that defied easy description but nonetheless set Jim's pulse racing in quiet, unexpected rhythms.

# Chapter 10
# Roomies

Jim's first night at Brock's house was permeated with an odd mixture of comforting familiarity and intriguing strangeness. The guest room, bathed in soft lamplight, boasted crisp white linens and a deep blue comforter that seemed to whisper promises of sleepless nights spent in blissful forgetfulness, inviting him to dissolve the chaos of the past week.

As he lay there, eyes tracing the subtle patterns of the ceiling, his thoughts drifted to the symphony of faint sounds that filled the quiet space—the rhythmic hum of the refrigerator echoing like a distant heartbeat, the occasional creak of weathered floorboards that spoke of the house's history, and somewhere down the hall, Brock's low, measured murmur as he conversed on the phone.

Turning on his side, a wave of uncertainty crept over him like a soft fog. It had been years since he had ever shared a living space with anyone— not since the carefree days of college—and the prospect of navigating this new arrangement felt as daunting as it was exhilarating.

Yet, a spark of anticipation pulsed quietly beneath his apprehension, making his heart flutter at the thought of sharing not just a roof but moments of life with Brock. He reassured himself that the rush was merely the excitement of a new chapter, a neat distraction from the upheaval of recent times. Still, deep within, he sensed that there might be more to this change than a simple deviation from the old routine.

As days melted into a steady rhythm, Jim and Brock gradually embraced cohabitation with an almost disarming ease. Their mornings began with the comforting aroma of freshly brewed coffee, a silent ritual where whoever rose first would boil the pot, offering a subtle nod of domestic harmony.

Brock's mornings were punctuated by the clatter of his protein shake blender and the sizzling of eggs, while Jim favored the gentle warmth of toast slathered in rich jam and complemented by a vibrant mix of whatever fruit graced the fridge. Their small talk flowed effortlessly—

snippets of conversation about work commitments or local happenings woven between the clinks of ceramic mugs meeting the countertop.

Yet beneath their smooth daily routines, there pulsed a subtle, unspoken tension—a gentle hum of anticipation like the crackle of static electricity in the air. It was not a tension that wove discomfort but rather a tantalizing undercurrent that made the fine hairs along Jim's neck stand on end whenever Brock brushed past him in the hallway or when their hands met unexpectedly while reaching for the same dish.

In the evenings, after a day filled with the steady rhythm of work and the lively bustle of daily tasks, both would often retreat to the sanctuary of the living room. There, amid the softened glow of ambient light, they unwound with the clink of beer bottles and the flickering images of a movie, sharing long stretches of companionable silence. Despite the ease and familiarity of these moments, Jim couldn't help but notice the occasional, fleeting glance Brock directed his way—a suggestive look as though he were studying Jim's every nuance or pondering thoughts just beneath the surface, thoughts not yet voiced aloud.

One balmy evening, roughly two weeks after they'd started sharing the same space, Jim found himself at the well-worn kitchen counter, meticulously dicing a rainbow of vegetables for a stir-fry while Brock, with a casual yet furtively intense air, rummaged through the chilly depths of the refrigerator in search of a beer. The room was alive with the warm, spicy aroma of garlic and ginger, intermingling with the faint tang of freshly chopped herbs, while the gentle sizzle from the stovetop played an understated symphony in the soft, ambient light of the kitchen.

"You know," Brock remarked, his voice relaxed but carrying a subtle, almost imperceptible edge, "I didn't expect things to slip so effortlessly into place. Having someone else here, I mean—it's just easier than I thought it might be."

Jim paused, lifting his gaze from the steady rhythm of his chopping, his knife momentarily suspended in mid-air. There was a raw honesty in Brock's tone, a hint of unspoken truths that made Jim feel as though he were about to cross a long-avoided bridge into something unknown.

"Yeah," he replied softly, the sound mingling with the clatter of freshly sliced peppers, "I guess it just fits. It's like we've known each other for so long... maybe that's the reason."

"Maybe," Brock agreed, though his tone suggested he was wrestling with uncertainty as much as with conviction. Retrieving a bottle opener with practiced ease, he popped the cap off his beer, the soft hiss of escaping carbonation punctuating the quiet space between them like a whispered secret. "But you have to admit," he continued, his voice dipping into a lower register full of hesitant wonder, "it's not exactly ordinary. I mean, us just syncing up seamlessly like this."

Jim's knife hovered momentarily above the cutting board, an electric flush of heat creeping up his neck as his skin prickled with acute awareness. He kept his attention fixed on the vegetables, feeling the texture of each slice under his steadying grip, and replied with a careful smile, "Normal is vastly overrated. Besides, I'd choose this 'easy closeness' over something dull and awkward any day."

A deep, resonant chuckle escaped Brock, vibrating softly through the kitchen and reverberating inside Jim, settling in like a trusted murmur of reassurance.

"Fair point," Brock conceded, taking a contemplative sip of his beer. After a weighted pause, he added in a tone laden with unspoken emotion, "It's just...I'm really glad you're here."

Those words hung suspended in the warm, incense-scented air, imbued with a quiet intensity that neither of them was quite ready to fully voice. As Jim reached for the bottle of soy sauce, its cool glass contrasting with the heat of the sizzling pan, his pulse quickened perceptibly.

"Well," he said, his tone attempting nonchalance while betraying a trace of vulnerability, "thanks for letting me stay. It's definitely a lot more homely than any hotel room could ever feel."

Brock then moved closer, his presence a comforting, unspoken warmth as he leaned casually against the counter, his arm brushing softly against Jim's shoulder—the intimate pressure sending a cascade of subtle shivers through him. "You're not just a guest," he murmured in a lowered, intimate cadence, "You're welcome here as long as you need to be."

Jim swallowed hard, the aromatic steam from the pan curling around his face like gentle tendrils of memory as he stirred the vibrant vegetables with deliberate care. There was a profound intimacy in Brock's words, a delicate stirring of a deep, hidden ache and longing that Jim had painstakingly kept under wraps since moving in. He could feel Brock's eyes, warm and searching, fixed intently on him, their weight almost as tangible as the heat from the stove, and for a suspended moment, it seemed as if the rest of the world had dissolved, leaving just the two of them enveloped in this shared secret space.

"Thanks," Jim managed, his voice dropping to a tender murmur far quieter than intended. He risked a fleeting glance over his shoulder, catching Brock's steady, knowing gaze. For a heartbeat, silence prevailed as tension coiled tightly between them, much like a drawn bowstring on the verge of release. Then, with a gentle step back, Brock broke the spell, and Jim allowed himself a quiet exhale, the moment receding into comfortable, unspoken understanding.

The days continued to slip by like sand through an hourglass, and with each passing moment, the quiet, poignant moments of longing seemed to multiply like stars appearing in the twilight sky. Jim found himself watching Brock when he thought the other man wasn't paying attention—captivated by the way Brock's jaw tensed with determination when he was lost in thought, the way his hands moved with a rough yet graceful precision when he was working on something around the house. It was the little things that caught Jim's attention, the subtle ways Brock's guard would drop when he was at ease, revealing fleeting glimpses of the man behind the easy-going facade like sunlight breaking through clouds.

There were times when they'd sit together on the couch, a movie playing softly in the background, and Jim would feel the gentle brush of Brock's arm against his, the warmth radiating through the thin fabric of his shirt like sunlight through a window. It was innocent enough, a natural consequence of sharing a small space, but each touch sent a shiver down Jim's spine, igniting the embers of something that was steadily becoming impossible to ignore, like a fire longing to blaze.

For Brock, the experience was just as intense, though he kept his feelings tightly controlled, hidden behind the carefully constructed veneer of their comfortable daily routine. He would catch himself stealing glances at Jim—mesmerized by the way the soft evening light danced over the curve of his jaw, the way his eyes crinkled at the corners when he laughed at one of Brock's jokes like waves breaking gently on a shore. He found himself noticing the smallest details: the faint stubble on Jim's chin, the subtle rise and fall of his chest when he was sleeping in the guest room, the door slightly ajar like an invitation.

But he didn't act on the magnetic pull between them. As much as he longed to close the distance, to reach out and touch, there was a part of him that feared shattering the delicate balance they had found. It felt safer to linger in the liminal space, to let the unspoken tension simmer quietly without forcing it to a boiling point. Yet, every time Jim laughed at one of his jokes or brushed past him in the hallway, the temptation to push just a little further grew stronger like a tide slowly rising against the shore.

Late one night, Jim found himself once again in the dimly lit kitchen, unable to find solace in sleep. The anticipation of his parents' arrival in just two days kept his mind restless. As he prepared a cup of tea, the steam rose in delicate, curling wisps, painting ethereal patterns in the cool air.

Suddenly, Brock appeared in the doorway, his hair tousled from sleep, casting a shadow over his face. His T-shirt draped loosely over his broad shoulders, and he rubbed a hand over his face, squinting against the harsh glare of the kitchen light.

"Couldn't sleep?" Brock inquired, his voice gravelly and thick with the remnants of sleep.

Jim shook his head, the teabag bobbing gently in the steaming water like a tiny boat adrift. "Yeah, just restless, I guess. Mom and Dad will be here the day after tomorrow. I'm excited to see them, but a little anxious too, with all that's going on." He offered Brock a small, tentative smile. "You want some tea?"

Brock moved closer, his presence comforting in the stillness of the night. He leaned casually against the counter, considering the offer. "Sure, why not," he replied, his voice softening to a gentle murmur, the kind reserved for the quiet hours when the world held its breath and secrets felt like they could slip free from their bonds.

As Jim handed Brock the mug, their fingers brushed lightly, a fleeting touch that neither of them hurried to break. The contact lingered, the warmth of Brock's skin seeping into Jim's own, and in that fragile moment, it felt as though something intangible had shifted, a boundary crossed under the gentle glow of the kitchen light.

Jim's breath caught in his throat, his pulse echoing loudly in his ears. He searched Brock's eyes, seeking some sign, some silent acknowledgment that he wasn't alone in this tender yearning, that the longing he harbored wasn't unrequited. And in the depths of Brock's gaze, he thought he caught a glimpse of it—a flicker of shared desire, an unspoken need mirrored back at him.

But then Brock took the mug and stepped back, a playful smile curling at the corners of his lips as he turned toward the inviting expanse of the living room.

"Come on," he suggested in a hushed tone. "Let's watch something. Maybe a bad late-night movie will help you sleep. I'm taking tomorrow off. Been pushing myself pretty hard at the site and just need a breather. So I don't have to get right back to bed."

Jim followed, a turbulent mix of hope and frustration swirling within his chest. As they settled onto the couch, the familiar tension between them thrummed like an electric current, crackling just beneath the surface, waiting for one of them to finally reach out and bridge the gap.

# Chapter 11
## Laundry Day

By the time Brock finally stirred, the sun reigned high in the sky, its vibrant rays streaming through delicate, translucent curtains that draped softly over his bedroom windows. Today, there were no appointments or demands punctuating his schedule—just the unhurried luxury of endless possibility. He stretched slowly, relishing the hushed solitude of an empty house that held no echoes of hurried footsteps or ticking clocks. The thought of devoting an entire day to utter relaxation felt like an indulgent reprieve, one he was determined to savor fully.

After a leisurely, unpressured breakfast, he drifted into the master bathroom, eyes immediately drawn to the commanding presence of the enormous tub nestled in the corner opposite the walk-in shower. The deep, curvaceous basin—with its gleaming chrome fixtures and an array of water jets—had always seemed like a lavish escape he could never fit into his routine until now.

Brock turned the taps and allowed the water to cascade in a torrent of steaming heat, the atmosphere quickly becoming infused with the rich, woody aroma of mahogany teakwood bubble bath, a scent that evoked both warmth and tranquility. With deliberate ease, he discarded his clothes and stepped into the foamy embrace of the bath, sighing deeply as he sank into the soft, enveloping water.

The heat permeated his body, coaxing his tense muscles into a state of release as his eyelids fell shut, surrendering to the gentle drift of his thoughts. The frenzied pace of the past several weeks melted away under the influence of this serene ritual. With Jim now sharing the space of his home, a new pattern of life had subtly emerged—a rhythm that felt unexpectedly natural and comforting. There was an unspoken intimacy between them, a mutual recognition conveyed through shared laughter and effortless conversations that filled quiet moments with a profound sense of understanding.

Yet beneath this surface of ease, an understated current of tension pulsed silently. Brock could sense it in the occasional, lingering glance from Jim—a spark of something deeper and more mysterious in his eyes that hovered just a fraction too long to be dismissed. Shaking his head in an attempt to banish the thought, Brock allowed himself to sink deeper into the bubbles, the warmth from the water gradually easing the sting of unspoken words and unresolved feelings.

As he reclined further into the steaming bath, the water swirled around him in a languid dance, each water jet massaging his fatigued muscles with delicate precision. The heat worked its alchemy, seeping into his skin and systematically easing the knots that had built up in his back and shoulders. He rested his head against the smooth edge of the tub, eyes fluttering closed as he exhaled in a measured, contented rhythm. The soft, lingering scent of mahogany teakwood merged with the rising steam, filling the space with an earthy, heady fragrance that elevated the serene quiet of his sanctuary.

In this cocoon of warmth and solitude, his thoughts inevitably drifted back to Jim. Unbidden yet welcome, vivid images flooded his mind— Jim's lean, muscled form, his skin radiant with a light sheen of post-workout perspiration, and that unmistakable twinkle of mischief in his eyes that dared Brock into silent challenges. Brock could clearly picture the way Jim's hair, damp and artfully disheveled, framed his face and how his playful smile harbored promises of deeper, unspoken emotions just beneath the surface.

Meanwhile, Jim was out on an assignment with Amanda, the lead detective and his partner. The day had unfolded seamlessly until an unexpected summer downpour ambushed them while he was assisting someone in changing a tire on the side of the road. The sky, once clear, had transformed into a cascade of heavy droplets that hammered down relentlessly.

By the time Jim completed the task, he was utterly drenched; the rain had soaked through his uniform until it adhered to his skin like a second, clammy layer. As they navigated their way back to the station, he shivered involuntarily, the frigid moisture seeping into his very bones, leaving him chilled to the core.

"You look like a drowned rat," Amanda teased, her eyes sparkling with amusement as she glanced over at him with a teasing smirk. Her words were lighthearted, contrasting the heavy atmosphere outside. "Why don't you head home and change? I can handle things for the next hour or so."

"Yeah, thanks," Jim replied, shaking droplets from his hair with a resigned chuckle as he peeled off his saturated socks and boots, which squelched unpleasantly as he removed them. "I'm no good to anyone like this." His voice carried a hint of gratitude mixed with the discomfort of sitting in drenched clothes.

Back at the house, Brock finally emerged from the bath, feeling thoroughly relaxed. A frown creased his forehead as he remembered he had thrown all the towels into the laundry last night and hadn't bothered to fold and bring them back upstairs. The hamper sat empty in the bathroom, which meant he would have to head downstairs to the laundry room in his current state.

He padded downstairs, naked and still warm from the bath, his skin tingling as he descended the staircase. As he rounded the corner of the kitchen into the laundry room, he slid on the slick tile floor, surprised to see Jim, also completely naked, standing with his back to him as he loaded his wet uniform into the washer.

Jim turned at the sound of Brock's approach, his eyes widening in surprise. In an instant, they collided—Brock's bare chest bumping into Jim's damp skin. The momentum of the sudden impact sent them both off balance and instinctively, they reached out to steady each other.

Brock's hands gripped Jim's shoulders while Jim's hands reached around to meet on Brock's back, their bodies pressed close, their torsos pressed firmly together. The warmth of Brock's recent bath meeting the coolness of Jim's rain-chilled skin.

For a moment, they froze, breathing heavily from the sudden embrace, their eyes locked. Brock could feel Jim's heartbeat against his own, the rapid thrum echoing the unspoken desire that had been building between them for months. The air was thick with tension, the world outside the small room forgotten as they held onto each other, as if afraid to let go.

Jim's hand slid down to Brock's lower back, his touch sending a shiver up Brock's spine. "Brock..." Jim whispered, his voice hoarse, caught somewhere between hesitation and longing.

Brock's response was wordless. His grip tightened, pulling Jim closer until their lips met in a fierce, impassioned kiss. The contact was electric, a spark that ignited the months of repressed desire, the longing they'd both tried to deny. Their mouths moved hungrily against each other, tasting and exploring as if they were starved for this connection.

The heat of the kiss deepened, Brock's fingers threading into Jim's wet hair, tugging him closer still. He could taste the rain on Jim's skin and feel the chill of the water droplets trickling down his back, but all that mattered was the fire coursing through him—the fire that had been smoldering quietly for too long and now raged out of control.

Jim responded with equal fervor, his hands roaming over Brock's body, tracing the muscles and contours he had only dared to glance at before. Then they both realized at the same time their cocks were both hard. Jim ground into the firm muscle of Brock's thigh while Brock's cock pulsed, trapped between their stomachs, the head reaching up to his belly button.

Their kiss broke only for a second, both of them gasping for air. Brock's forehead rested against Jim's, his voice breathless and raw. "You're home."

They came together again, the kiss deeper this time, more tender but no less urgent. As their bodies melded, Jim could feel the heat radiating off Brock's skin, the softness of his lips contrasting with the firmness of his embrace. The scent of mahogany teakwood from Brock's bath mingled with the fresh, clean smell of rain still clinging to Jim, creating a heady, intoxicating mix that seemed to envelop them.

Brock guided Jim backward until his back pressed against the cool metal of the washing machine, his hands running down Jim's sides, feeling the damp skin beneath his fingertips. Jim's breath hitched as Brock's mouth trailed down to his jaw, his neck, leaving a trail of soft, open-mouthed kisses that sent waves of heat pooling low in his belly.

The sensation was overwhelming, a rush of pleasure that made Jim's knees feel weak. Then Brock took Jim's cock into his hand, admiring it. "This is the most beautiful dick I've ever seen." But before Jim could even process the words and think of a response, Brock dropped to his knees and took Jim's throbbing cock into his mouth. The sensation radiated throughout Jim's body.

Brock settled onto his knees and reached around to gently caress Jim's plump bubblebutt while his head bobbed on Jim's leaking cock. With each movement, Brock took more and more of Jim's length into his warm, wet, inviting mouth until his lips brushed against the prickly patch of Jim's low-trimmed pubes and the head of Jim's cock brushed against the back of Brock's throat.

"Oh. My. God!" was all Jim could utter as Brock picked up the pace, swirling his tongue around the shaft and creating a rhythm as he alternated the pressure of his suction from gentle and teasing to intense and driven. Jim's fingers found Brock's damp hair and tangled into the thick fringe. He leaned his head back and moaned out in pleasure. Then, suddenly realizing he was about to erupt, he tensed and tried to push Brock's head away.

"I'm gonna cum, Brock. I'm…"

Brock increased his intensity and slid a hand around to cup Jim's balls as he pulsed his release down Jim's throat. The warm salty mush pushed him to suck even harder. Then Brock was aware that Jim's legs were trembling as were his hands holding his head.

When Brock finally withdrew, he smiled up at Jim. "I need to get a towel." he laughed. Then moved in to kiss Jim's neck.

"We should… go upstairs," Jim managed to say, his voice breaking slightly as Brock's lips brushed over a particularly sensitive spot just below his ear. "Before we… do more right here."

Brock pulled back, his eyes dark with an emotion that sent a thrill racing through Jim. He took Jim's hand, their fingers interlocking, and nodded.

"Yeah," he agreed, his voice husky. "Let's go."

Upstairs, the bedroom door closed behind them with a quiet click. They didn't bother turning on the lights; the late morning light streaming through the curtains was enough. In the dimness, their movements were slow and unhurried, a stark contrast to the frenzy of their first kiss in the laundry room. There was a new awareness between them now, a silent agreement to let themselves feel everything they'd been holding back.

As they lay together on the bed, the world outside ceased to exist. It was just them, the warmth of each other's skin, the soft murmurs and breathless whispers that filled the room. Every touch as they explored each other's body. Every kiss felt like a promise, a declaration that neither of them needed to hide anymore.

Jim took a moment to just take in the physical beauty of the robust man lying next to him. The gleam of lust and longing in his blue eyes. His eyes roamed lower, taking in the ruggedness of his hairy muscular body; his eyes paused briefly on the soft roundness of Brock's belly. Jim couldn't explain it, but it was so sexy to him for some reason.

Then his eyes finally rested on the glorious rock-hard dick standing proudly. It was bigger than Jim's. He let out a brief gasp of surprise and desire. He extended his hand and took hold of Brock's manhood. His fingers were not quite able to connect as he encircled the girthy shaft with his trembling hand.

A guttural moan escaped his lips as he leaned in closer. He gripped the throbbing cock with his other hand, and still, the dark engorged head protruded from his two-fisted grip. Jim licked his lips as he moved to taste the glistening bead of precum crowning the tip. He looked up into Brock's burning eyes.

"I want to…I don't know…tell me what to do." Jim whispered in a husky tone.

Brock's grin was encouraging as he exhaled slowly. "Just do whatever you want to. You'll be amazing at it. I just know."

Jim started by licking up and down the thick length while he stroked it slowly. He let out a breath it seemed to him he'd been holding since the day he met this gorgeous man. Then he opened his mouth and took in the head of the first dick, other than his own, he'd ever held. His lips stretched, and he was cognizant of his teeth as he fit the throbbing head into his mouth. He allowed himself to savor the taste and inhale the scent. It was clean, woodsy, and masculine. He swirled his tongue around the head, savoring the slightly salty bitter taste. Then he released one of his hands and moved his head to see how much he could take into his mouth.

The act was so erotic, so exciting. Jim's entire body was trembling and tingling with fulfillment. He pulled his head back up, then pushed the cock even deeper into his mouth, the head brushing the back of his throat. He felt the tears forming in the corners of his eyes, so he withdrew again, but only long enough to breathe in through his nose and plunge back down, letting the bulbous head hit the back of his throat again. His right hand stroked his lover's cock as he lavished his wet mouth up and down on it at the same time. He reached down with his left hand and began to stroke his own cock. He continued, building the pace and the pressure of his mouth until he and Brock were both moaning with passion and pleasure.

Then suddenly, their passion found its climax, Jim shooting up onto his stomach as Brock withdrew from his mouth and shot all over Jim's chest as well. Their passion mixed as Brock pulled Jim into a tight embrace, and their mouths found each other again.

When they finally pulled apart, sticky and sated, lying side by side, their breaths still ragged, there was a sense of relief mingled with the lingering heat. Brock turned his head to look at Jim, his eyes searching for something in the depths of Jim's gaze.

Jim reached out, tracing a finger along Brock's jawline, his touch light and affectionate. "I guess laundry day was more exciting than usual," he said, a hint of laughter in his voice.

Brock's lips curved into a slow smile as he took Jim's hand and brought it to his lips, pressing a gentle kiss to his palm. "Yeah," he agreed softly, his eyes never leaving Jim's. "Definitely more exciting. I'm glad I grabbed this before we headed up," he teased as he retrieved a towel off the bedside table and began cleaning them up.

And for the first time in a long while, the unspoken tension between them was replaced with something else—something that felt like the beginning of whatever came next.

Jim's mind felt like a storm of abrasive thoughts as he finished his shift, each memory from the day colliding in his head like a relentless, swirling vortex. Every detail seemed both heightened and blurred at the same time—his skin still buzzed with the ghostly warmth of Brock's touch, and the memory of their kiss clung to him like the echo of a half-remembered dream.

Even as his rational mind attempted to piece together the fragments of that charged moment in the laundry room—the abrupt, fated collision; the raw, desperate intensity of Brock's kiss; the intimate passion that had unfolded in Brock's bed—logic and reason evaporated, leaving behind a tangled maze of questions. What now? What did this mean for their friendship, for him? Did this mark the beginning of a newfound attraction, or was there something deeper stirring within him, something that defied neat categorization?

The sharp buzz of his phone snapped him out of the tumult, its vibration slicing through his reverie. He glanced down at the screen and saw his mother's name glowing, innocent and familiar. With a deep, steadying breath, he answered, striving to mask the chaos inside.

"Hey, Mom."

Her voice burst through the line with comforting warmth. "Jim, honey! Your dad and I just got to Spence's house. Chandler and Spence have been cooking up a storm, and it smells heavenly here. We can't wait for you to join us."

At these words, a sinking feeling churned in his stomach. The thought of facing his family—and the ever-watchful eyes of Spence and Chandler—after the tumult of his morning felt suddenly overwhelming. The casual family dinner he had eagerly anticipated now loomed like a gauntlet, each familiar face a reminder that nothing remained unchanged.

"Uh, that sounds great, Mom," he managed, his voice wavering just enough to betray his inner turmoil. "I'm just finishing up my shift, so I'll head home to change and be over soon."

"Good! We've missed you so much, and I'm excited for you to try Chandler's homemade cornbread—it's supposed to be famous. See you soon, darling." Her tone, so drenched in the comforting love and familiarity of a lifetime, only deepened the knot in his chest.

Hanging up the phone, Jim exhaled slowly as if attempting to disperse the clashing emotions swirling inside him. The looming family dinner, with its warm lights and expectant smiles, felt like an arena where nothing would be as it seemed.

He drove home with a racing mind and clammy hands, the blur of passing roads echoing the jumbled cascade of thoughts tumbling in his head. When he finally pulled up to the house, his hands gripped the steering wheel so tightly they left imprints, and he tried in vain to smooth out the wrinkles of anxiety on his face as he stepped out of the car.

But nothing could have prepared him for the sight that greeted him when he opened the front door. There, in the softly lit living room, stood Brock. Dressed in dark jeans that hugged his legs and a lavender dress shirt with the sleeves casually rolled up to reveal the sculpted curves of his forearms, Brock looked like a figure straight out of a high-fashion magazine. His hair, still damp from a recent shower, was slicked back into a style that emphasized his chiseled features. He was undeniably striking—so effortlessly alluring that his presence transformed the familiar space, making everything about the evening even more complicated.

"Hey," Brock said, his voice calm yet imbued with a gentle warmth that stirred a shiver along Jim's spine. "Chandler invited me to dinner too. I figured I should dress up a little." A hint of a smirk played on his lips— the kind that usually lightened Jim's mood with laughter, but today only deepened the restless fluttering in his chest.

"Right," Jim replied, carefully restraining his gaze from admiring the way the vibrant color of Brock's shirt brought out the piercing blue in his eyes. "I didn't know you were coming."

"Chandler called a bit ago and mentioned your parents were in town," Brock explained, his tone mixing nonchalance with undertones of anticipation. "Figured it'd be a good time to meet everyone. Plus, free food." His smirk softened into a more genuine smile, though Jim sensed an unspoken tension hanging between them—like Brock was delicately testing the waters, trying to gauge the shifting ground of their relationship.

Jim's throat felt parched, his mind swirling with emotions. "Yeah, makes sense." Clearing his throat, he cast a fleeting glance up the staircase. "I'm just gonna change real quick."

As he hurried upstairs, he felt Brock's steady gaze following him—a silent, caring presence. In the quiet seclusion of his bedroom, Jim closed the door behind him and leaned against it for a moment, pressing his eyes shut in an effort to gather himself. His heart pounded wildly against his ribcage, and his skin radiated a feverish heat, as though the adrenaline from their earlier encounter was still surging through his veins.

Everything was unfolding so rapidly—too rapidly. Now Brock was there, about to meet his parents, who were gathering for dinner with Spence and Chandler like a scene from a picturesque family reunion. But with all these emotions churning inside him, Jim wondered how he was supposed to navigate the maze of his own stewing feelings.

He rifled through his closet in search of something that could strike the perfect balance between appropriate and effortless. Finally, his eyes settled on a fitted gray button-down paired with dark slacks—a look that could pass for casual, yet still polished enough for an encounter with his parents.

As he meticulously buttoned his shirt, he caught a glimpse of his reflection in the mirror: his hands trembled ever so slightly, and the tight lines around his eyes betrayed his internal struggle. Was it anxiety, excitement, or simply the overwhelming confusion of it all? He couldn't say for sure.

The thought of facing everyone at Spence's—especially Brock—made his chest feel constricted. Would Spence be able to read him like an open book? Ever since they were kids, Spence had possessed an uncanny ability to see right through him, to peel away the layers of his carefully constructed walls.

Jim could already imagine Spence's knowing grin, perhaps even a raised eyebrow or a subtly pointed remark to indicate that his inner turmoil was as visible as day. It was as if the secrets he and Brock shared were painted in bold, unmistakable colors across his skin, visible only to Spence's perceptive eyes.

"Get it together, Jim," he muttered softly to himself, raking a disheveled hand through his hair. Drawing a steady, calming breath, he resolved to venture back downstairs.

Down in the living room, Brock remained seated on the edge of the sofa, his attention absorbed by his phone. Upon seeing Jim approach, he set the device aside and rose, his expression shifting from playful to profoundly serious.

"You okay?" Brock asked in a low, genuine tone, as if he could sense the storm of emotions swirling beneath Jim's calm exterior.

"Yeah, just… a lot going on," Jim replied, avoiding Brock's earnest gaze as he moved toward the door. "We should probably get going."

"Jim," Brock said, stepping closer until the space between them was nearly non-existent, his voice soft and intimate. In that moment, Jim froze, his pulse quickening once more as Brock's quiet presence enveloped him from behind. "About this morning… we don't have to figure everything out right now, okay? It happened, and… I don't regret it."

Those words were a soothing balm on Jim's troubled spirit, yet they did little to completely ease the knot coiled tightly within his chest. Slowly, he turned, meeting Brock's earnest eyes. "I don't know what it means yet," he admitted, his voice barely above a whisper. "And with my parents here, and everything with Spence and Chandler… I just don't know how to act like nothing's different."

Brock's eyes softened even further, his expression radiating compassion and understanding. "We don't have to pretend. Whatever's happening, we'll just take it one step at a time. Tonight, let's just get through dinner."

Jim nodded, a silent thank you passing between them as the reassurance began to replace the pang of anxiety. It was a small moment, yet it carried the weight of an unspoken promise—a promise that together, they would navigate this shifting terrain of feelings and uncertainties.

As they left the house and slid into Jim's truck, the nervous flutter in his stomach gradually eased into something gentler—a tentative hope, or perhaps the unmistakable thrill of the unknown. The drive to Spence and Chandler's residence was enveloped in a quiet hush, not born of discomfort, but of mutual anticipation and the dawning realization that life was on the cusp of transformation.

Jim's grip tightened on the steering wheel as they pulled up to the warmly lit house. It was time to confront the dinner and brace himself for the inevitable cascade of questions—both from the outside world and from the depths of his own turbulent heart.

Glancing over at Brock as they reached the front porch, their eyes met in a silent, profound exchange that communicated volumes without a single word. Whatever awaited them behind that door, they would face it together—one careful, determined step at a time.

# Chapter 12
# Family Dinner

Jim and Brock stood on the timeworn wooden porch as the cool, gentle caress of the evening air brushed against their skin, carrying with it a hint of dew and distant honeysuckle. Their eyes met in a brief, uncertain glance, laden with the weight of unasked questions and unspoken feelings.

Behind the open front door, the cheerful tapestry of conversation and lilting laughter spilled out into the night, a magnetic promise of warmth and welcome waiting just inside. Although family gatherings had always carried the comforting familiarity of home, tonight felt different—charged with subtle tension and lingering questions born from the morning's sudden, intimate revelations.

As Jim reached out toward the doorbell, his hand trembled ever so slightly, a silent confession of his inner turmoil that he wasn't even sure Brock had noticed. Before he could press the button, the door swung open and there stood Jennifer, her glowing, golden eyes lighting up with joyful recognition. Her smile was radiant as her bouncing braids framed a face bursting with delight, and she leapt forward into Jim's waiting arms.

"Uncle Jim! Uncle Brock!" she chirped in a tone so bright it warmed the cool air itself. Jim's heart soared at her unbridled enthusiasm. With a fluid, affectionate motion, he lifted her up, spinning her around as her giggles rang out like musical chimes. He wasn't quite sure when Jennifer had started calling him and Brock "uncle," but the innocent sweetness of it made even the awkwardness of the evening seem charming. Meanwhile, Brock couldn't resist gently tousling her braids as she wrapped her tiny arms around Jim's neck.

"Hey there, kiddo," Brock said in a deep, relaxed tone, his voice soaked in warmth and ease. "You been keeping everyone in line tonight?"

Jennifer's face lit up even further as she grinned cheekily. With a nimble skip, she slid gracefully down to the floor and tugged at the hem of both men's clothes, urging them into the house. "I tried, but Auntie Helen brought cookies, so everyone got distracted!" she declared, her voice bubbling with mischief and childlike wonder.

Stepping inside the foyer, Jim was instantly enveloped by the comforting embrace of his childhood. The familiar hum of his parents' laughter washed over him like a gentle tide. His mom emerged from the gathering, arms wide as if to embrace the entire world. Before he could utter a word, she had wrapped him in a firm, loving embrace that only a mother could bestow.

The hug was both a sanctuary and a reminder of countless evenings filled with unspoken compassion, with the subtle aroma of lavender lotion mingling with memories as it danced around him.

"There's my boy," she murmured softly against his shoulder, her voice warm and soothing, "It's been far too long."

Jim sunk into the embrace, feeling the accumulated tension of the day ebb away. "It has, Mom," he agreed quietly, returning the hug as he noted the delicate creases around her eyes, deepening beautifully as she smiled.

Not long after, his dad stepped forward, his broad hand coming down to clap him on the back in a hearty, solid hug that reverberated with pride and nostalgia. "Good to see you, son. You've been keeping busy, huh?" he said, his deep-toned words full of genuine interest and affection.

"Busy enough," Jim responded with a half-smile as he stepped back, his eyes dancing with both relief and tentative humor. "I'm really glad you both could make it."

Taking a step forward into the warm light of the foyer, Jim introduced Brock with a casual ease born of familiarity. "Mom, Dad, this is Brock Curry. My…best friend and, for now, my temporary roommate. Brock, these are my parents, Bill and Helen Williamson."

"Very nice to meet you folks," Brock rumbled in a deep, approving tone as he extended a firm handshake to Bill. When he turned to greet Helen, the charming woman pulled him into a warm, enveloping hug, her smile as radiant as a summer sunrise.

"And we are just thrilled to meet you, Brock," she exclaimed, her voice lilting with excitement. "Jim has gone on and on about you, and aren't you just a mountain of a man! Jim didn't mention how incredibly tall you are," she teased, gazing up at him with playful admiration.

Both Jim and Brock felt their cheeks warm in an unspoken acknowledgment of her words before they slipped into the inviting living room to greet Spence and Chandler.

The house throbbed with the familiar chaos of family life: the rhythmic clinking of silverware mingled with the gentle hum of overlapping conversations; bursts of laughter, pure and spontaneous, echoed from Chandler and Spence as they put the final touches on preparations. The dining room was already alive with whispered excitement when Jennifer, with a lightness that belied her small stature, skipped back into the room, her high voice announcing the arrival of Jim and Brock like a herald of good fortune.

Spence appeared from around the corner, drying his hands on a well-worn dish towel, his eyes sparkling with mischief and warmth. Grinning as he spotted Jim, he then cast a deliberately playful glance at Brock—a look that sent a chill of being observed too intently racing up Jim's spine.

"Look who decided to show up," Spence declared, pulling Jim into a quick, brotherly hug that felt as comfortable as a familiar patchwork quilt. "Your mom and dad are practically begging for all the stories— hope you're ready."

With a playful roll of his eyes, Jim retorted, "I'm sure you've already told them plenty."

The dining room was suffused with the soulful aroma of Southern cooking—the sweet, earthy fragrance of cornbread, the savory, roasted notes of vegetables, and a faint, tantalizing whisper of smoked meat. Chandler soon appeared, balanced gracefully with a dish in his hands, his welcoming smile as hearty as the meal before them.

"Just in time," he said, his voice laced with genuine cheer. "You two, grab a seat; dinner's ready."

Jim and Brock found their places at the long, polished table, their eyes meeting once again in a glance heavy with unspoken sentiments and deep, inner conflicts. Plates were passed, laughter mingled with conversation, and for a fleeting moment it all felt remarkably ordinary— a tapestry of family rituals and shared histories that was as soothing as it was timeworn. Yet beneath that veneer of normalcy, an electric undercurrent of anticipation lingered, as though the very air waited for someone to speak the truth of what lay beneath.

Jim's mom turned toward him with a curious smile that broke into his reverie. "So, Jim, tell us about work. Any big cases lately? And how are those repairs on your apartment coming along?"

Jim's gaze shifted to his carefully arranged plate, the weight of the question momentarily stilling his thoughts. "Work's good—staying busy with a few cases here and there, nothing too major at the moment. And the apartment's coming along; there are still bits and pieces to finish up, but it's getting there. The landlord said things are behind schedule, so it might be another month or so."

Brock interjected with a serene smile, adding his perspective. "But you know, he's got a place to call home as long as he needs it. It's a pretty big house, after all."

"And Brock," Jim's dad leaned forward, his tone both inviting and inquisitive. "How's the real estate business treating you? I heard there's a big project on the horizon."

Brock set down his fork with deliberate care, nodding slowly. "Yeah, I'm working on converting an old warehouse near the town square. It's going to be a vibrant, mixed-use space—retail on the ground floor and loft apartments above. It's a major undertaking, but I believe it'll bring new life to that corner of the town. And we've got Chandler running point as our chief electrical engineer. I must say, he's been doing a stellar job."

"Sounds incredibly ambitious," Jim's mom said, nodding with thoughtful approval. "And you bought Spence's old house too, didn't you?"

"Yeah," Brock replied with a modest smile. "I've always had a soft spot for Craftsman-style homes, and when I saw Spence's place online, I didn't hesitate."

As the conversation meandered from the new warehouse project to fond memories of Spence's former home, Jim sensed the intensity of attention start to shift away from him, though he couldn't help noticing Spence's eyes lingering on him with quiet, probing curiosity. The moment was ephemeral, however, quickly replaced by his mom's renewed flurry of questions.

"Jim," she began, her tone casual yet laced with an unmistakable undercurrent of curiosity, "it's really wonderful to see you and Brock so close. I don't recall you having just one best friend when you were growing up. Sure, you had plenty of friends, but not one person I'd call your best friend."

Just as Jim's mouth attempted a response, Spence interjected with a playful grin. "Jim and I were probably the closest thing to best friends he ever had," he said, his voice teasing as he recalled old escapades. "Although, if truth be told, I was always the one nudging him into the occasional bout of mischief."

Jim shot Spence a pointed look, his cheeks heating with a mixture of embarrassment and affection. "That's one way to put it," he replied, a half-smile betraying his chagrin.

Brock chuckled softly, the sound blending with the low hum of familial conversation, while Jim felt his mom's keen gaze upon him once more— as if she were silently sifting through his words for hidden meanings.

After the hearty dinner, as the clamor of dishes being cleared gave way to the soft clinks of coffee cups and dessert platters in the living room, Jim's dad pulled him aside. The older man's thoughts seemed as deep and measured as the steady glow of a lantern, his eyes locked onto Jim's with an intensity that foretold a serious conversation. Jim had sensed this moment coming, yet its arrival still carried the weight of inevitability.

"Jim," his dad began in a low, earnest voice, "I couldn't help but notice how close you and Brock are. Is there… something more between you than just friendship?"

A tight twist churned in Jim's stomach. He swallowed hard, his voice caught somewhere between honesty and hesitation. "We're just… best friends, Dad. We have a lot in common, and we simply hang out a lot—that's all there is to it."

His dad's eyes narrowed slightly, as if trying to gauge a truth hidden beneath Jim's words. "You know you can talk to us about anything, right? Your mom and I only ever want you to be truly happy."

"I know, Dad," Jim murmured, offering a small, tight-lipped smile that revealed both resignation and relief. "But there's nothing more to say. We're simply friends."

"Alright," his dad said softly, clapping a supportive hand on his shoulder in a gesture that tried to bridge the gap between unspoken understanding and acceptance. "If you say so."

As Jim rejoined the rest of the family, his heart thumped unevenly when he caught sight of his mom and Spence in a hushed conversation near the doorway. Slowing his steps to better catch their words, he listened as his mom's voice dipped into a secretive tone.

"You don't think…?" his mom whispered, her tone a mix of hope and mischief. "I mean, wouldn't it be exciting if—"

Before she could finish, Spence interjected gently, though a playful note still laced his voice. "Aunt Helen, it's too soon to jump to conclusions."

"I just think it might be something to keep a close eye on," she murmured, glancing over at Jim before lowering her voice further. "Who knows, I might have just met my future son-in-law tonight."

Spence offered a noncommittal shrug, his eyes momentarily flicking to Jim with a knowing look that made Jim's cheeks burn with both amusement and discomfort.

Later, as the evening's festivities wound down and the house settled into a reflective calm, little Jennifer climbed softly into Jim's lap, wrapping her small arms around his neck like a cherished keepsake. "Goodnight, Uncle Jim," she whispered sleepily, her words a gentle lullaby in the quiet room. Then she turned to Brock, who stood nearby with a kind smile, and added, "Goodnight, Uncle Brock."

Jim's mom, standing not far away, chuckled softly and murmured, "Out of the mouths of babes." Her comment hung in the air like an alluring challenge, stirring the unspoken emotions between Jim and Brock. Their eyes met once more—this time charged with an intensity that spoke of uncertainty, temptation, and the weight of unspoken destinies. Jim realized, with disquieting clarity, that he needed to define what was unfolding between them—if indeed it could ever be defined.

Later, as they left Spence and Chandler's house under the starlit sky, Jim's chest tightened with a blend of uncertainty and the possibility of something new. His parents had seen it, Spence had seen it, and even little Jennifer had sensed the shifting dynamics between him and Brock—dynamics that he himself was still wrestling to understand. Now, with two days off from the everyday, he knew he'd have to confront these tangled emotions and clarify their meaning.

Climbing into the truck, Jim glanced over at Brock, whose expression mirrored his own—a blend of tender hope and quiet apprehension. In the hushed confines of the vehicle, Brock's soft voice finally broke through, "Guess we have a lot to talk about."

Jim's grip tightened on the steering wheel as he nodded slowly, the quiet determination in his eyes belying the storm of thoughts raging within. "Yeah. We do."

# Chapter 13
# What Now?

The ride back to Brock's house was laden with a heavy, charged silence as the crisp night air slipped in through the cracked car windows. The engine's low, insistent purr broke the quiet while Jim's hazel eyes remained fixed on the road, his fingers drumming a restless beat on the steering wheel.

Brock sat stiffly beside him, his mind a turbulent storm of raw, unspoken emotions that twisted relentlessly within him. The evening had unfolded with a frenetic energy—or at least as much energy as one could muster after a tumultuous, almost explosive family dinner. Yet, unvoiced questions churned between him and Jim, hanging like a dense, oppressive fog.

When they finally pulled up, Jim parked in the driveway and let the engine growl softly for a moment before shutting it off as if to punctuate the quiet tension. He exhaled a deep, release-laden breath as if he had been clinging to it for an eternity.

"Thanks for coming tonight," he said, his gaze flickering to Brock with a mixture of gratitude and hesitance.

"Yeah, of course," Brock replied, his voice steady yet edged with a razor-sharp uncertainty. The conversation at dinner, or maybe the passionate warmth of Jim's family, had rattled his emotions into a frenzy. And then there were those knowing smiles from Jim's mom whenever she mentioned them together—a silent confirmation that only deepened the turmoil inside him.

Jim swung open the door and stepped onto the gravel-strewn path, each crunch underfoot echoing the unspoken intensity of the moment. The porch light bathed the entrance in a searing glow, tossing elongated, dramatic shadows across the wooden planks.

Jim fumbled with his keys, a brief moment of vulnerability when Brock almost reached out with a steadying hand—but he hesitated. By the time the door swung open, Jim had wrested back his composure, his eyes smoldering with conflicted determination.

Inside, the house was cloaked in a heavy silence broken only by the relentless tick-tock of an ancient grandfather clock. Jim carefully closed the door behind them, the lock clicking into place as if sealing away their uncertainties. They stood in the entryway, the air crackling with anticipation and the weight of unspoken truths. Jim's eyes darted anxiously around the room, searching desperately for something solid to anchor his swirling thoughts.

"Brock…" he began quietly, a tremor in his voice as if testing the gravity of what lay ahead. "I—I need some time to think… before we decide on our next steps. Whatever that means."

Brock's heart sank, each beat a heavy thud of uncertainty, though he fought hard to mask his inner turmoil. He forced a reassuring smile, though his mind seethed with anxious questions: Is Jim truly ready for this? Does he yearn for me as fiercely as I do for him? The uncertainty gnawed at him, a relentless predator in the back of his throat, making him wonder if he had pressed too far or if Jim's feelings were simply too fragile to grasp.

Drawing closer, Jim's features hardened with a mixture of confusion and a tender vulnerability, like a man caught between duty and desire. Before any further words could dare surface, Jim reached out, his hand trembling as it gently cradled Brock's face. The kiss that exploded between them was laden with intensity—a tentative collision of need and desire, an exploration fraught with both hesitation and burning reassurance. In that moment, each touch, each soft press of lips, screamed with unspoken promises.

As they slowly pulled apart, Jim's thumb traced a lingering, electrifying line across Brock's cheek. The look in Brock's eyes—brimming with questions, mixed with a fragile hint of fear—spurred Jim on. "Don't give up on me," he whispered, his voice nearly lost in the charged silence. "I just…I need time to think."

Brock swallowed hard, the knot in his chest loosening ever so slightly. "Take all the time you need," he managed to say, though the raw ache in his tone betrayed the storm of emotions within him.

With a small, grateful smile, Jim turned toward the darkened staircase, his footsteps soft against the wooden floor as he ascended to his room. For a long, breathless moment, Brock stood frozen, watching him vanish upward, the weight of the night pressing down like an irrevocable verdict.

Eventually, Brock exhaled a long-held breath and trudged to his own room, the burdens on his shoulders making them sag. In the dim light of the space, a faint glow from streetlights seeped through the window, creating ghostly, shifting silhouettes over the floor. Collapsing onto the edge of his bed, he ran a hand through his hair, trying in vain to summon clarity amid the chaotic rush of doubts. Was Jim really ready for this passionate gamble? Or was he simply caught in his own maze of confusion and desire? Yet, despite the brutal uncertainty, a cautious hope still simmered within him. He could still taste the lingering warmth of Jim's kiss, the way that gentle hold had ignited a fragile flame of something deep and irrevocable.

Across the hall, Jim lay in bed, his eyes fixed on the ceiling, each thought a maelstrom of possibilities. The memory of Brock's tender yet charged kiss lingered, a vivid reminder of a connection that transcended impulsive lust, reaching into the realm of desperate need for reassurance. It was overwhelming, a torrent he hadn't anticipated, and now that it enveloped him, it terrified him.

His mind raced back to the vivid evening at his parents' house—the sly questions, the heavy-eyed glances, the shiver-inducing moment when his mother murmured, "Out of the mouths of babes," as Jennifer had casually called them Uncle Jim and Uncle Brock. Perhaps her words held a seed of truth, or perhaps they were simply an echo of his own frantic thoughts.

A sudden buzz from his phone yanked Jim from his tangled reflections. It was a text from Brock: *Goodnight. I'm here whenever you're ready.*

Jim stared at the screen, feeling the pulse of their intertwined fates, before replying: *Goodnight, Brock. And thank you.* Setting the phone aside, he rolled over and swallowed himself beneath the blanket, a cocoon of fleeting warmth.

Their futures shimmered with uncertainty, yet tonight had been a ferocious step forward—raw, unsteady, but undeniably real. As sleep threatened to claim him, Jim's thoughts circled back with fierce clarity to Brock's tentative smile to the searing memory of that first kiss. It wasn't a promise etched in stone, merely a blazing beginning. And for now, that incendiary spark was enough.

# Chapter 14
## Stranger in Town

Jim's alarm buzzed relentlessly on his phone at 5:30 AM, slicing through the quiet gloom of early morning and yanking him from a night steeped in restless tossing. With heavy, reluctant arms, he reached over and smothered the clamor of the phone; his limbs were weighed down by exhaustion and lingering dreams.

The hours before had been filled with a ceaseless dance of thoughts—images of Brock, the residue of last night's electrifying kiss, and a mixture of longing and confusion that left more questions than resolutions in its wake. With a sigh that carried the weight of his conflicted emotions, he rubbed the sleep from his eyes and slowly extricated himself from the embrace of his bed, gathering his uniform from the chair as if it were a talisman for the day ahead.

Venturing into the kitchen, Jim was met with an enveloping silence that seemed to echo his inner turmoil. Brock's door remained closed, its stillness belying any sign of life or the comforting chaos of shared mornings.

Jim's hand hovered hesitantly over the cool metal of the doorknob, caught between the instinct to check on him and the mindful decision to grant Brock the solitude he needed. In that quiet moment, he resolved to let his friend sleep; both of them, after all, were in desperate need of time and space to wade through their tangled thoughts.

Stepping out into the relentless Alabama summer, Jim was hit by the oppressive heat that seemed almost tangible—a thick, humid shroud hanging over the quiet neighborhood. The air shimmered with the intensity of the rising sun, making each breath feel weighted and slow. With no time to wait, he climbed into his patrol car. The rumble of the engine provided a fragile anchor to reality, offering a semblance of concentration amid the inner chaos. Today was the final shift before a short reprieve with his parents—a two-day escape planned meticulously for reconnection, free from distractions and complications... or so he hoped.

By mid-morning, the radio began crackling to life with a series of urgent calls. Amanda, his steady and observant partner, sat by his side as she calmly detailed the incoming reports, her voice a soothing counterpoint to the rising tension in the car.

"Another sighting of this stranger," she remarked, her tone edged with an unmistakable hint of unease. "That makes four today."

"Sounds like people are spooked." Jim turned at the next intersection, heading toward the location of the latest sighting. "Description's the same every time—tall, dark clothes, baseball cap pulled low. Just watching places."

Amanda tapped her pen against her notepad. "You know what's strange? Three of these sightings have been near your apartment complex."

Jim's hands tightened on the steering wheel. "You thinking what I'm thinking?"

"That maybe our mysterious stranger has something to do with the fire?" Amanda's voice dropped lower. "The timing is a little off. These sightings started a few weeks after the blaze."

"But Fire Chief Rogers did say it looked like arson." Jim's mind raced through the details Rogers had shared—multiple ignition points, accelerant trails, the gas can in the bathtub. "Professional job too. Someone who knew what they were doing."

Jim's grip tightened on the steering wheel as he asked, "What's the description this time?"

"Same as the others," Amanda replied, her brow creasing as she recounted the details.

"Tall, wearing dark pants and a dark hooded shirt. Which is really bizarre given it's hotter than hell out here." She shook her head lightly, her auburn curls bouncing with the motion as if in silent disbelief. "Who in their right mind wears a hoodie in August?"

"Let's keep it open as a possibility that this stranger is somehow related to the fire. Once we have more information, we can decide if we pursue the connection or if we have two troubling cases.

Jim's mind raced as the patrol car weaved through the humid streets. Every call they pursued revealed the same elusive figure: a shadowy presence, always skirting the edges of perception, lurking near back alleys or slinking behind abandoned storefronts.

Every time he evaded capture on camera, his features were obscured by the darkness of his hood or his body angled just so as to vanish from view. It was as if he possessed an almost preternatural intuition for dodging the relentless eye of surveillance.

Their first destination was Old Man Prescott's hardware store, a venerable establishment with creaky wooden floors and dusty shelves that echoed with history. Inside, they huddled around a grainy black-and-white monitor to scrutinize the security footage—a brief glimpse of the stranger, a dark silhouette momentarily illuminated by streaks of sunlight before he slipped out of the frame like a fleeting ghost.

"Damn," Amanda murmured, her eyes narrowing as she focused on the elusive figure. "He's a slippery one."

Leaning in closer, Jim's frustration simmered beneath his calm exterior. The footage displayed the man as nothing more than a vague outline—a shadow against the luminous backdrop of the alley, his face forever turned away and hidden beneath the hood.

"He knows the cameras are there," Jim observed, shaking his head slowly. "He's deliberately avoiding them."

They poured over additional footage from other locations around town, each clip painting the same enigmatic picture: the stranger emerged at the periphery of the lens, his movements deliberate and evasive, as if he were choreographing a silent dance of evasion.

The local shop owners reported increasingly disturbing losses—initially trivial items like loose screws and faded trinkets, then escalating to essential supplies: lengths of rope, rolls of duct tape, bundles of garbage bags, and even a hunting knife.

The most alarming revelation came from Mr. Danberry, whose voice trembled as he recounted how a prized shotgun had inexplicably vanished from his truck overnight.

"A shotgun?" Amanda echoed, her tone suddenly laced with concern. "This is more than just petty theft."

Jim nodded, a tight knot of anxiety coiling in his stomach. "We need to figure out what this guy is really after. And fast."

Under the relentless midday sun, which beat down with a merciless intensity, Jim and Amanda continued their investigation. Sweat beaded on their brows as they drove through the sweltering heat, questioning locals whose brows furrowed in confusion at the mention of the elusive intruder.

Everyone described the stranger similarly—a man who didn't quite belong, shrouded in an enigmatic air that clashed starkly with the suffocating weather.

After a brief stop at a rustic diner, with its neon-lit sign flickering against the fading daylight, they settled in for a late lunch. The clink of ice in their glasses of iced tea punctuated the silence, and amid a particularly long sip, Amanda's eyes fixed on Jim. "You're awfully quiet," she noted softly. "Everything alright?"

Jim met her gaze, the lines on his face revealing a storm of thoughts. "Yeah… just a lot on my mind." His voice trailed off, refusing to divulge more, though Amanda's attentive silence spoke volumes about her own buried concerns.

No sooner had they finished than another call erupted through the radio. This time, the stranger had been spotted at the edge of town, skulking around a desolate lot behind the old grocery store.

A surge of adrenaline quickened Jim's pulse as he pulled the patrol car out of the diner's parking area. "Let's hope we get there in time," he muttered, his voice a blend of urgency and caution.

As the sun began its slow descent, casting long, dramatic shadows across the cracked asphalt, the duo arrived at the vacant lot. The area was hauntingly quiet, the only sound being the soft, persistent buzz of cicadas in the distance. Jim's eyes swept across the desolate expanse—a scattering of old, crumbling foundations and rusted barrels that whispered remnants of past industry.

While they ventured further into the lot, Jim's boot brushed against something unexpected amid the scattered debris. Bending down, he discovered a fragment of black fabric protruding from behind one of the dilapidated barrels. With a careful crouch, he retrieved a dark hooded sweatshirt, its fabric damp with perspiration and crumpled as if discarded in haste.

"Looks like he was here," Amanda said, her voice filled with a mix of curiosity and concern as she picked up a nearby empty water bottle, turning it over in her hands. "But why would he leave this behind?"

Jim's gaze swept over the scene again, a chill creeping along his spine despite the stifling heat. There was something profoundly unsettling about the moment—a silent assurance that they were not alone. An inexplicable tension hung in the air, as if an unseen presence lingered just beyond the corner of their perception, watching their every move with eerie intent.

"We should check with Danberry again," Jim suggested in a low, tense tone. "Make sure there's nothing else missing."

As they slowly made their way back to the patrol car, the oppressive heat seemed to melt away into the background, replaced by a creeping dread that clung to Jim's thoughts. It felt as though they were teetering on the brink of an unseen abyss—a precipice from which danger might suddenly surge.

In that heavy silence, a small, nagging voice in the back of his mind questioned, What if this stranger isn't just a petty thief? Is this stranger somehow connected to the arson at the apartment complex? What if he's here for something—someone—far more sinister?

For the first time in what felt like an eternity, Jim was gripped by a raw, undeniable fear. Flashback to the junkyard investigation gripped him. He exchanged a look with Amanda, whose eyes mirrored his own urgency and the dark, uncertain edge of the day's unfolding events.

"Let's figure out who this guy is," Amanda said firmly, breaking the silence with a determination that resonated in the quiet afternoon air.

"Before something really bad happens."

Jim nodded, his jaw set in steely resolve, as they climbed back into the patrol car. The day had been a labyrinth of unanswered questions, yet one thing was unmistakably clear—whatever was unfolding had only just begun. And he vowed, in that charged moment, that neither he nor the town under his guard would be caught unawares.

# Chapter 15
# A Brush with Danger

As the day wound down, the late afternoon light stretched its golden slant across the asphalt, casting long, wavering shadows that danced along the quiet streets. Jim was just about to radio into the dispatcher and clock out when a crackling call shattered the calm—a security breach had been detected at the new warehouse project on the outskirts of town. A sudden, icy weight settled in his stomach.

"Amanda, we've got an alarm at the construction site," he said, his tone tight with urgency as he flipped the sirens on.

In moments, the patrol car's flashing lights sliced through the fading twilight as they sped down Main Street, the sound of the engine a steady drumbeat against the silence of the evening.

Approaching the sprawling complex, Jim's unease mounted. The warehouse was a colossal structure of cold concrete and imposing steel beams, looming like a modern fortress devoid of warmth. It stood deserted and eerily silent, the usual bustle nowhere to be seen. They parked near a weathered chain-link fence and shut off the engine, the stillness amplifying their tension.

"Let's hope this is just a false alarm," Amanda murmured, her eyes scanning the quiet perimeter with cautious suspicion.

Jim nodded and stepped out, drawing his flashlight, its narrow beam slicing through the dimming light. "Stay alert. I'll cover the east side; you check the west. It might be the guy we've been tracking all day," he instructed in a hushed voice.

The night air was oppressively hot, wrapping around him like a heavy cloak that made his skin glisten with sweat. Every step toward the half-finished warehouse sent a shiver of anticipation down his spine. His flashlight cut a precise arc across the rough gravel and scattered remnants of construction equipment, each fragment illuminated in stark detail. Rounding a silent corner, Jim's eyes fell upon a solitary figure standing by a partly-opened side door—Brock.

Instantly, Jim's pulse quickened, pounding like a rapid drumbeat in his ears. Brock was there, pacing with a frantic energy; his face was ashen, and his eyes shone with a mix of agitation and relief.

"Brock?" Jim called softly, quickening his pace. "What are you doing here?"

Startled, Brock turned around, relief washing over his features as soon as he recognized Jim. "Jim, thank God," he stammered, his voice trembling with residual fear. "The alarm went off just after I left. I rushed back as soon as I got the notification on my phone. I wasn't sure what to expect."

"What did you find?" Jim asked, his eyes scanning the area for any signs of movement in the growing shadows.

"Nothing's missing," Brock replied with a furrowed brow.

"But..." He paused, swallowing hard as he pointed shakily toward a small office space at the far end of the warehouse.

"The place I'm using as an office—it's been ransacked. Someone tore through everything; plans, paperwork... all of it is scattered everywhere. I don't keep any cash in sight. Nothing of any real value, outside the mountain of power tools, which were untouched. Someone was looking for something. But what?"

Jim surveyed that small space. Each of the drawers from the desk had been pulled out, and their contents dumped and scattered. The file cabinet had been pried open and treated similarly. Even the trash can had been dumped out, and the contents were strewn about. The concept sketches had been ripped off the wall.

A chill crept up Jim's spine as he edged toward the doorway. Inside, the room was a disaster of disarray: blueprints lay crumpled like discarded leaves, documents were strewn haphazardly across the dirty concrete floor, and a once-sturdy file cabinet had been knocked over. The papers, caught in a weak draft, fluttered restlessly, creating a dance of erratic shadows in the meager light.

Amanda reappeared beside them, her gaze sharp and assessing as she took in the chaotic scene. "Looks like someone was looking for something," she said, her tone heavy with suspicion. "And it might just be the same perpetrator we've been following."

Jim moved closer to Brock, who looked visibly shaken. Lowering his voice, he placed a reassuring hand on Brock's shoulder. "It's going to be okay," he murmured. "We'll figure this out. You didn't see anyone on your way back, did you?"

"No," Brock replied, his voice barely above a whisper. "Just... everything was like this when I got here."

For a fleeting moment, as Jim's hand rested on Brock's shoulder and their eyes locked, an unspoken intimacy filled the space between them—a warmth that contrasted sharply with the chill of the night and the chaos surrounding them. In that brief heartbeat, the urgency of their duty faded into a palpable connection. Each lost in the silent recognition of something more than just camaraderie.

Brock stepped closer, his voice dropping to a tender murmur. "Jim... thank you. For being here." There was a glimmer in his eye, a spark of gratitude intertwined with longing that Jim had seen before—one that resonated with the growing beat of his own heart.

Just as the moment threatened to overtake them, Amanda's voice cut sharply through the silence. "Hey, I'm going to check the perimeter again. Just to be sure," she said briskly, glancing at the pair before disappearing around a corner.

Jim cleared his throat, reluctantly letting his hand fall from Brock's shoulder, the fragile connection dissolving with the abrupt return to duty. "We... we need to finish up here," he said, striving to regain his composure. "I'll take your statement and file a report. Extra patrols will be out here tonight."

Brock's face faltered for a moment as he nodded slowly. "Right. Of course."

Even as Amanda's footsteps faded into the encompassing shadows, a quiet, lingering spark remained between Jim and Brock—unspoken words hanging heavily in the air, a reminder of their shared vulnerability amid the chaos. But now was no time for private thoughts; there was a job to be done, and the dangers of the night demanded their full attention.

Jim didn't get home until well after midnight, exhaustion weighing on him like a burden as he fumbled with the keys at the front door. The familiar silence of the house, wrapped in darkness, felt almost somber. He trudged up the creaking stairs, a small, desperate hope flickering within him that maybe—just maybe—Brock would still be awake. Yet, upon whispering his way to Brock's room, the closed door and the thin ribbon of light seeping beneath it betrayed the truth: Brock was already lost to sleep.

A long, heavy sigh—one Jim hadn't realized he'd been holding—escaped him before he slowly drifted into his own room. There, in the embracing darkness, time seemed to stretch on interminably as his mind bounced between the recent, unsettling break-in and the strange, lingering sensation of Brock's presence—so near, yet so sorely out of reach.

# Chapter 16
# A Sharp Dressed Man

The dawn broke with a delicate blush, casting a soft glow over the world as Jim slipped away from the warmth of his room at Brock's craftsman, a sense of urgency pulling him into the quiet morning. His parents had planned a cozy day together, but an insistent whisper in his mind urged him to divert his path, to seek out Brock once more. It wasn't just the unsettling report that haunted him; it was the fierce curiosity curling like smoke in his chest, igniting a hunger he couldn't ignore.

As he arrived at the construction site, the air thick with humidity and the scent of wet earth, Jim's eyes locked onto Brock, who stood near the entrance. He was flanked by another man, a striking figure radiating an air of polished sophistication. Clad in a meticulously tailored charcoal gray suit that seemed to mock the sweltering heat, the stranger's jet black hair was slicked back with a precision that made Jim's fingers itch to run through it, to unravel the pristine facade.

A brilliant white smile beamed bright in contrast to the well-groomed, sharply edged ebony mustache and beard. The man's demeanor exuded confidence, a quiet power that sent a jolt of something dark and possessive coursing through Jim.

Brock's nod was gentle yet hesitant, and Jim could see the flicker of unease in his eyes as he conversed with the impeccably dressed intruder. A surge of anger mixed with an unsettling jealousy clawed at Jim, tightening around his chest like a vice as he parked his car with a force that echoed his inner turmoil. The humid air wrapped around him, heavy and suffocating, amplifying the rapid thrum of his pulse, not from excitement, but from a primal urge to stake his claim.

At the sound of his approach, Brock turned, his face transforming with a radiant mixture of relief and surprise. "Jim," he breathed, his warm voice wrapping around Jim like a familiar embrace. "I didn't expect to see you here today. I figured you'd be with your folks. Is everything okay?"

Jim's gaze flickered toward the stranger, who had just begun to drift away from Brock's side, his movements smooth and deliberate as he slipped into one of the nearly finished warehouses. "Who's that?" Jim asked, striving for a casual tone, but the tremor in his voice betrayed the storm brewing within him.

"That's State Inspector Gary Mitchell," Brock explained carefully, his brow furrowing slightly. "He's here to review the progress on the project and sign off on the next set of permits. I called in a favor to have him come before business hours. Cost me a pair of courtside Hawks tickets. If not, we'd be waiting for another 6-8 weeks to fit into his schedule."

But even as Brock spoke, Jim felt a gnawing instinct that something was off. Watching Gary move through the site with an almost predatory grace, each deliberate step and furtive glance toward Brock ignited a fire of unease deep within him. And Brock had given him tickets to a Hawks game. *What the fuck!* It was as if the air crackled with unspoken tension, a current that threatened to pull them all under.

Perceptive to the turmoil brewing between them, Brock took a step closer, his presence a comforting balm against Jim's rising storm. "What is it?" he asked softly, his eyes searching Jim's face, probing for the truth behind the veil of his emotions. "Jim, you seem… upset."

The weight of Brock's concern was a double-edged sword, both grounding and electrifying. Jim felt the heat of his gaze, a connection that blazed through the tension, igniting a longing that threatened to overwhelm him. He'd never been the jealous type, ever. "I just—" he began, but the words faltered as he wrestled with the raw intensity of his feelings, the need to protect what was his, clashing with the reality of the situation. The air between them thickened, charged with unspoken desires and a sense of impending confrontation, leaving Jim teetering on the edge of something profound and inevitable.

"I'm not," Jim protested, though his strained voice revealed otherwise. "I just wanted to check in on you. After last night. You were already in bed when I got back to the house last night and up and gone this morning before I even woke up."

Brock's eyes softened as he reached out, his fingertips brushing lightly against Jim's arm in a gesture of comfort. "I'm okay," he murmured.

"You really didn't have to worry. I knew you were exhausted after last night and figured you deserved to sleep in."

Jim nodded, though the searing jealousy in his chest made each nod feel like an admission of defeat. Determined to clear his muddled thoughts, he reluctantly decided that a session of family bonding might drown out the darker feelings stirring inside. "I should get going," he said, forcing a smile. "Family day."

With a lingering, regretful look, Brock let go, and Jim turned back toward his car, deliberately not daring to glance back one more time.

As Jim drove back toward town, his knuckles whitened against the steering wheel. The image of Gary Mitchell's predatory smile and the way his hazel green eyes had lingered on Brock played on repeat in his mind, stoking a fire he didn't fully understand. The rational part of him knew he was being ridiculous—Brock was a successful businessman who dealt with inspectors and officials regularly. But the primal part of him, the part that had awakened since their night together, wanted to turn around and make it clear that Brock wasn't available.

As he approached Spence's farmhouse, he passed Chandler, who was headed to the warehouses, and offered a wave. He took a deep breath and exhaled. He knew he had to clear his head before spending the day with his parents. They deserved his full attention during this short visit.

# Chapter 17
# Camaraderie

Brock finished up with the inspector and headed into his office before the crew arrived. The cold shoulder treatment he'd received from Jim had him reeling. Jim was hot one minute and cold as ice the next. *What the hell?* He focused on organizing the files and documents he'd collected and shoved into the file cabinet after last night's break-in. He needed the distraction.

The pale light of early morning was warming the sky when Chandler's truck groaned to a halt on the gravel lot of the construction site. He stepped out, clutching his thermos and paper bag, the cool, crisp air nipping at his nose.

As Chandler strode toward the office—a back corner glass enclosure with a weathered 'Office' sign swinging above its door—he spotted Brock through the frosted window, slumped in the chair with his head resting in his hands.

Brock shifted, hunched over a sprawl of blueprints, his dark ginger beard catching the soft glow of the desk lamp. The rugged man's usually confident posture was absent, replaced by a slump that suggested a weight heavier than the steel beams he so often hoisted.

Chandler hesitated for a moment, taking in the unusual sight. Brock was the epitome of a self-made man, always composed, with his intense demeanor and armor against the world. To see him this way stirred a new sense of camaraderie within Chandler.

"Morning boss," Chandler called out as he pushed open the door, hoping his voice would bridge the gap between them without startling the bear of a man.

Brock looked up, his soft blue eyes revealing a hint of surprise before they settled back into their calm, inviting gaze. "Hey, Chandler. You're in early."

"Could say the same about you." Chandler raised the thermos with a knowing smile. "Brought some coffee. Figured we could use a decent cup before the day kicks off."

"Appreciate it." Brock's response was brief, but there was warmth in his tone that welcomed the gesture.

Chandler poured the steaming liquid into two mugs he found in a cabinet, the aroma filling the small space. He handed one to Brock, who wrapped his large hands around it, the heat seeping into his skin.

"Trouble sleeping?" Chandler ventured, leaning against a filing cabinet. Brock's gaze drifted momentarily to the blueprints before returning to Chandler.

"Something like that," he admitted, taking a slow sip of the coffee. It was rare for Brock to concede even the smallest vulnerability.

"Mind if I join you?" Chandler gestured to the chair across from Brock.

"Please." Brock's nod was almost imperceptible, but it was an invitation nonetheless.

Chandler settled in, the two men sharing the silence comfortably for a few moments, sipping their drinks. The office was sparse, functional, much like Brock himself—no frills, just the bare essentials, but everything with a purpose. The quiet intensity that typically surrounded Brock seemed muted now, replaced by an openness that Chandler recognized as an unspoken cue to conversation.

"Anything on your mind?" Chandler asked, breaking the stillness. His words were casual, but his gaze held a steady, supportive focus, ready to listen to whatever might be weighing on Brock's broad shoulders.

Brock let out a breath he seemed to have been holding, his eyes remaining fixed on Chandler. He looked like a man standing at the edge of a precipice, deciding whether to retreat or leap.

"Actually, yeah," Brock said, the trace of resolve in his voice suggesting he was ready for the latter. "There's something I've been trying to sort out..."

Chandler nodded, giving Brock the space to let the words flow in their own time. This was new territory for both of them, but Chandler sensed that whatever Brock was about to share, it mattered—and he intended to be there, fully present, for whatever came next.

Brock's hand trembled slightly as he set his coffee cup down, the black liquid barely disturbed. He ran a calloused finger along the rim, seemingly gathering his thoughts before his gaze lifted, meeting Chandler's steady eyes.

"Back in the day," Brock started, voice rough like gravel being turned over after a heavy rain, "I thought I found the real deal. Someone who felt like home." His lips curled into a bitter smile, pulling at the edges of his silver beard. "Turns out, fidelity was a foreign language to him." Brock powered through recounting the basics of his relationship with Jason Waters.

Chandler leaned forward, elbows on thighs, projecting an aura of quiet solidarity. He knew better than to interrupt; this was Brock's moment, and he needed to let it unfurl at its own pace.

"Faithful" seemed to hang in the air between them, a word loaded with disappointment and pain. Brock's jaw tightened, muscles working under the skin as if chewing on the memories.

"Ever since then," Brock continued, looking past Chandler now, to a place filled with shadows and echoes of his past, "I've kept it casual. Real casual." A self-deprecating chuckle escaped him, but there was no humor in it. "Bath houses, sex clubs... You name the app, I had it."

His confession hung between them, unadorned and raw.

"Never the same guy twice. No strings. No chance for another heartbreak." Brock's hand formed a fist, knuckles whitening against the desk's surface. "Emotion and sex... I pulled them apart like threads from fabric. Thought it made me stronger."

Chandler remained silent, his presence a solid comfort, a witness to the fortress Brock had constructed around himself. Brock's blue eyes flickered back to Chandler, carrying a depth that spoke of storms weathered and seas navigated alone.

Brock's gaze drifted out the window to the burgeoning light of dawn, painting the construction site in hues of gold and amber. A crane stood silhouetted against the awakening sky—a stark reminder of the life he had built: structured, predictable, controlled. That is, until Jim.

"Jim was...different," Brock admitted, his voice barely above a whisper, betraying a vulnerability that surprised even himself. He turned from the window, his eyes finding Chandler's. "I didn't intend for it, you know? I wasn't looking for anything deep. But with him, everything felt different."

Chandler watched Brock closely, noting the subtle shift in his demeanor. The man who had walked through fire to build walls around his heart was now confessing an unexpected crack in his armor.

"Before I even knew about his struggle or where he stood," Brock continued, a fondness seeping into his tone, "there was this pull towards him. It was more than just physical—it was like... like gravitating towards warmth when you've been cold for too long."

"Jim talked to Spence and me," Chandler said gently, breaking into the silence that followed. "He's got his own battles, Brock. This small-town mindset, it's a lot for someone to take on, especially someone like Jim."

"Did he say...?" Brock's question hung, unfinished, his eyes searching Chandler's for an answer he wasn't sure he wanted.

"Enough to connect the dots." Chandler leaned back in his chair, choosing his words with care. "He's not blind to what's between you two. Or at least, what could be. It's not easy for him either—this isn't about not feeling the same way. It's about the weight of those gazes, the whispers, the judgment."

"Intimate..." Brock murmured, almost to himself, as if saying it aloud would make it real, solidify the connection that he'd been craving yet distancing himself from simultaneously.

"More than once," Chandler affirmed softly, acknowledging the depth of their shared experience without needing to spell it out. Brock's hand trembled as he reached for his coffee cup, absorbing the implications of Chandler's revelations.

"More than once," he repeated, allowing himself to believe—to hope— that amidst the complexity of their entangled lives, there existed the possibility of something genuine, something worth risking the fortress he had so meticulously maintained.

Brock leaned against the cool metal frame of the window, staring out at the skeletal structures that rose from the construction site. The morning air carried a crispness that hinted at the impending change of seasons, and with it, a shift in his own life that left him unsettled.

"Small towns," Chandler began, breaking the contemplative silence as he joined Brock by the window, "they have this way of holding onto you, you know? Everyone thinks they know who you are, what you're about. It's suffocating when the person you thought you were... isn't who you turn out to be."

Brock turned from the window, his gaze settling on Chandler. He could see the empathy in the man's eyes, the understanding that came from shared experiences—different, yet somehow the same.

"Jim's got this whole town's history wrapped around him like a blanket," Chandler continued, "and stepping out of that comfort zone for something-or-someone he's unsure about... that takes courage."

"Courage," Brock echoed, the word tasting bitter on his tongue. He gripped his coffee cup tightly, as if it could anchor him in the storm of emotions that threatened to sweep him away. "We've slept together, Chandler. And it was more than I could have imagined." Brock's voice dropped to a whisper, each word heavy with significance. "But it's not just about the sex. There's something deeper, and it scares me."

"Jim feels it too. That much is clear," Chandler assured him, leaning against the window frame in a mirror of Brock's earlier posture.

"Does he?" Brock's eyes searched Chandler's again, seeking assurance, seeking hope. "Because I'm falling for him, Chandler. Hard. And I don't know how to be with someone who's still questioning everything he's ever known about himself."

Chandler nodded, solemn in his understanding. "It's a tough road, but Jim's not walking it alone. And neither are you." He placed a hand on Brock's shoulder, a silent vow of support.

"Promise me something?" Brock asked, his voice barely above a murmur as he met Chandler's steady gaze.

"Anything."

"Keep this between us," Brock said, his plea etched with vulnerability. "I don't want to push him or make things harder."

"You have my word," Chandler replied, his grip on Brock's shoulder firm and reassuring. "This conversation stays right here, in this office."

"Thank you," Brock breathed out, feeling a fraction lighter. With Chandler's promise, he allowed himself a sliver of optimism amidst the tangle of fears.

Brock shuffled the papers on the desk, a mindless task to steady his thoughts. He glanced up at Chandler, who had settled into the chair across from him, coffee cup cradled in his hands. The silence stretched between them, filled with the hum of the office air conditioner and the faint sounds of the construction site outside coming to life.

"Been out since my late teens," Brock finally said, breaking the stillness. He ran a hand through his beard, a gesture that anchored him. "Proud of it, too. But Jim... he's got a whole world weighing on his shoulders."

Chandler took a slow sip of his coffee, setting it down with measured care. "When Spence and I started getting close, there was plenty to navigate. He was Jennifer's teacher. Small town, remember?" His eyes held a flicker of memory, a hint of the hurdles they'd overcome. "It wasn't easy."

"Sounds complicated," Brock murmured, leaning back in his chair, the leather creaking under his weight.

"Was," Chandler agreed. "But love isn't that easy. It just is. And when something is meant to be..." He trailed off, locking eyes with Brock, unspoken understanding passing between them. "You can run all you want, but love, real love, it finds you. No matter what."

Brock absorbed the words, feeling them resonate deep within his chest. He nodded slowly, a sense of solidarity forming. Here was someone who understood the cost of love, the risk of it.

"Thanks, Chandler," he said, voice lined with a newfound determination. "I guess sometimes you just have to fight for what's worth it, huh?"

"Every time," Chandler replied, the corners of his mouth lifting in a knowing smile.

# Chapter 18
# Revelations

The visit with his parents offered only a fragile respite from his inner turmoil. Their cheerful smiles, light-hearted chatter, and even the playful splashes in the new pool that Spence and Chandler had installed behind the farmhouse were little more than temporary distractions. Despite the warmth of these moments, Jim's mind inevitably circled back to Brock and that mysterious, impeccably dressed man.

By the time he finally left his parents, the setting sun bathed the sky in a breathtaking, golden glow, pulling him magnetically toward Brock's house. He needed answers. He needed clarity. A whisper inside warned him of the absurdity of his suspicions, yet another, fiercer voice burned with relentless doubt.

When he arrived at Brock's house, the driveway lay empty and quiet, heavy with unspoken promises. Disappointment settled like a stone in his stomach as he pulled out his phone and dialed a familiar number, his heart hammering with anxious uncertainty.

"Spence? It's Jim," he said when his cousin picked up. "I know I just left your house, but…feel like meeting for a beer?"

Spence's voice was bright and warm on the other end. "Sure, man. I'm always up for a beer. Meet you at Hank's in ten?"

Jim agreed, already feeling a measure of relief at the idea of talking to someone who might help him make sense of everything. Maybe Spence would know what to say to cut through the uncertainty, the jealousy, and help him face whatever was waiting between him and Brock.

The bar was dimly lit with a warm, amber glow that softened the hard edges of its worn furnishings. A low hum of overlapping conversations mingled with the rhythmic clinking of glasses, creating a background melody that was both familiar and oddly comforting. Tonight, Hank's Tavern held a sparse crowd—a few regulars lingering casually at the bar, and a couple of timeworn booths where locals sought refuge from the rigors of the day.

In one secluded corner booth, Jim sat across from Spence, his fingers idly caressing the condensation on his half-finished beer, though he scarcely sipped it. His mind was a storm of thoughts, a heavy swirl of emotions pressing against his chest like an invisible weight.

Spence, leaning forward with genuine concern etched into every line of his face, broke the silence. "You look like you're about to burst, man. What's going on?" His voice was soft yet probing, inviting Jim to unburden himself.

Taking a deep, steadying breath, Jim set his bottle down on the table, his eyes locking onto the intricate patterns of the wood grain as if it might reveal hidden secrets. "It's Brock," he began hesitantly, the word hanging in the air with a mix of vulnerability and fear. "I… I'm attracted to him." His voice was low and almost inaudible, but the declaration echoed loudly in the small, dim space around them.

Spence offered no immediate rebuke or judgment; instead, he responded with a slow, understanding nod that encouraged Jim to continue. "Go on," he urged gently.

Jim's fingers absently rubbed the back of his neck as he struggled to articulate his inner turmoil. "I don't really know how to explain it," he admitted, his tone laced with uncertainty. "I've never felt this way about a guy before… Hell, I wasn't even aware I could feel like this." His eyes met Spence's, his brow creased in confusion and raw vulnerability. "But when I'm around him… everything about him just gets to me. The way he looks at me, the sound of his voice, even his damn smile—it all pulls me in. He's…he's sexy."

A soft smile began to form on Spence's lips, his expression blending warmth and empathy. "You're falling for him," he observed simply, the earnestness in his voice wrapping around Jim like a comforting blanket.

A hot rush of embarrassment flushed Jim's face as he ran a trembling hand through his hair. "I don't know," he muttered, his voice dropping to a confidential whisper. "I kissed him," he confessed slowly, eyes betraying both wonder and apprehension. "It wasn't planned. It just… happened. And ever since, I haven't been able to shake it from my mind." His admission hung in the air, carrying an unspoken truth that the encounter had gone farther than just the kiss.

Spence leaned back in his seat, his gaze turning thoughtful as he absorbed every word. "And how did Brock respond?" he inquired, his tone laced with curiosity and concern.

A small, almost incredulous chuckle escaped Jim as he recalled the moment in visceral detail. "He didn't push me away," he said, his voice softening into recollection. "He kissed me back. But... then I pulled away." His jaw tightened as he admitted the confusion that still tangled his heart. "I wasn't sure what I was doing. And to be honest, I still haven't figured it out." He shook his head, battling the storm of emotions within. "Then today, when I saw him with that state inspector—I felt that fire of jealousy ignite. It caught me completely off-guard... the anger that surged through me."

Spence tilted his head slightly, pondering Jim's confession before speaking in a tone that blended insight with empathy. "Jim, it sounds like you're not just attracted to Brock. It's like you're scared, too, because this is all so new, stirring up parts of you that you weren't prepared for. Believe me, I understand."

Jim's eyes flickered with hesitant hope as he looked at Spence, his voice reduced to a fragile whisper. "How did you know?" he asked almost timidly. "I mean... how did you come to terms with being... you know, gay?"

Spence's gaze softened, memories and a touch of melancholy dancing in his eyes. "It wasn't easy," he admitted, his voice thick with recollection. "I remember when I was 14, and you were the first person I ever came out to. You were so supportive—I still cherish that. But I kept it hidden from everyone else until after graduation. That period was filled with fear and anxiety, every day a battle against my own insecurities. And then, there was the fallout with my dad—he exploded, and that rejection still lingers in my heart."

His eyes shimmered with the residue of old pain. "But after that, I chose to embrace who I truly am. Whether it was college life or coming back here to work, I finally found acceptance, genuine love, and even found Chandler. All of it happened because I was brave enough to be my authentic self.'"

Jim's chest tightened as the weight of his own uncertainty pressed down on him. "I just… I don't really know what this is supposed to look like for me," he admitted, his voice cracking under the strain of emotion. "I don't know how to navigate through this."

With a steady, reassuring gesture, Spence reached across the table and placed his hand on Jim's arm. "There's no right or wrong way, Jim," he said softly. "It's perfectly okay to feel unsure, to be scared. All that matters is that you're honest with yourself and with Brock. If there's something genuine between you two, take it one step at a time. There's no need to rush."

After a moment of reflective silence, Jim lifted his gaze, the resolve in his eyes growing stronger. "I want to talk to him," he declared, his voice steadier now, imbued with newfound determination. "I want to see where this could go, even if I'm just taking it slow. I just can't have everyone knowing, not yet."

Spence's gentle smile widened, filled with heartfelt warmth. "That's perfectly alright. You don't need to have everything figured out right now. Just be honest with him, and I have a feeling you'll find that he understands more than you might think."

Jim's car ground to a halt in Brock's driveway as dusk bled into a deep, bruised twilight, the sky crisscrossed with violent strokes of indigo and smoldering crimson. The house loomed in brooding silence, punctuated only by a solitary, flickering light in the window. Each step up the worn steps sent his heart into a frantic sprint, his hand quivering as he fumbled with the key to the creaking door.

The door swung open with a reluctant groan, and there stood Brock—hair disheveled by the night air, eyes shadowed with recent storms. Surprise melted from his features, replaced by a cautious gentleness as he parted to allow Jim entry.

"Hey," Brock murmured, his tone heavy with underlying tension as he surveyed Jim escaping into the dark hallway. "I wasn't sure where you'd turned up."

"I know," Jim replied, wrestling with the tremor in his hands as he shoved them deep into his pockets. "I had to step back and clear my head...I grabbed a beer with Spence. I'm sorry," his words came out measured but intense, "for earlier at the site—I didn't mean to let the jealousy get the better of me."

Brock's lips curved into a wistful, pained smile. "It's not the first time, Jim," he said, folding his arms as if defending against an ever-present, cold threat. "You're not the first man to wear jealousy like a scar."

Stepping closer, Jim's eyes burned with both remorse and curiosity. "What do you mean?" he probed, his voice edged with urgency.

Brock's hesitation was palpable as he exhaled a heavy, sorrowful sigh. "My last relationship… it crumbled because he betrayed me—again and again," he confessed, each word laced with intense heartache. "I grew numb to the fight, convinced I was forever battling for his flickering affection. Eventually, I stopped fighting altogether."

The raw vulnerability in Brock's admission struck a fierce chord in Jim. Moving closer still, his hand reached out, trembling as it rested on Brock's arm. "I'm sorry," he whispered, his tone aching with sincere regret. "You never deserved that pain."

Brock's eyes dropped to the hand on his arm, their silent contact laden with unspoken histories before he finally locked his gaze with Jim's. "I'm not telling you this to wound you," he said, voice low and guarded. "It's the reason I keep my heart locked away—I can't bear another fracture."

Jim's chest constricted with the impact of Brock's truth, the quiet agony in his words reverberating through him. "I understand," he admitted, voice soft yet fierce. "I'm a stranger in these turbulent waters… but I care about you, Brock. I can't risk ruining this connection." He inhaled deeply, his thumb gliding tenderly along Brock's skin. "Let's take it slow… unravel this mess together. If you'll let me."

Brock's eyes, previously shadowed, warmed as he inched nearer, the distance between them evaporating. "I'd like that," he murmured, his tone husky with hope. "I'm ready to savor this pace." Pausing, he added,

"No need to force fate—I just want to see where this intense path leads us."

Jim's nod came like a breath of exultant relief as he closed the final gap. Leaning into the overwhelming gravity of the moment, their lips collided in a kiss that was both tender and charged—a kiss that whispered fierce promises and fierce understanding, unhurried yet insistent, as two souls dared to navigate the storm together.

As they slowly drew apart, Brock's forehead rested gently against Jim's, and they lingered in the profound stillness of the moment. "Come upstairs?" Brock murmured, his breath warm and whispering against Jim's cheek. Jim's heart pounded as he nodded, replying softly, "Yeah, let's go."

Brock led Jim up the creaking wooden staircase, where each step felt soft and familiar beneath their feet. The quiet house resonated with every creak and subtle shift of the aged floorboards, each sound intensifying the pulsating anticipation between them. With Brock's warm, steady hand securely in his own, Jim was guided down a shadowed hallway toward a room at the far end of the corridor.

Inside Brock's bedroom, Jim absorbed every detail of the space. The room was spacious and uncluttered, bathed in the gentle glow of a bedside lamp that cast a luminous, golden hue across every surface. The inviting bed lay unmade, its crisp white sheets now artfully rumpled as though freshly left in a tender embrace. A faint but lingering aroma of sandalwood mingled with the subtle scent of freshly laundered linens, imbuing the room with an intimate warmth.

Turning slowly to face Jim, Brock's eyes revealed a flicker of vulnerability—a delicate, uncertain gleam that tugged at Jim's heart. Without breaking their unyielding gaze, Brock lifted the hem of his shirt with deliberate slowness, peeling it away to reveal a robust, masculine torso adorned with a natural hint of hair. In a measured pause, his breathing quickened as he started unbuttoning his jeans, letting them fall to the floor and leaving him clad only in charcoal boxer briefs. His unwavering gaze held Jim's, silently inviting him to step deeper into this intimate realm.

Jim's throat tightened as he drank in the sight: Brock's skin, bathed in the soft lamplight, glowed warmly, and a delicate blush tinged colored his cheeks. The room's air seemed to thicken with a potent mixture of uncertainty and desire. With a slow, steady nod, Jim began to undress; his motions were tentative and unrefined, as if he were stepping onto new, uncharted ground.

When both were reduced to their boxer briefs, Brock reached for Jim's hand once more—his touch gentle, yet insistent—and led him toward the bed. The cool sheets rustled under their combined weight as they climbed in together, the atmosphere buzzing with anticipation. Brock slid under the covers onto his side, facing Jim, who mirrored his position. The proximity of their bare skin, separated only by a whisper of fabric, ignited a thrilling blend of intimacy and longing in Jim's chest.

For a few heartbeats, silence reigned, broken only by the soft rustling of sheets and even, measured breaths. Then, with a tender familiarity, Brock's fingers drifted into Jim's hair, tenderly combing through each strand. "You okay?" he asked, his voice barely rising above a whisper— a soothing murmur in the quiet room.

Jim offered a hesitant nod, the nervous tension in his chest laid bare as he replied, "Yeah… just so much racing in my head."

Brock's gaze softened, his fingers still delicately tracing through Jim's hair as he murmured, "I get it. This is new for you, just as it is for me— at least, it's been a long time since I've felt this way." His voice wavered slightly, laden with the weight of past hesitations. "I never thought I'd let someone get this close after my last relationship. But with you, it feels… different."

Moved by the honesty in his words, Jim reached out, his hand settling on Brock's hip. The warmth of Brock's skin seeped into his palm as he whispered, "You make it feel so different. I never imagined I'd be here, like this… with a guy. But I can't stop wanting it. I can't stop wanting you." His voice dropped to a husky murmur, his eyes raw with sincerity.

Brock exhaled in a shaky breath, drawing even nearer until their foreheads nearly touched. "I'm glad you didn't try to hold back," he murmured, his fingers lightly trailing down to caress Jim's jaw, memorizing the contours with every gentle stroke. "Because I've been wanting you too."

The charged words hung between them, thick with desire and unspoken promises. Jim's heart pounded as every brush of Brock's skin and every slight movement of the sheets seemed to echo his own yearning. He could feel the radiating heat of Brock's body, the subtle flex of muscle as Brock's hand wandered to Jim's lower back, drawing him even closer until their chests nearly met. Even the soft, tantalizing contact of their throbbing dicks connecting through the thin barrier of boxer briefs hinted at the intense, unspoken passion that crackled in the space between them.

"Tell me what you're curious about," Brock murmured huskily, his deep voice resonating through Jim's body and sending a heady, electric thrill surging down to his core. "Or, tell me exactly what you want." There was a wild glimmer in Brock's eyes—a delicious mix of daring command and gentle invitation—that made Jim's stomach knot with delicious anticipation.

Jim gulped, his throat suddenly parched. "I…I want to know what it feels like," he admitted slowly, his fingertips trailing a burning path along Brock's broad shoulder and down his sculpted arm. "I want to feel every inch of you—so raw, so intensely." His words trembled on the edge of becoming a confession, heavy with longing. "I'm not even sure how to ask for it."

Brock's lips curved into a knowing, teasing smile as he inched closer, placing a featherlight kiss on Jim's temple. "You don't have to be perfect with words," he whispered, his warm breath making Jim's skin tingle with desire. "Just let yourself feel every moment."

That simple invitation sent shivers cascading along Jim's spine. In a heartbeat, he closed the distance, pressing his entire body against Brock's. Beneath the soft sheets, limbs intertwined and desire ignited, their hard cocks pressed teasingly against one another. Jim's hand slid confidently to the base of Brock's neck, drawing him into a slow, profoundly deep kiss that spoke of unbridled longing without haste or desperation—a sensuous exploration that promised endless pleasures yet to come.

Brock's wandering fingers traced deliberate, lingering paths over the planes of Jim's back, leaving sparks in their wake. As their kiss deepened, Brock's breath caught, and an intensity built between them that was as fervent as it was tender.

When they finally parted slightly, Jim's forehead rested against Brock's in an intimate closeness as both panted, their skin glistening with the sheen of passion. "I've never been this vulnerable," Jim confessed softly, his voice thick with emotion. "But with you, it's like magic. I love kissing you—every kiss feels like a revelation. And your body… you're so powerfully manly, so irresistibly masculine, and yet so stunningly beautiful. I want to explore every inch of you—touch you, taste you."

A mischievous grin danced over his lips. "I still remember the first time I devoured that enormous, unruly cock of yours—I was lost in it. I want to do it again, over and over. I want you to savor it as much as I enjoyed every inch of you when you took me deep."

Brock's own grin deepened into a provocative smile. "We can indulge in that endlessly. I loved giving you head, and honestly, if I hadn't known any better, I'd never have guessed it was your first time going down on a man. You were impressive—hell, I can only imagine the wild heights you'll reach with a bit more practice," he teased, his tone both playful and lustful.

There was more they wanted to share, yet Brock could feel Jim's desire to savor every electrifying moment. "I need to take it slow," Jim whispered, earnest and raw in his desire. "I want to cherish every bit of this with you. Be patient with me as I learn, and I hope you'll guide me along the way."

Brock's eyes softened, and he lifted his thumb to caress Jim's cheek tenderly. "Take all the time you need," he promised, his voice gentle yet unwavering. "I'm here. I'm not going anywhere."

For a long, languid moment, they lay there in a cocoon of shared warmth and whispered promises. Jim could feel Brock's hand steady on his chest, matching the beat of his own heart, taming the storm of thoughts inside him. A long-held breath finally escaped as Jim closed his eyes, immersing himself completely in their intense, unhurried connection.

"I'm curious about everything with you," Jim murmured huskily, his hand exploring Brock's thick, hairy chest in slow, deliberate strokes. "Especially about waking up right here with you."

Brock's smile broadened into a slow, tantalizing arc of desire. "I'd love that," he replied softly, pulling Jim even closer until there was no room between them. "And maybe... tomorrow morning, I'll make you breakfast. We can talk—or just stay wrapped in each other's heat," he added, his voice dipping into a sultry whisper. "Or maybe we'll just linger in bed a little longer."

Jim hesitated for a playful moment before confessing, "I've got plans with Mom and Dad tomorrow—it's Saturday, and everyone's free. Care to join us?"

"They're going to have a million questions," Brock chuckled darkly.

"Maybe tomorrow we'll trade in questions for answers," Jim replied with a teasing glint. "But first, I can't sleep with this raging boner keeping me up." His tone was mischievous as his hand slipped under Brock's waistband. "Seems like you're in the same boat. Mind if I ask for something a little, well... childish?"

Brock grinned teasingly, a sparkle of lust in his eyes. "Just because you're a decade younger doesn't mean you're too immature for a little fun," he shot back, the promise of rough, playful passion hanging in the air.

"Brock's voice dropped huskily, "How about we jerk off together? I can't stop fantasizing about watching you pleasure yourself—the sight of you driving yourself wild is irresistible. And I know I'd be stroking my own hard cock as I devour every inch of that sexy display."

A wicked smile played on his lips as he carelessly tossed the comforter off the bed's end. Rising slowly, he padded toward the bathroom and soon returned with a pair of plush towels. Just before reaching the bed, he halted, his blue eyes smoldering with raw desire. With deliberate sensuality, he flung the towels onto the mattress. Seductively, he slipped his thumbs into the waistband of his boxer briefs and slowly pulled them down over his chiseled thighs until they pooled at his feet.

Turning his back to Jim, he offered him a tantalizing view of his immaculately sculpted ass. Then, with an almost languid bend, he stooped to retrieve the fallen underwear. In that moment, his crack parted ever-so-slightly to reveal the delicate pink curve of his enticing pucker. Pivoting back to face Jim, he grasped his impressively throbbing erection and began to stroke it slowly, his unwavering gaze boring into Jim's soul.

Jim couldn't help himself. He shed his own boxer briefs, licked his palm, and started massaging his own pulsing cock. Brock let his other hand wander smoothly over his torso, his fingers threading through the thick, swirling locks of hair until they came to rest on his nipple, pinching and teasing the frosted cinnamon nub that was rock hard and inviting. Their eyes locked in a sultry battle, and as Jim quickened his hand movement, Brock correspondingly increased his pace.

Sliding over to join him on the bed, Brock reached into the top drawer of the nightstand and retrieved a bottle of lube. With a slow twist, he unscrewed the cap and slicked up his index finger. A sharp intake of breath escaped Jim as he watched Brock press the cool, glistening lubricant against his skin before sliding his finger inside himself. A soft moan escaped Brock's lips as he welcomed the intrusion, every movement saturated with unbridled lust. Jim's eyes absorbed every explicit detail.

"Can I have some?" Jim rasped, his voice thick with longing.

In response, Brock extended the bottle, letting cool droplets fall onto Jim's waiting fingers. Without the need for excessive words, Jim mimicked Brock's actions. Slowly, deliberately, he circled his own slickened hole, feeling sensations that were tantalizingly new yet overwhelmingly erotic. Gently, he pushed his finger past the first knuckle, marveling at the delicious intensity. With every graceful stroke, he eagerly watched Brock reciprocate.

Brock had already introduced a second finger to the mix, pleasuring himself in a perfectly synchronized rhythm—his hands working both his throbbing cock and his inviting hole simultaneously. Jim's eyes widened as he observed Brock burying his fingers deeper, pushing with purposeful intensity until one finger plunged all the way in. The intrusion brushed against a hidden knot deep inside—a sensitive prostate—and Brock let out an explosive whimper of delight. The surge of pleasure overtook him entirely as he neared his climax, his eyes locking with Jim's.

"Yes, baby. Let go! Cum for me, Jim. Let it all out!" Brock commanded, his voice a sultry whisper of domination and desire.

At his cue, Jim's finger flicked the secret pleasure spot inside himself, igniting the most ecstatic orgasm he had ever experienced. His entire body shuddered violently as his release burst forth—thick streams of cum splattering across his chest and pooling in his hand. In the final moments, he caught sight of Brock reaching his own explosive peak, ropes of thick, white cum coating the swirling chest hair on his torso.

Between gasps and laughter, Jim admitted, "That was so fucking intense! I've never come like that before!"

Brock only managed a deep, knowing smile. He reached over to gather the towels, passing one to Jim as they both began to clean up. Jim then collapsed into Brock's warm, inviting embrace.

In the tender quiet that followed, Jim chuckled softly, his breath mingling with Brock's as he murmured, "I really enjoyed that." His voice dripped with relief and simmering desire. The darkness around them wrapped them in a secret world—a private, sensuous haven where whispered confessions sailed unchallenged by the mundane outside.

Their limbs entwined, and as time ticked by, Jim felt the weight of his anxieties melt away, replaced by a slow-burning, pulsating warmth deep inside his chest. Uncertain of what tomorrow might hold or how this passionate journey would evolve, for now, he was perfectly content to lie there in Brock's arms, lost in the possibility, surrendered to the intense, sexually charged connection that was only beginning to unfold.

# Chapter 19
# A Day with Mom and Dad

The morning light crept into the kitchen as the sun poured through the window, bathing the room in a golden glow. Jim stood before the counter, carefully pouring coffee into his favorite mug, its steam mingling with the warmth of the day and echoing the gradual unfolding of his thoughts.

The previous night had been a restless tapestry of emotions: he had replayed every fleeting surge of excitement, every subtle pang of doubt until he embraced one stunning truth—he needed more with Brock. That realization pulsed within him, both electrifying and daunting, yet wholly genuine. Today, he decided, was the day he would invite Brock to share an ever-deepening piece of his life, beginning with a lunch date with his parents.

As Brock entered the kitchen, the air seemed to brighten further. Dressed casually in a pair of well-fitted jeans and a soft, gray shirt that accentuated his broad chest with effortless grace, Brock carried an aura of relaxed confidence. When he smiled—a mischievous, boyish grin that effortlessly disarmed Jim—the latter's heart fluttered with an intimate mix of admiration and nervous anticipation.

"Hey, you," Jim greeted, his voice a careful blend of steadiness and warmth.

"Hey yourself," Brock replied, drawing in close for a brief, lingering kiss that sent shivers cascading through Jim's spine. "Ready for this big day?"

Jim chuckled, though the laughter trembled with underlying nerves. "Ready as I'll ever be," he managed, his voice betraying his excitement.

The Magnolia Diner buzzed with life as they arrived, its interior saturated with the mouthwatering aroma of fried eggs, sizzling sausage, and the freshly baked comfort of biscuits. Jim's parents were already waiting in a cozy booth by the window, his mother meticulously fussing with a napkin while his father scanned the menu—a menu he had memorized years ago, now worn and cherished like an old secret.

Taking a slow, deep breath, Jim became acutely aware of every nuance around him. He noticed the gentle scraping of silverware, the soft murmur of conversations layered within the hum of the diner, and the delicate way Brock's fingers brushed against his as they settled into the booth across from his parents. This seemingly minor contact felt like an anchor, grounding him in the reality of his newfound happiness.

"Mom, Dad, how's your morning so far?" Jim began, his voice mingling question and invitation.

Jim's mother brightened instantly, her eyes sparkling with delight as she reached eagerly across the table with a hand that radiated warmth. "Oh, it's so wonderful to see you boys! And Brock, we're just over the moon to have you join us today."

Brock's smile deepened in response as he returned her affectionate squeeze. "Glad I could join y'all," he said, his tone as sincere as it was enthusiastic.

Her reply came with a conspiratorial wink that made the moment even more enchanting.

Brunch unfolded in a joyful medley of conversation and laughter, seasoned with stories of Jim's childhood—stories only a parent could recount with a mix of pride and gentle embarrassment. As Brock listened intently, his laughter rose at all the perfectly timed punchlines, his eyes crinkling in delight at every humorous detail, even when the tales bordered on mortifying.

When Jim's father recounted the legendary escapade of Jim trying to flee with his cousin's pet frog as a comical sidekick, the memory drew chuckles from both Jim and his aged heart, melting away remnants of tension.

Leaving the diner later felt symbolic to Jim, as if they had crossed an invisible line into a realm of new possibilities. His parents had embraced Brock with genuine warmth, infusing Jim with a burgeoning confidence in what the future might hold for them all.

The afternoon unfurled with a movie matinee at a nostalgic theater; the nearly empty screening room allowed the classic noir's shadows and contrasts to mirror the quiet intensity between them. Jim noticed how, during moments of tension on screen, Brock's fingers would gently search for his, their hands intertwining with an understated promise. Each silent touch carried the exhilarating weight of a blossoming intimacy—a romance unfolding in its own graceful, understated crescendo.

Next, they ventured to a mini-golf course, where sunlight danced on the green and laughter spun through the air like playful confetti. Every missed putt and playful accusation of "cheating" between them painted their afternoon with teasing banter and gentle competitiveness. Jim found himself inexplicably enchanted by the way Brock's eyes sparkled when he laughed—those moments when their gazes met lingered just a heartbeat too long, charged with a tender acknowledgment of their shared spark.

As the sun began its slow descent, casting long, languid shadows across the mini-golf course, they made their way to Brock's place for dinner. In the cozy kitchen of a stranger's home turned intimate sanctuary, Jim felt unprecedented ease. He helped Brock slice vegetables, their hands colliding in subtle, electrifying exchanges. Every accidental touch sent tiny sparks racing up his arm, and each time Brock's eyes met his, a wordless conversation of affection passed between them.

During dinner, emboldened by the warmth of the day, Jim cleared his throat and began to speak, his voice layered with both nervous energy and a deep-seated need for honesty. "So... Mom, Dad," he started, pausing to gather his thoughts as he looked across the table at his parents still basking in the remnants of the day's excitement, "Brock and I are... talking about what it might mean to be more than just friends."

His mother's eyes widened with joyful surprise before softening into radiant delight. She reached out, enclosing his hand within her own in a gesture both comforting and affirming. "Oh, honey, that's just wonderful. And Brock," she continued, turning kindly towards him, "we're so thrilled to welcome you into Jim's life. You're clearly someone very special."

Brock's cheeks flushed with a gentle rosy hue as he murmured a heartfelt, "Thank you, Mrs. Williamson," his tone imbued with warmth and genuine emotion.

Jim's father gave an approving nod. "We just want you both to be happy, son," he stated, his expression thoughtful as he added, "So, Thanksgiving plans? Think we might see both of you down in Florida?" His unexpected question, peppered with a hint of playful expectation, sent a thrill through Jim, confirmed by the glimmer of pleasant surprise in Brock's eyes.

"I think we'd like that," Jim replied steadily, a bashful smile playing on his lips. "Yeah, I think we'd like that a lot."

After dinner, his parents departed with enveloping, affectionate hugs, his mother whispering with earnest joy, "Hold on to this one," as she embraced him tightly.

Turning toward Brock, Jim's heart swelled with both unspoken pride and a profound sense of relief. "You were incredible with them. My folks absolutely loved you," he confessed, his words soft yet filled with meaning.

Brock's hand moved to rest reassuringly on Jim's thigh. "That means so much," he said, his voice imbued with tenderness. "And I have to say… I loved them too. They're truly good people."

Jim's voice dropped to a tender murmur, as if each word was weighed with all his newfound emotion. "I feel like… I'm finally where I'm meant to be. And that's because of you."

Brock's eyes softened further as his thumb traced small, loving circles along Jim's thigh. "I feel the same," he murmured. "It's like we're slowly assembling something beautiful… one piece at a time."

A comfortable silence fell between them as they absorbed the depth of what the day had woven into their hearts. Then, as if drawn by an irresistible gravity, Jim leaned in and captured Brock's lips in a kiss that spoke volumes of gratitude and unrestrained yearning. Brock responded with matching eagerness, his fingers tangling in Jim's hair as he deepened the kiss, drawing him ever closer until nothing separated them.

"Come here," Brock whispered against Jim's lips, his voice rich with mischief and promise.

Hand in hand, they ascended the stairs with an ease that spoke of intimate familiarity. Shoes were cast aside, and soft kisses trailed down the hall until they reached the sanctuary of a bedroom. Here, the air was thick with shared anticipation—there was no trace of earlier nervousness, only a simmering desire and the quiet thrill of discovery.

They undressed slowly, each garment shed like the unveiling of secret layers, savoring the intimate moments as more of themselves was revealed. Finally, when they lay side by side in the tender cocoon of each other's arms, a profound peace descended upon Jim—a deep, soul-satisfying contentment that whispered of homecoming.

In the gentle dark, fingers intertwined in a silent vow, Jim's voice broke the quiet with a soft murmur. "This... whatever we're building together... I want it to last."

Brock nodded, drawing Jim even closer until their foreheads rested in a delicate, shared caress. "Me too," he whispered, his voice thick with emotion. "And I truly believe that if we stay honest and trust one another, we can weather anything."

They settled into a serene silence, wrapped in the delicate embrace of the night, the soft sounds of the world outside forming a lullaby to their hearts. As sleep slowly edged over Jim, he realized with a joyful certainty that, for the first time in many years, he was exactly where he belonged.

# Chapter 20
# Perceptions

Jim sensed it immediately—the furtive sideways glances, the hushed whispers that abruptly stopped as soon as he entered a room. On his way to the police station, his stomach churned with anxiety, each step urging its own silent question. In Brookstone, a community bound together by unspoken rules, even the faintest hint of change was like an undeniable scent to a hound on a hunt. It didn't take long for everyone to deduce that the atmosphere between him and Brock had morphed into something unspoken and complex.

Swallowing hard, Jim squared his shoulders as he crossed the threshold of the station, relying on a carefully crafted mask of composure to protect him against any veiled remarks. Before he could even get to his desk, Officer Carl greeted him, his smirk betraying more than just a friendly hello.

"Morning, Jim," Carl drawled, leaning back in his chair with a knowing glint in his eye. "Seems like you've been keeping busy, huh?"

The weight in Jim's gut surged, but he forced a shrug, letting his tone sound as casual as possible. "You know how it is, Carl. Just the usual bustle."

Carl's chuckle carried an edge as he replied, "Oh, I heard you've been spending a lot of time with Brock lately. Even had him visiting all over town, including with your parents yesterday. Looks like you two have gotten quite close."

A sharp, cautionary look flashed from Jim, silently questioning whether Carl's words were meant to provoke him. The uncertainty stung, yet he maintained his calm. Settling at his desk, he responded evenly, "Good friends are hard to find. He's proven to be a real Godsend while my apartment complex is under repair."

Even as he spoke, Jim knew that his words did little to dispel the rumors that seemed to be spiraling around him, each comment and side-note adding fuel to the fire of whispered gossip. The morning trudged on with tense, carefully measured dialogues, each conversation feeling like a probe into his personal life. By lunchtime, the oppressive atmosphere had become too heavy to bear, and Jim longed to escape.

During his break, his trembling hands reached for his phone, dialing Brock's number. When Brock answered, the gentle cadence of his voice immediately dulled the sharper edges of Jim's anxiety.

"Hey," Brock greeted warmly, his tone imbued with understanding. "How's your day treating you?"

Jim hesitated before replying, "Fine… mostly," though the uncertainty in his voice did not go unnoticed.

"What's eating you?" Brock pressed, concern lacing his words.

A long, exasperated sigh filled the silence on the line. "One of my coworkers saw us together yesterday… and he had a lot of harsh things to say. Not exactly the kind of feedback I was hoping for."

Brock's heart sank deeply at the news. "I see. That must have been rough, Jim."

In a rush of hurried words laced with desperation, Jim confessed, "Brock, I…I don't know. Maybe we should just keep things low-key for now?" His tone revealed a man who felt cornered, swallowing tight fear with every syllable.

The suggestion struck Brock like a physical blow. The notion of retreating, of hiding who they truly were again, tightened his chest painfully. He paused before carefully choosing his response. "I get it, Jim. Truly, I do. People love to talk, and it's just unbearable sometimes. I'm not exactly thrilled about facing the town's judgment either. But—" his voice faltered as emotions warred inside him—"I just can't help but feel that we shouldn't be made to feel ashamed for being ourselves."

Silence hung between them for a heavy moment before Jim finally answered in a barely audible tone. "It's not about shame, Brock. I've seen what happens when people in this town start whispering—how they treated Spence and Chandler. I'm scared, Brock. If the chatter turns to harsher judgments… I'm not sure I can be strong enough."

Brock exhaled slowly, wrestling with an urge to insist that they stand together against the tide of gossip. Yet he understood the paralyzing fear that had gripped Jim—fear he himself had known since his own turbulent past. "Let's take it day by day," he proposed softly, his voice steadier than he felt. "We don't have to broadcast our lives for everyone to see, but hiding completely might be marring who we are. We can find a balance... just together."

After a pause weighted with mutual understanding, Jim's voice returned—quieter, but carrying a bittersweet note of relief. "Okay, Brock. I think... I think I can manage that."

When Jim returned to Brock's place later that evening, the weight of the day seemed to melt away the moment Brock swung open the heavy wooden door, revealing a welcoming smile that normally banished all worries. Yet, tonight, there lingered a subtle tension etched into Brock's features—a faint crease of worry slowly creasing his brow, like a whispered secret caught in the soft glow of the hallway light.

"Is something else going on?" Jim inquired, settling onto the plush leather sofa in the living room as Brock poured two richly colored glasses of wine. The room held a quiet intimacy, the only sounds being the gentle clinking of glass and the murmured hum of a song playing in the background.

Brock hesitated, his fingers idly tracing the delicate rim of his glass as if seeking answers in its smooth curve. "Ms. Nancy, the neighbor, mentioned something strange," he began, his voice low and laced with concern. "She said she'd seen someone, a stranger, hanging around the house a few times lately when both of us were away." His words seemed to hang in the air, thick with uncertainty.

Jim's instincts immediately sharpened, and he set his glass down with deliberate care, his eyes narrowing with a mixture of curiosity and concern. "What did she say exactly?" he pressed, the seriousness of the situation casting a focused intensity into the room.

"She didn't get a clear look," Brock replied, running his hand through his hair as though trying to untangle the worry there, "just a vague description. She mentioned a tall figure in dark clothes lingering around the backyard, close to the property's edge. And—get this—she commented dryly that I ought to have a 'cop friend' for safety." His attempted laughter was hollow, an echo of disbelief, and he massaged his forehead as if trying to ease the creeping unease. "I can't shake off the feeling that something isn't right."

Reaching across the short distance between them, Jim clasped Brock's hand firmly in his own, his touch warm and reassuring. "Amanda and I were tailing a stranger ourselves a couple of days back. He was as elusive as a shadow, slipping through the cracks and making off with some odds and ends. But what's most concerning is our suspicion that he also made off with a hunting knife and a shotgun. I'll inform Amanda about his persistent appearances. Just promise me that if you see anything or anyone, you'll reach out immediately."

Brock's eyes softened as he nodded, his grip on Jim's hand tightening with gratitude. His thumb brushed slowly over Jim's knuckles, conveying silent thanks and a shared determination. "Thank you, Jim. I might be letting paranoia get the better of me, but having you here makes all the difference."

For a heartbeat, they existed in a cocoon of mutual solace, the worries of the day receding into the quiet background noise of their intertwined lives. Jim felt his heart swell with a fierce protectiveness—a sudden, unexpected surge of emotion—and silently vowed to do whatever it took to keep Brock safe, even if whispered rumors and shadowy figures lurked just beyond their doorsteps.

As the two ascended the creaking wooden stairs, leaving behind the residual hum of the day—the sidelong glances, half-smiles, and murmured gossip—the serenity of the space wrapped around them like a well-worn blanket. At the top of the stairs, with only the soft ambient light of a dying day and the steady rhythm of shared breaths, Brock reached out and interlocked his fingers with Jim's. The touch was both delicate and electric, a tangible promise that transcended mere words, forged in the quiet depths of mutual understanding.

Jim turned to face him, his blue eyes glinting with warmth and a playful spark, yet tonight they also shone with vulnerability. "You know," he murmured, his voice a gentle caress as he squeezed Brock's hand, "I think half the town is placing bets on what exactly this means."

Brock's deep, resonant chuckle filled the space between them, a sound both comforting and enigmatic. "Let them talk. Tonight, it's just you and me," he whispered, leaning forward so that his lips lightly grazed Jim's forehead. The soft press of his kiss lingered, as if to imprint him with the gentle, reassuring rhythm of his breath. Jim's skin was filled with the intoxicating aroma of sandalwood, mingling with a unique scent that was unmistakably his, a fragrance that always stirred something deep within Brock, a stirring that was far more profound than mere desire. "I prepared something special for you," Brock added softly, the promise hanging between them like a treasured secret waiting to unfold.

They stepped into the bedroom, and Brock gently pulled Jim into his arms, wrapping them around him, his hands sliding over Jim's back and down to cup his firm round ass cheeks, pressing their bodies close. Jim melted into the embrace, resting his head against Brock's shoulder, his fingers tracing the lines of Brock's broad chest. Brock could feel his heartbeat quicken as Jim's touch roamed slowly, exploring, savoring.

Jim's voice was barely a whisper. "I've wanted this for so long." His hand slipped up, curling around the back of Brock's neck as he looked up, their faces close, breaths mingling. "You have no idea."

Brock's hand caressed Jim's cheek, his thumb brushing lightly over his cheekbone. "I think I do," he said softly, his blue eyes darkening as he took in Jim's face, memorizing every detail. He leaned down, capturing Jim's lips in a slow, deep kiss. It was tender but filled with a hunger that had been building for weeks, months even, a promise of the connection they both craved.

Jim's lips parted under his, welcoming his tongue, meeting him with equal intensity. Their kiss deepened, their bodies pressing together as Brock's hands roamed over Jim's back, feeling the heat radiating from him, the steady rhythm of his breathing quickening as they lost themselves in each other. Every touch, every movement felt deliberate, savoring, as if they wanted to make every second stretch on and on.

As they pulled back for air, Jim's fingers lingered on the buttons of

Brock's shirt. He hesitated, his eyes meeting Brock's, a question unspoken but understood. Brock nodded, his gaze steady and reassuring. "Take your time," he whispered. "We don't have to rush."

But Jim shook his head with a soft smile. "I don't want to hold back tonight."

With that, he slipped each button open, his fingertips brushing against the firm muscle and coarse hair of Brock's chest, sending small sparks of anticipation flickering along his skin. Brock shrugged off the shirt, letting it fall to the floor as he reached for Jim, guiding him closer, his hands sliding under the hem of Jim's uniform shirt, feeling the warm, toned skin beneath, every ripple of his six pack evident beneath the dusting of hair. He took his time, letting his hands move up slowly, memorizing the way Jim's body responded, the soft intake of breath, the slight arch of his back. When his thumbs grazed Jim's nipples, he let out a breathy moan.

Their bodies pressed together as Brock pulled Jim into another kiss, this one deeper, more urgent, their hands exploring, discovering, the last barriers of clothing slipping away until there was nothing between them but warmth and want. Brock's hands found their way to Jim's ass, pulling him close, feeling the strength of him, the solidness, the way their bodies fit together so perfectly. Their hard cocks pressed against one another. Brock's firmly against Jim's stomach while Jim's ground into Brock's massive thigh.

Jim's fingers traced the line of Brock's jaw, his voice soft and breathless. "I love the way you look at me…like you're seeing all of me."

Brock's lips found the curve of Jim's shoulder, pressing slow, lingering kisses along his skin, savoring every taste, every touch. "Because I am," he murmured against his skin, his voice thick with emotion. "You're everything I want, Jim." His eyes burned with a deeper intensity now. "I want you inside me."

Jim's eyes searched Brock's for only a moment. "I…I want that too." A shy smile fell over his face. "I…? You…?"

Brock's smile was warm and encouraging. "I'll make sure it's perfect. I want to feel you inside me, not latex."

Jim looked intently into Brock's eyes with so many questions.

"I understand if you want to use condoms. But I'm on PrEP and tested every three months. My last test was all clear, and I haven't been with anyone in over 6 months. And before that, I always used condoms. Even with Jason. Somehow, I always knew he was cheating. But, I trust you, feel a different kind of connection and really want to feel you inside me. But only if you are okay with it."

Jim's face flushed, and a grin spread over his face. "I also get tested every three months for work. Have only ever had protected sex in the past. Which, other than my right hand, hasn't been anyone for almost a year. And yes, you big sexy bear, I want to be inside you with nothing between us."

They moved to the bed, and Brock retrieved the lube from the nightstand. "You have to prep me, get me ready for your dick."

A blush crept across Jim's face. "I...I watched a video and the guy ate the other guy's ass to get him warmed up. Can I try that?"

"Unexpected!" Brocked half-tease, half-praise his lover. "I'd love that. Can I show you exactly what I like?"

Jim looked at him quizzically for a moment before Brock flipped him over and sliding a hand under his tummy, lifted his beautiful, plump ass into the air. Before Jim could utter another word, a warm tingling sensation radiated from his most intimate part throughout the rest of his body. Brock's tongue gently grazed against his pucker, sliding up and down, round and round.

Electricity shot through Jim, his cock pulsing and leaking as the sensation warmed and excited him. He drew in a shaky breath. Brock's hands firmly held his cheeks apart, gripping, kneading them as his tongue flicked and swirled pleasure Jim had never imagined.

"Oh, God!" Jim managed to mutter. That was Brock's que to take it a step further. He pressed his face hard between Jim's round globes and slowly slid his tongue inside Jim's quivering pucker. A heightened level of the new sensation for Jim. Brock lapped and licked, tongued and teased Jim's hole until Jim's legs trembled. Slowly, gently, Brock withdrew. Easing Jim over onto his back and moving up to kiss his neck, his ear lobe, his shoulder.

"What'd you think?" Brock's voice was low and husky.

"Holy fuck! I never, I mean, Holy fuck!"

Brock chuckled. "Want to try on me?" he asked as he rolled over, exposing the beauty of his voluptuous ass to Jim.

Jim reached out and grasped each of the round mounds; his eyes had ogled so many times. There was a light dusting of reddish brown hair, soft to the tough, and sexy as hell to Jim. When he parted them, he was surprised to find a smooth waxed area surrounding Brock's pink pucker. Tentatively, he leaned in and let his tongue explore.

The taste was a mix of clean shower gel and a manly scent that was all Brock. The act was intimate, so sensual. As much as he'd enjoyed Brock lavishing attention on his hole, this was just as appealing. He was able to pleasure his lover in that same way. He reached around and found Brock's shaft. He stroked the girth slowly as his tongue played. He tried to imagine what all Brock had done to bring him so much pleasure and mimicked it. He obviously was doing something right because Brock was gripping the sheets and growling low, rumbling murmurs of Jim's name and other indistinct phrases. Jim smiled to himself and worked even harder at pleasuring his man.

After a few minutes, Brock looked over his shoulder and instructed Jim to lube his fingers.

"Slide one in," he coached. Jim followed the instruction, and Brock moaned with approval.

"Another," he groaned.

Jim complied, fucking Brock's tight hole with his fingers remembering the sensation he felt as he finger fucked himself watching Brock do the same. His cock was achingly hard and leaking.

Brock pulled away temporarily and rolled onto his back, pulling Jim on top of him. He parted his legs and bent his knees, and looked desperately into Jim's blue eyes. "I need you inside me."

Jim hoisted Brock's legs onto his shoulders, gripped his own cock and lined it up with Brock's wet pucker. He reached over and poured a generous amount of lube onto his dick and stroked it a couple of times to make sure it was amply coated.

Then, ever so gently, he started to push inside. The warm wet tightness was incredible as it engulfed his cock slowly, inch by inch. He looked into his lover's eyes.

"Okay?" he questioned. Brock answered by taking hold of Jim's hips and gently pushing him away until only the tip of his shaft was still inside him. Jim, about to retreat completely, fearing he'd hurt Brock, felt Brock's fingers digging into his ass as he pulled forcefully, plunging Jim balls deep into Brock.

"Oh, fuck yes!" Brock shouted. "Fuck me Jim. I need it. I need you!" Jim withdrew slightly, then pushed back in. Brock's hands setting the pace, gripping Jim's ass, pushing and pulling until he set a rhythm that was pushing them both closer and closer to the edge. J

im pounded into Brock with intensity. He'd never experienced pleasure to this degree. Whether because it was his first time without a condom, his first time fucking a guy, or because it was Brock that he was fucking, he couldn't be sure. Maybe a combination of all three. But this was by far the best sex he'd ever dreamed of.

They moved together, their bodies tangling in a dance that felt both new and familiar, filled with quiet laughter and whispered words, each touch, each kiss taking them deeper. The room was filled with the soft sounds of their breathing, the rustle of sheets, the gentle rhythm of their bodies moving in sync, losing themselves in each other. Bock's body began to tremble and the inner ring of muscle clamped down on Jim's cock. The intensity pushed Jim over the edge as he shot hard, filling the condom deep inside his lover. Only when the pulsing waves of pleasure began to subside did he realize Brock had also cum, shooting his load over both their stomachs and chests.

As they finally lay wrapped in each other's arms, their breaths slowing, their bodies still humming with the afterglow of their shared intimacy, Brock held Jim close, feeling the steady beat of his heart against his chest. Jim's head rested on his shoulder, his fingers tracing lazy patterns in Brock's chest hair.

In the soft quiet of the night, Brock pressed a kiss to Jim's forehead, his voice a gentle whisper. "That was amazing. This is amazing. You and me, Jim. I want all of this, every day."

Jim's hand found his, their fingers intertwining as he looked up, his eyes bright with unshed tears. "Then I'm yours, Brock. Completely."

# Chapter 21
# Clashing Loyalties

Jim stepped into the station with the chill of early morning clinging to his skin. The air was thick with an undercurrent of tension, and he could almost taste the apprehension. Amanda greeted him immediately, her brow furrowed with urgency as she held a stack of worn case files teetering in her arms. Their brief greeting evaporated into the background when she launched into the latest update, her voice low and determined.

"Two more reports," she said in a hushed tone as she flipped open her well-thumbed notebook. "Another round of sightings, and more stolen goods. The most recent inventory? Zip ties, a battered suitcase, and—get this—a cache of handgun ammunition. People are terrified, Jim. If this guy is stockpiling weapons and supplies, we could be staring down a genuine threat.

Jim felt the gravity of her words settle into his chest like a heavy stone as he followed her into the cramped workspace. Together, they huddled over monitors, methodically sifting through grainy video footage from local stores and scrutinizing a map dotted with reported sightings.

Each frame was a brushstroke in an unfinished painting—the elusive stranger just out of reach. Jim's eyes darted back and forth, absorbing every detail with meticulous concentration, hopeful that a single angle or fleeting shadow might reveal their suspect's true face.

"Look at this," Amanda murmured, her finger pointing to a dim corner of the video where a man in a dark hoodie loitered by the checkout line. "He's picking up a bottle of whisky here, right after he was seen lurking in that other neighborhood two blocks over. The guy's cautious, yet he's dropping breadcrumbs—a pattern, maybe."

They plunged into a frenzied hour of piecing together disparate timelines, meticulously marking down locations on the map and parsing every minute detail the footage could possibly divulge. Yet amid the intense focus, Jim became aware of a subtle shift in the atmosphere.

Colleagues exchanged furtive glances and whispered behind cupped hands, their voices merging into an indistinct murmur that bordered on conspiratorial speculation. The distractions gnawed at his concentration, turning his focus into a battle against the rising tide of unease.

Just as he and Amanda were locking onto a possible route the man might be exploiting to glide stealthily around town, the chief's voice cleaved through the ambient office noise like a cold blade.

"Williamson, a word in my office?"

Amanda's eyes flickered with curiosity as Jim rose from his chair, each step down the sterile hallway weighed down by unspoken concerns. The chief's office was a study in precision—a pristine space adorned with commendations and family photographs, a chronicle of steadfast loyalty and public service. The chief himself, seated behind an imposing desk, exuded an air of controlled authority, his expression a carefully honed mask of inscrutability.

"Jim," the chief began, reclining slightly as he regarded him with calculating eyes, "I've been hearing things. Whispers. Discontent in these halls." He crossed his arms, fingers interlaced as if to contain his disquiet. "But that's not why you're here today. I'm considering you for the detective position opening at the end of the month."

Jim's heart pounded like a drum against his ribs, a mixture of hope and apprehension surging through him. He had long dreamed of a shot at this promotion, yet the chief's measured tone hinted at complications beneath the surface of this seemingly straightforward opportunity.

"You've done solid work here, Jim," the chief continued, voice measured but earnest. "You're diligent, astute, and unyielding in your pursuit of the truth. But I need to know—you're 'man' enough for this role. I need to be certain that you can leave your personal life at the door, that nothing can cloud your judgment."

Jim's jaw tightened as those words sank into him, echoing all the furtive whispers that had circulated around the station. The low, murmured barbs about his relationship with Brock, the raised eyebrows whenever Brock had appeared unexpectedly—a subtle yet relentless barrage of doubt. Now, even the chief's measured inquiry hinted at those same concerns.

"I am," Jim managed, his voice steady despite the turmoil beneath. "My personal life doesn't interfere with my work, Chief."

The chief's piercing gaze never wavered. "It's just… there's concern that your personal entanglements might be complicating matters here. The job demands an unwavering detachment, Jim. I need to be sure you're not letting any relationships affect your decisions."

Jim clenched his fists at his side, summoning every ounce of self-control. "Understood. I give you my word—my commitment to this job is absolute."

The chief nodded slowly, though a faint trace of scepticism shimmered in his eyes. "Very good. Just keep your priorities in line, Jim."

Leaving the chief's office, Jim's frustration burned beneath his composed exterior like a simmering fire. He inhaled deeply, trying to refocus on the tasks awaiting him. Amanda had resumed their work with relentless determination, yet their mind was still haunted by the chief's insinuation and the judgment-laden glances of their colleagues.

A few hours later, while he meticulously organized a scattered pile of notes, the front door creaked open, and there was Brock, standing there as if he were a burst of sunlight in the otherwise murky room. Brock's relaxed demeanor was at odds with the palpable tension; his small bag containing takeout containers was a token of casual domesticity. His smile was warm and inviting, but in an instant, silence fell like a heavy cloak over the station as every eye turned in their direction.

Jim felt a cold twist in his gut as the weight of the chief's words and the silent accusations of his peers pressed down on him. With every step Brock took towards him, his pulse raced faster, and a cold sheen of sweat broke out on his brow.

"Thought you might be hungry," Brock said softly, his tone laced with gentle humor as he tried to dismiss the stares. Yet Jim's response was distant and stiff, his body taut with discomfort.

"Thanks," Jim muttered, barely managing to catch Brock's eyes as he accepted the bag without so much as a glance. The strain was evident in every line of his posture.

Brock's smile faltered, replaced by an unmistakable hurt as he searched Jim's face for any sign of warmth. "Jim… you okay?"

Jim forced a nod, his voice tight as he offered a quick, "I'll see you later." The air between them crackled with unspoken tension, and Brock hesitated, his eyes lingering on Jim with a plea for reassurance. Finding none, he slowly nodded, his smile vanishing like morning mist, and he turned to leave.

After Brock's departure, Amanda sidled up to him, raising a questioning eyebrow. "You okay? That looked… rough."

"Yeah," Jim replied, stuffing his hands into his pockets as if trying to hide his inner turmoil. "It's just… complicated."

The remainder of the afternoon dragged on, each minute laden with strained glances and hushed whispers that seemed to claw at Jim's resolve. By the time his shift finally ended, every nerve in his body was on edge. Desperate to mend what was fraying at home, he drove to Brock's place, hoping to smooth over the tension. Yet as soon as he crossed the threshold, the atmosphere in the room told him everything was already amiss—Brock's eyes were still red-rimmed, his posture rigid with unresolved hurt.

"What happened back there?" Brock's voice was low and tight, every word revealing his inner turmoil. "You practically brushed me off."

Jim exhaled heavily, running a weary hand through his disheveled hair. "It's just… everyone's talking. The chief is questioning my commitment to the job. And some of the other guys… they're making comments. It's like a storm of doubts, all piling up at once."

Brock crossed his arms, his gaze unwavering. "So… what? You're ashamed of us?"

A flame of frustration ignited in Jim's chest, his voice rising ever so slightly. "No! It's not like that at all. But it's unbearable, Brock. Every step I take at work, it feels like I'm constantly under scrutiny, like people are waiting for me to slip—to let our relationship cloud my judgment."

Brock's tone sharpened, betraying his wounded feelings. "So what's the solution then? Should we keep hiding? Pretending we're just friends until this all blows over?"

Jim paused, searching Brock's eyes for a spark of understanding. "I don't want to hide. I don't want to pretend anything. But I also don't know if I have the strength for this kind of constant pressure right now."

They stood in a heavy silence, the weight of unspoken words filling every corner of the room. Finally, Jim shook his head, his eyes drifting away. "I just... I need time to clear my head. Maybe I'll crash over at Spence and Chandler's tonight."

Brock's anger softened slightly, the harsh lines of hurt giving way to a look of deep sadness. "If that's what you need."

Jim reached for his phone, then hesitated, torn between leaving and trying to salvage the closeness they once shared. At the door, he paused, his eyes lingering back on Brock, full of quiet resignation and hope all at once.

"I'm not giving up on us," he said softly, his voice barely above a whisper. "I just need a little space... to figure this out."

Brock nodded slowly, the faint glimmer of understanding mingling with lingering pain in his eyes. "I'll be here, Jim. Just... don't take too long."

With a heavy heart and a mind swirling with doubts, questions, and the fragile hope for clarity, Jim stepped out into the night, leaving behind the stark reality of his fractured world.

The door closed with a soft click that echoed through Brock's chest like thunder. He stood motionless in the living room, staring at the space Jim had just occupied, the silence of the house suddenly oppressive. His shoulders slumped as he exhaled a breath he hadn't realized he was holding.

"Damn it," he whispered to the empty room.

Brock sank onto the couch, elbows on his knees, head in his hands. The memory of Jim's face at the station—that flash of shame, of hesitation—twisted in his gut like a knife. He'd seen it coming, had felt the tension the moment he'd walked through those doors, but he'd pushed ahead anyway. Stubborn. Always so stubborn.

"What did you expect?" he asked himself. "That he'd just throw his arms around you in front of everyone?"

He knew he wasn't being fair. Jim was still finding his footing, still struggling to reconcile the man he'd been with the man he was becoming. Brock had been there himself, years ago. He remembered the stares, the whispers, the way some people had pulled away when he'd first come out. But he'd had time to build his armor, to learn which battles were worth fighting and which weren't. Jim was still raw, still figuring it all out under the scrutiny of a small town that seemed determined to make everything their business.

Brock pushed himself up from the couch and wandered into the kitchen, opening the fridge without really seeing what was inside. The takeout he'd brought for Jim sat on the counter, untouched. He closed the fridge door and leaned against it, eyes drifting to the window where the last rays of sunset painted the sky in hues of amber and purple.

Outside, a car drove past on the quiet street, its headlights briefly illuminating the kitchen before disappearing around the corner. Brock pushed himself away from the fridge and moved to the window, peering out at the darkening neighborhood. Something caught his eye—a shadow moving near the edge of his property, just beyond the reach of his porch light. He squinted, trying to make out the figure, but it melted away into the gathering darkness.

A chill ran down his spine. Was that the stranger Ms. Nancy had mentioned? Or was his mind playing tricks on him, conjuring threats from the shadows because he was already feeling vulnerable?

He stepped back from the window and pulled out his phone, his thumb hovering over Jim's name. He wanted to call, to tell him about what he'd just seen, but pride held him back. Jim needed space, and Brock had to respect that.

As Jim drove away from Brock's place, the evening air seemed to press in on him from all sides. He rolled down the window, hoping the cool breeze might clear his head, but his thoughts remained tangled and heavy. The road ahead blurred slightly as his eyes welled with tears he refused to let fall.

His phone buzzed. A text from Spencer: "Door's open when you get here. Beer's cold."

Jim felt a surge of gratitude for his friend's simple understanding. No questions, no judgment—just an open door and cold beer. He turned onto the familiar street where Spencer and Chandler lived, their farmhouse a beacon of normalcy in his increasingly complicated life.

Spencer greeted him at the door with a beer already in hand. "Rough day?" he asked, his voice casual but his eyes concerned.

"You could say that." Jim took the beer and followed Spencer into the living room, where Chandler was lounging on the couch, a baseball game playing on low volume. He gave Jim a nod, then tactfully stood up.

"I'll give you guys some space," Chandler said, squeezing Spencer's shoulder as he passed. "Got some papers to grade anyway."

Jim sank into the worn armchair, taking a long pull from his beer. The familiar surroundings—Spencer's collection of vintage concert posters, the slight scent of Chandler's fancy candles, the perpetually crooked coffee table—offered a strange comfort.

"So," Spencer said after Chandler had disappeared upstairs. "You want to talk about it, or you want to pretend we're just having beers and watching the game?"

Jim stared at the condensation forming on his bottle. "The chief called me into his office today. Said there've been complaints about my 'personal conduct.'

" Spencer's face darkened. "About Brock?"

Jim nodded, taking another swig of beer. "Not directly, but it was clear what he meant. Said he was considering me for that detective position, but needed to make sure I was 'man enough' for the job." He made air quotes with his fingers, his voice bitter. "That I needed to keep my priorities straight."

Spencer leaned forward, his eyes narrowing. "That's bullshit, Jim. Complete bullshit."

"I know," Jim sighed, running a hand through his hair. "But then Brock showed up at the station with lunch, and everyone was staring, and I just... froze. I couldn't even look him in the eye." His voice cracked slightly. "You should have seen his face, Spence. I hurt him."

"So what are you going to do about it?" Spencer asked, his tone gentle but firm. "Because I've gotta tell you, Jim, this isn't going to get easier. The town will always talk. People will always stare. That's not going to change."

Jim set his beer down, the bottle making a dull thud against the coffee table. "I know that," he said, his voice strained. "But I wasn't prepared for how it would feel... to have everything I've worked for suddenly hanging in the balance because of who I'm with."

Spencer leaned back, studying his cousin's face. "You mean the promotion?"

"It's not just about the promotion," Jim said, standing up to pace the small living room. "It's about respect. The guys at the station—they used to look at me like I was one of them. Now they look at me like... like I'm someone they don't recognize anymore." He stopped, his back to Spencer. "But with Brock... when I'm with him, I feel like I'm finally being honest. Like I'm not pretending anymore." He turned, his expression torn. "But I don't know if I can handle losing everything else I've worked for."

Spencer was quiet for a moment, studying his cousin with a thoughtful gaze. "You know what I think?" he finally said, his voice gentle. "I think you've spent so long being who everyone else wanted you to be that you're afraid of what happens when you finally choose yourself."

Jim sank back into the chair, the weight of Spencer's words settling over him. "What if I make the wrong choice?"

"The wrong choice," Spencer said, leaning forward, "would be choosing what makes other people comfortable instead of what makes you happy." He reached for his beer, taking a thoughtful sip. "When I came out, I lost things. I lost my dad's approval, and I lost friends I thought would always be there. But you know what I gained? I gained Spence, my self worth. I gained a life that's honest and real." He gestured toward the ceiling, where the faint sound of Chandler moving around upstairs could be heard. "And I gained him."

Jim looked down at his hands, turning Spencer's words over in his mind. "I'm afraid," he admitted quietly. "I'm afraid of losing who I am."

"No," Spencer said firmly. "You're afraid of becoming who you really are." He reached across and placed a hand on Jim's shoulder. "The question is, who matters more? The guys at the station who judge you, or Brock, who loves you just as you are?"

Jim's head snapped up. "Love? We haven't... we haven't said that."

Spencer gave him a knowing look. Spencer smiled warmly, giving Jim's shoulder a reassuring squeeze. "Maybe not in words yet. But I've known you my whole life, and I've never seen you look at anyone the way you look at Brock." He stood up, stretching his arms above his head. "Listen, I think you need some time alone to process everything. Sometimes the answers come when we're not trying so hard to find them."

"Thanks, Spence," Jim said, grateful for the space.

"No problem. The guest room's made up for you. Take all the time you need." Spencer glanced upstairs with a barely concealed smile. "I should head up. Chandler's probably waiting for me."

As Spencer climbed the stairs, Jim sank deeper into the armchair, letting his cousin's words settle over him. He moved to the guest room. His mind was slowly making the decisions his heart had already chosen.

# Chapter 22
# A Leap of Faith

Jim's night at Spence and Chandler's had been a violent storm of unrest. Sleep was a distant ally, chased away by relentless images of Brock and the crushing weight of lingering doubts from their last conversation. Every moment was sharpened by the tension poisoning his work, his colleagues, even the thin veil of his personal life.

As dawn's first light clawed its way through the window, Jim surrendered to the wakefulness. His heart pounded like a war drum, its desperate rhythm echoing one resolute thought—he had to find Brock. They had to confront this menace together. Jim shot Brock a quick text. He waited patiently, but after five minutes the message remained unread.

In the barely awakened town, Jim left Spence and Chandler's with a patient fury. He steered his SUV down familiar, restless streets, every shadow and silence amplifying the gnawing unease in his gut. Rounding the corner toward Brock's, his heightened senses screamed that something was dreadfully off. The house itself was a mausoleum of darkness, completely unlit. It was barely dawn, but Brock was usually an early riser. When Jim rapped on the door, no reply came.

"Brock?" he shouted, his voice slicing desperately through the quiet of the early morning.

Frustration mounting, he knocked again with louder urgency before finessing the key from his pocket and stepping in. The oppressive silence inside twisted his stomach into knots. Room by room he combed through the house, each empty space intensifying the disquiet that now bordered on panic. Finally, his racing mind brought him back to his SUV. Something was terribly wrong—everything was out of place, and he needed answers, and fast.

Determined, Jim pivoted toward the warehouses. He knew Brock's construction crew would soon be assembling there, the epicenter where plans were made and lives were built from sweat and promise. Pulling into the site felt like stepping into the eye of a brewing storm. He spotted a few faces he recognized from Brock's team, busy unpacking supplies and scrutinizing work orders as if trying to stave off an impending calamity. Yet Brock was nowhere to be seen.

"Hey, Jim," one crew member called out, his tone laced with an unsettling uncertainty. "You here to see Brock?"

"Yeah. You seen him this morning?" Jim replied, his voice taut with barely concealed tension.

The man's shake of the head was the only reply. "Nope, not yet. Thought he'd be here by now. We've got a full day ahead—drywall and flooring in the east wing. But he's always early; this is late for him."

A creeping dread slithered up Jim's spine. Managing a curt nod, he hurried back to his SUV. His pulse pounded as he raced back by the house. He moved to the garage and opened the heavy wooden doors. Brock's Yukon was gone. No need to search the house again. *Where could he be*? The uneasy question kept repeating in the back of Jim's mind. He jumped back in his SUV. His desperation grew; he retraced his route, speeding past all those places where Brock might have stopped for coffee or a quick breakfast for the crew. Every empty stop tightened the noose of anxiety. Returning to the warehouses, his stomach twisted into despair. Brock still had not arrived.

Just as the weight of impending doom was about to force him into action—dialing Amanda to confess that something was very wrong—his phone vibrated violently on the console. The screen flashed Amanda's name, and he pressed the button on the steering wheel, answered instantly, his voice raw with urgent intensity.

"Jim, where are you?" Amanda's voice carried an urgency, tinged with an edge that made his stomach twist uncomfortably.

"I'm out by Brock's job site, trying to find him. Why?"

"Ol' man Conway found a brand new, fully loaded Yukon, that sounds exactly like Brock's, abandoned on a dirt road. Conway was headed out to Granger Lake to go fishing and thought someone might need some help when he saw the car on the side of the road. He pulled over, but there was no one around and no evidence of car trouble. He called it in, and Brock's the only one with a vehicle like that around here. It's about ten miles north of town, near that stretch by the service road to the old mill. Know it?"

Jim's heart skipped as he heard the news. "I'll meet ya there." He hung up, his mind racing, and steered the SUV northward as he tried to call Brock again, straight to voicemail.

When he reached the location, Amanda's patrol car was already stationed behind Brock's vehicle. The old dirt road was rough, its surface cracked and faded, lined with wild, overgrown weeds and shrubs that tangled with the red clay. The early morning sunlight cast long, eerie shadows through the dense canopy of trees, which loomed with a quiet, foreboding mystery. As Jim parked in front of Brock's Yukon, he felt the weight of the moment pressing down.

Amanda was waiting, her eyes sharp and focused as they met his. Without uttering a word, she gestured him over to the passenger side of the vehicle.

"Jim…" she hesitated, her breath forming a faint cloud in the cold morning air. "His phone is in the car, and I found something else."

Jim's heart sank further. "What else?"

"There's a rough arrow drawn into the dirt here, just outside the passenger door. Looks like it was made with a heel, like he was trying to leave a sign. It's pointing into the woods."

Jim's pulse quickened, his mind a flurry of thoughts. "I know that area. There's an old hunting cabin out that way, about a mile in. Hardly anyone goes there anymore." He crouched down to examine the mark, the arrow's lines etched clearly in the dust. Brock's cell phone lay on the passenger seat, its screen dark, a thin layer of road dust hinting at its recent abandonment. Brock had been in that car, and he'd tried to leave a trail.

Jim looked up, meeting Amanda's intense gaze. "If he left this sign, he wanted someone to find it. Let's head to that cabin."

"Well, we need to check it out," Amanda replied, her voice steady but laced with tension. "You ready?" she asked, drawing her service weapon with a swift, practiced motion.

"Already on my way," Jim responded, determination hardening his resolve.

The walk into the woods was eerily silent, each footfall hushed by the thick carpet of leaves and pine needles that blanketed the forest floor. The air was a cool shroud, heavy with the scent of damp earth and the rich, green aroma of moss that clung to every surface. As Jim and Amanda ventured further into the dense forest, branches reached out like skeletal fingers, clawing at their clothes and snagging their skin. The towering pines loomed above, their dark silhouettes weaving a canopy that seemed to press down upon them, closing them into a world of shadow. Despite the morning's deceptive calm, Jim's senses were alive, every nerve taut, hypersensitive to the slightest rustle or crack.

After what felt like an eternity of weaving through the oppressive maze of trees, Jim finally glimpsed the faint outline of the cabin ahead. It stood in a small clearing, its weathered wooden frame leaning like a weary sentinel, the roof slumping under the accumulated burden of years without care. A chill of apprehension settled over him as they neared, the silence around them deepening into an unnerving void.

Amanda edged closer, her voice a mere breath against the stillness. "Doesn't look like anyone's been here in ages," she murmured, though the hairs on the back of Jim's neck prickled with a sense of unease that whispered otherwise.

With a tentative touch, he pushed the door open, the hinges shrieking in protest, their rusted joints groaning as if awakening from a long slumber. As he stepped inside, the floorboards creaked ominously under his weight, and the air hit him like a stale wave, laden with dust, mildew, and something sharper—an acrid metallic tang that set his teeth on edge.

"Over here," Amanda called out softly, her flashlight slicing through the murk to reveal the room's grim secrets. Jim followed the beam to a shadowed corner where a small pile of supplies lay discarded: a half-empty water bottle, a crumpled pack of trail mix, and a piece of fabric, torn and stained, that matched the shirt Brock had been wearing yesterday. Jim's heart thudded painfully in his chest, a knot of dread twisting his insides.

"This isn't good," he muttered, his voice tight with anxiety. His mind raced with questions and possibilities, each more troubling than the last. Brock had definitely been here, perhaps even sought refuge for the night. But the unsettling question loomed larger and more insistent: where was he now?

As Jim knelt to examine the fabric, his fingers trembled slightly. He could still smell Brock's cologne on it—that distinctive cedar and citrus scent that lingered on his own clothes after their evenings together.

The knot in Jim's stomach tightened. He stood abruptly, scanning the cabin's interior with renewed urgency. "Brock!" he called out, no longer concerned with stealth. His voice echoed through the empty space, answered only by the settling of old wood.

They meticulously searched the dimly lit cabin, scrutinizing every corner, every shadowed nook with growing frustration, yet there was no trace of Brock himself. As they retraced their steps to the main room, an eerie sound shattered the oppressive silence—a faint, rhythmic tapping that seemed to echo from the depths of the forest beyond.

Amanda's eyebrow arched in suspicion, and they exchanged a wary glance, the tension between them palpable, before cautiously stepping onto the creaky porch. The tapping grew louder, more insistent, as if summoning them, originating from somewhere behind the cabin, hidden in the encroaching darkness. Jim's heartbeat pounded like a drum in his chest, each thud resonating in his ears as they edged along the side of the weather-beaten building, only to halt abruptly at the unexpected sight before them.

An old, tattered tarp, its edges frayed and fluttering in the breeze, concealed something large and ominously lumpy. The tapping noise, now almost a whisper, seemed to retreat as they inched closer. With a deep, stealing breath, Jim crouched down, reaching out with trembling fingers to lift a corner of the tarp. Beneath it lay a rudimentary shelter, crafted hastily from branches and leaves, a testament to survival in dire circumstances.

And inside it lay Brock, bound yet seemingly untouched by harm, a gag loosely fastened around his mouth. His eyes snapped open at the sight of Jim, a torrent of relief washing over his face, though the terror of his ordeal still lingered in his gaze.

"Brock!" Jim fell to his knees, his fingers working swiftly to loosen the rough, frayed ropes that bound Brock's wrists. The ropes left deep, angry red marks on Brock's skin. "What happened? Who did this to you?"

Brock coughed harshly as the gag was pulled from his dry, cracked lips, his voice coming out raspy and strained. "I—I don't know. I went to take that garbage out last night after you left." His eyes, wide and glistening with a mix of fear and confusion, met Jim's.

"Someone jumped me outside the house, hit me on the back of the head, hard. The next thing I know, I'm waking up here in a truck. My hands were bound, gagged, and a blindfold was over my eyes. A harsh voice commanded me to get out of the car. I couldn't see anything. The voice told me to shift my position to face at an angle from the doorway of the vehicle and then told me to walk straight until he told me to stop. Once I knew the direction, I dug my heel into the dirt. I managed to scrape that arrow into the dirt, hoping someone… hoping you would find me. I tripped and fell. Then I felt myself being covered, and the voice told me not to move. And I lay here until I hear your voice. That's when I started tapping my boot on the ground."

Amanda knelt beside them, her eyes scanning Brock with a careful, assessing gaze. "Did you see who it was at any point?" she asked, her voice steady but edged with concern.

Brock shook his head, frustration and helplessness etched into the lines of his face. "No… I didn't see his face. Just a dark hoodie, maybe a hat. He was big, though—strong enough to knock me out. I could hear him going in and out of the cabin. But then I heard your voice and I started tapping. Just hoping and praying you'd hear me." Tears welled up in his eyes and spilled down his cheeks.

Jim tightened his grip on Brock's trembling hand, offering support as Brock struggled to stand, his legs unsteady beneath him. Jim pulled Brock into a tight embrace and then a scorching kiss. He didn't care what

Amanda thought. He was just so relieved they'd found Brock. The overwhelming relief that washed over Jim was tinged with a lingering unease. Someone had left Brock here, tied up and defenseless, in the desolate silence of the woods. It felt like a message, a warning of something sinister lurking just beyond their sight, an unseen and unpredictable threat.

As they trudged back towards the vehicles, the forest seemed to close in around them, each shadow whispering secrets. Brock leaned heavily on Jim, his body still quivering from the harrowing ordeal. Jim wrapped a reassuring arm around him, grounding them both in the simple, steady rhythm of their footsteps crunching against the forest floor.

When they reached the edge of the forest, Jim paused, casting a lingering glance back into the quiet, brooding woods as if trying to sense the presence that had slipped through their grasp.

"We'll figure out who did this," Jim promised, his voice low but filled with an unwavering determination.

Brock looked up, his eyes reflecting a deep sense of gratitude and trust. "I know we will, Jim. I know."

The oppressive silence of the forest seemed to swallow Jim, Amanda, and Brock as they cautiously retreated toward their vehicles, every rustle of leaves underfoot echoing in their ears. But the tranquility was violently disrupted by an unexpected, piercing metallic clang that reverberated through the trees. In a heart-stopping moment, Jim's eyes widened in terror as he saw Amanda collapse to the forest floor, a shadowy figure towering above her, clutching a shovel with menacing intent. The air thickened with tension as a gun was suddenly trained on Jim's chest, its cold glint promising danger.

"Don't even think about it. Drop your weapon, asshole," the figure snarled, voice rough and dripping with malice. "Thumb and forefinger only to remove your gun. Slowly."

Jim's hand hovered, paralyzed, inches from his holster, his mind racing as he took in the threat before him. The man's face was a tapestry of menace—an unkempt scraggly beard, eyes rimmed with exhaustion and fury, and deep, bitter lines etching a life of hard experiences. Recognition dawned on Jim as he heard Brock's strangled gasp, the sound slicing through the tension like a knife. The pieces fell into place, turning the situation even more perilous as the hidden connections unraveled with each passing second.

"Dad?" Brock's whisper trembled in the charged silence, his wide eyes reflecting a mix of disbelief and raw terror. In that charged moment, his father's gaze burned with equal parts disdain and calculating greed.

"Surprised to see me, sonny boy?" he drawled, every syllable dripping menace, his voice the gravely signature of a lifelong chain smoker.

Jim's mind raced in frantic confusion. Every instinct urged him to adjust his grip on his weapon, but before he could act, the man's finger tightened around the trigger. Jim's grip faltered; his gun slipped from his grasp, hitting the dirt with a muted, final thud that seemed to echo their impending doom.

A sinister smile curled on Brock's father's lips as he sneered, "Good choice. Now, handcuff her," he ordered, motioning toward Amanda's limp, unconscious form sprawled carelessly beside the patrol car. "And then you cuff yourself." The command reverberated through the heavy air.

Hands trembling with fury and dread, Jim obeyed. He fumbled with the cuff links around Amanda's inert wrists before snapping them loosely but securely, a disturbing finality sealing her fate. Not long after, he encircled his own wrists, the metallic clink of the restraints a grim prelude to what was to come. With almost clinical satisfaction, Brock's father turned his attention to his son.

Without warning, he yanked Brock in front of him, forcing the boy to become an unsuitable human shield. Brutally, he bound Brock's defiant hands with thick zip ties, each tug a testament to his cold control, and then wrapped another layer of duct tape around his wrists like a final suffocation of hope.

"You're making a mistake," Jim managed to choke out, his voice seething with suppressed wrath as he spoke. "The whole department's going to be looking for us." His warning hung in the air, laden with foreboding.

A dismissive scoff erupted from Brock's father as he hauled Brock even further in front of him, positioning his son as a shield against the world. "Oh, they'll look, sure," he taunted, his voice low and heavy with malice. "But they won't find you until it's too late." With a deliberate, chilling gesture of the gun, he forced Jim to march, like a beaten man, back toward the ominous hunting cabin looming in the distance.

Inside Jim's storming thoughts, every nerve was electrified with the desperate search for a sliver of hope, a hidden angle that might reverse their grim fate. Beside him, Brock's rigid shoulders and contorted expression betrayed a boiling mix of frustration and anger—a silent plea that Jim felt as a burning weight, urging him to save them both.

At the cabin, the door slammed open as Brock's father shoved them violently inside. With a degrading force, he pushed Jim to the cold, unforgiving floor. Standing above them, his eyes danced with deranged satisfaction, wild and glazed, as he took in the scene like a mad sculptor proud of his grotesque handiwork.

"You really think I was just going to let you walk around, rich and smug? After all I gave up to raise you?" he spat, his tone wavering between seething rage and desperate betrayal. "It's time for you to pay up, sonny boy. Time for my cut. Ten million sounds about right." Each word was a scalpel, slicing through the thin veil of normalcy.

Brock's retort came out in a stream of venom, pure and unfiltered: "What the fuck! You think I'd give you ten cents? You gave up nothing!" His voice cracked with the weight of accumulated hurt. "You only ever took. And you know it. I'm not giving you a fucking dime!"

The cruel sneer on Brock's father's face intensified as he gripped the gun tighter, his features twisting with anger. "You don't know anything! Everything you have, everything you built—it's because of me! I gave you a life! I put you on this path."

"On this path?" Brock's incredulous voice sliced through the tension. His eyes blazed with resentment as he retorted, "You put me on a path of survival. I fought tooth and nail to get where I am despite you, not because of you. I worked hard, day in and day out, to build something I could be proud of. You've done nothing but ruin lives—mine, Mom's, everyone's who was unfortunate enough to have you in their life."

At the mere mention of Brock's mother, a fleeting vulnerability flickered in his father's eyes, quickly smothered by bitter resolve. "Your mother," he scoffed, his voice laced with disdain, "was always on your side. Probably the reason you turned out to be a sissy boy. Always going on about how strong you were, how you'd do better without me. Maybe she's right." A twisted smile emerged as his words dripped with malice. "Maybe I don't need you alive, after all. You're probably vain enough to name her your beneficiary, aren't you? If I take you out of the picture, maybe she'll finally appreciate what I've done for this family."

Brock's face blanched, his jaw clenching in a silent, defiant promise of retribution. "If you touch her—" he began, voice trembling with protective fury.

A cold, rough laugh erupted from his father, cutting off Brock's protest.

"Touch her?" he sneered, his tone dripping with icy contempt.

"Brock, I'm well past 'touching' anything. I'm in debt, son. Real debt. People I owe aren't the forgiving kind. I need that ten million to disappear, or they'll make sure I do. Permanently." His voice quivered, just enough to reveal the underlying terror of his own predicament.

"Those loan sharks found me, you know," Brock's father said, his voice dropping to a near whisper as he paced the small cabin. "I was holed up in that empty apartment in your building." He gestured toward Jim with the gun. "Thought I'd found the perfect spot—abandoned after some water damage, management company too lazy to fix it up right away."

Jim's eyes widened with sudden understanding. "My apartment building. The fire..."

"Yeah, your precious little apartment." Brock's father laughed bitterly. "They tracked me there somehow. This big Russian guy and his goon. Kicked in the door while I was sleeping. I barely made it out the back window before they torched the whole place." His hand trembled slightly on the gun.

"They wanted to make sure I was dead. Figured burning me alive would send a message to anyone else thinking of skipping town with their money." He wiped sweat from his brow with a shaking hand. "I made it out the back window just before the place went up. Flames everywhere, smoke so thick I could barely breathe. I hid in the woods for three days, hoping they'd think I died in that fire."

"So you're the one who's been skulking around town," Jim said, the pieces finally clicking into place. "The stranger everyone's been reporting."

"Had to come back," Brock's father muttered, his eyes darting nervously to the cabin window. "Thought maybe they'd given up, figured I was dead. But they know. They're here somewhere, watching, waiting. I've seen their car—a black sedan with tinted windows—circling the neighborhoods. The interest on the money I borrowed compounds daily. Every fucking day, thousands of dollars. I need that money now, or we're all dead."

"We?" Brock challenged, struggling against his restraints.

"Yes, we!" Brock's father hissed, his eyes wild with desperation. "You think they'll stop with me? They'll come after anyone connected to me— you, your mother, even your cop boyfriend here. These aren't your average loan sharks. They're professionals. Killers."

He paced frantically, the floorboards creaking beneath his weight. "I've been watching you for weeks now, planning how to get to you. When I saw you with him," he jerked the gun toward Jim, "I knew I had to move fast. Figured a cop might complicate things."

"So that's why you took me to the cabin," Brock said, his voice steady despite the fear in his eyes. "To keep me isolated until I gave you the money."

His father nodded, sweat beading on his forehead. "Ten million, and I disappear forever.

Unable to hold back any longer, Jim's voice cracked through the tension. "You think this is going to fix anything? Kidnapping your own son?

Assaulting not one, but two police officers. You're only digging yourself deeper." His words, heavy with impending doom, floated unheeded in the charged air.

Brock's father's attention narrowed to focus solely on his son. "I can't believe you'd be so selfish," he growled, his voice low and menacing. "Sitting in your fancy office, raking in millions and millions while I have nothing. That money is mine. It's owed to me. You won't even miss that measly amount. I read the article on you in Forbes—more than half a fucking billion dollars! And you can't give your old man pennies in comparison, you ungrateful cocksucker."

"Nothing is owed to you," Brock shot back, his voice quivering with a mix of raw emotion and painful resolve. "You've done nothing but destroy everything around you."

As the tension escalated to a breaking point, Brock's father's face hardened like stone. Slowly, deliberately, he lifted the gun, aiming it unerringly at Brock's chest. Jim's heart thundered in his ears, each beat a desperate drum of impending disaster, while time itself seemed to slow as the future turned perilously uncertain.

"You're not going to live long enough to insult me again, sissy boy," his father hissed, his words hanging in the stagnant air like a death sentence, setting the stage for a climax soaked in foreboding dread.

In a single, desperate move, Jim lunged forward, shoving Brock out of the way just as the gunshot shattered the tense silence. A hot, searing pain exploded in Jim's shoulder like a wildfire, and he staggered back as his vision swam with a dizzying blur of colors. The acrid smell of gunpowder filled the cabin, mingling with the sharp, metallic tang of blood that hung heavily in the air.

Ignoring the fiery agony that pulsed through his body, Jim instinctively reached for his backup weapon, cleverly concealed at his ankle. Even with his hands cuffed, with a swift motion, he brought it up and fired, the gun's recoil jolting through him before Brock's father could react. The man staggered back, a look of disbelief etched across his face, clutching his chest as he crumpled to the floor, his features twisted in shock and pain.

"Jim!" Brock was beside him in an instant, his presence a beacon of urgency, pressing a firm hand against Jim's bleeding shoulder. Each breath Jim took was ragged, his chest heaving as his hand trembled while raising his radio, his voice a strained whisper calling for backup and an ambulance.

"Officers… injured… need immediate assistance…" His words faded as the relentless pain clawed at him, darkness creeping insidiously at the edges of his vision, threatening to pull him under.

As the world around him began to dim, he felt Brock's hand gripping his own, steady and strong, like an anchor in the storm. Even as the pain consumed him, Jim found a strange comfort in that touch, a poignant reminder that, despite everything, they weren't alone.

The last sound he heard before slipping into unconsciousness was the distant wail of approaching sirens, their mournful cry echoing through the stillness of the forest, a promise of help and hope.

# Chapter 23
# Hope and Healing

The steady beeping of the heart monitor was the first sound Jim registered as consciousness slowly returned. His eyelids felt heavy, weighted down by the lingering effects of anesthesia. The sharp smell of antiseptic filled his nostrils, and a dull, throbbing pain radiated from his left shoulder. He tried to move, but his body felt like lead.

"Easy there," came a soft, familiar voice. "Don't try to move too much."

Jim forced his eyes open, blinking against the harsh fluorescent lights. Brock sat beside the hospital bed, his face drawn with worry, dark circles beneath his eyes. His large hand enveloped Jim's, thumb gently stroking across his knuckles.

"How long?" Jim's voice was hoarse, his throat dry.

"About eight hours," Brock replied, reaching for a cup

of water with a straw. "Surgery went well. The bullet missed anything vital, but they said you'll need physical therapy for a while."

Jim sipped the water gratefully, the cool liquid soothing his parched throat. As awareness fully returned, memories flooded back—the cabin, Brock's father, the gun aimed at Brock's chest. He tried to sit up, wincing at the sharp pain that shot through his shoulder.

"Brock," he gasped, "your father—"

"He's alive," Brock said, gently easing Jim back against the pillows. "In custody at the county hospital. The shot you fired hit his lung, but they say he'll recover. He's facing multiple charges—kidnapping, assault on two officers, attempted murder."

Jim exhaled slowly, relief washing over him. "And Amanda?"

"Concussion, but she's going to be fine. She's here too, a few rooms down. Her parents are with her."

Jim nodded, relief flooding through him. He squeezed Brock's hand, noticing the dark circles under his eyes, the rumpled clothes. "You look exhausted. Have you been here the whole time?"

"Of course I have," Brock said softly, his voice rough with emotion. "I wasn't about to leave you."

Jim swallowed hard, the weight of everything that had happened settling over him. "You could have died," he whispered. "When I saw him point that gun at you, I just... I couldn't let that happen."

Brock's eyes glistened with unshed tears. "You took a bullet for me, Jim. Why would you do that?"

"Because I love you." The words tumbled out before Jim could stop them, simple and honest. The words hung in the air between them, and for a moment, Jim felt a flicker of fear—had he gone too far, too fast? But then Brock's face softened, his eyes brimming with emotion.

"I love you too," Brock whispered, leaning forward to press his forehead gently against Jim's.

"God, I love you so much it terrifies me sometimes." His voice broke slightly. "When I saw you fall, saw the blood... I thought I might lose you."

Jim reached up with his good arm, ignoring the twinge of pain as he cupped Brock's cheek. "It's going to take more than a bullet to get rid of me," he said, attempting a smile despite the pain.

Brock laughed softly, though it sounded more like a sob. "Don't joke about that. Not yet."

The door to Jim's hospital room creaked open, drawing their attention. Jim's parents entered quietly, worry etched into their faces. Helen's eyes were red-rimmed, and Bill's jaw was set with tension. Behind them, Spence and Chandler stepped in, carrying a modest bouquet of flowers.

"Oh, Jimmy," Helen whispered, rushing to the opposite side of his bed and carefully placing her hand on his uninjured arm. "Thank God you're awake."

"Hey, Mom," Jim said, his voice stronger now. "Dad. You didn't have to come all this way."

Bill moved to stand beside his wife, placing a steadying hand on her shoulder. "Of course we did. Spence called us as soon as he heard what happened." His eyes flickered to Brock, then back to his son. "Said you'd been shot protecting someone important to you."

Jim met his father's gaze steadily, a newfound resolve in his eyes. "Yes. I was."

Bill Williamson's face softened, and he nodded, a look of understanding passing between father and son. "You did good, son."

Brock shifted slightly, as if preparing to give the family some privacy, but Jim tightened his grip on Brock's hand, keeping him firmly by his side.

"Mom, Dad," Jim said, his voice quiet but steady, "I need you to know something. Brock isn't just my friend. He's... we're together." He paused, feeling the weight of the words, the reality of saying them aloud to his parents. "I love him."

Helen's eyes widened slightly, then a warm smile spread across her face. "Oh, honey," she said softly, reaching across the bed to place her other hand over Brock's and Jim's intertwined hands. "We know."

Jim blinked, surprise evident on his face. "You know?"

Bill chuckled, the sound warm and reassuring. "Son, we've known since dinner at Spence's. The way you two looked at each other..." He shook his head, smiling. "A father recognizes when his son is in love."

Relief washed over Jim, and he felt Brock's grip on his hand tighten slightly. Spence moved closer, setting the flowers on the bedside table.

"Told you they'd be fine with it," he said with a gentle smile. "The Williamsons are made of sturdier stuff than you give them credit for."

Chandler nodded in agreement, his arm slipping around Spence's waist. "And now that everything's out in the open, maybe we can finally get Jim to take some time off. He works too hard." He squeezed Spence's side affectionately.

A knock at the door interrupted their moment, and Chief Haines, the department, stepped in, his uniform crisp despite the late hour. His expression was solemn as he surveyed the room.

"Officer Williamson," he said, nodding respectfully. "Good to see you awake. How are you feeling?"

"Like I've been shot," Jim replied with a weak smile. "But I'll live."

The chief's expression remained serious. "I need to talk to you about what happened out there. When you're up for it."

Jim nodded, wincing slightly as he shifted. "I'm up for it now, sir."

Chief Haines glanced at the family gathered around the bed. "Perhaps we should speak privately—"

"With all due respect, Chief," Jim interrupted, his voice firm despite his weakened state.

"Whatever you have to say can be said in front of my family." His eyes met Brock's, drawing strength from his presence. "All of my family."

The chief seemed to notice their clasped hands for the first time, his eyebrows rising slightly before his expression settled back into professional neutrality. He cleared his throat.

"Very well. First, I want to commend you for your actions. You showed exceptional bravery in a life-threatening situation." He paused, his gaze steady. "The district attorney is moving forward with multiple charges against Raymond Curry—kidnapping, assault on law enforcement officers, attempted murder. He's not going anywhere for a long time."

Brock's hand tightened around Jim's, and Jim could feel the tension radiating from him at the mention of his father.

"What about Amanda?" Jim asked, concern for his partner evident in his voice.

"Detective Marks is recovering well," the chief replied. "Her concussion was mild. She's been cleared to go home tomorrow, though she'll be on desk duty for a week or so." He hesitated for a moment before continuing. "She's already given her statement, and it corroborates what Mr. Curry here told us happened. She also mentioned your quick thinking under pressure."

Jim nodded, relief washing over him. "Good. She's a damn good officer."

"That she is," Chief Haines agreed.

The chief moved closer to the bed. His posture seemed different—less rigid, more respectful as he glanced between Jim and Brock.

"I've got some more news you both need to hear," he said, lowering his voice. "We picked up that loanshark and two of his goons last night. Seems they were closing in on Curry's father when we intercepted them."

Brock straightened in his chair. "The mobsters?"

"Actually, they're already on their way back to West Virginia," the chief continued, crossing his arms. "We coordinated with authorities there who've been building a case against them for years. Turns out your father wasn't their only victim—they've got a rap sheet longer than my arm. Extortion, money laundering, assault... even a couple of suspected murders."

Jim's eyes widened. "So they're gone? For good?"

"If the West Virginia DA has anything to say about it, they'll be locked up for decades." The chief's expression softened slightly. "Seems like your father got himself tangled with some serious players, Curry. You're lucky to be alive—both of you."

Brock exhaled slowly, his shoulders sagging with relief. "Thank you, Chief. For everything."

The chief nodded, then turned his attention back to Jim.

He shifted his weight, seeming uncomfortable with what he needed to say next. "Jim, I owe you an apology."

The room fell silent, all eyes turning to the chief. Jim blinked in surprise. "Sir?"

Chief Haines cleared his throat again. "Before all this happened, I called you into my office. Made some… implications about your personal life interfering with your work. That was unprofessional of me." He shifted uncomfortably, his gaze briefly dropping to Jim and Brock's joined hands before meeting Jim's eyes again.

"Your actions out there proved me wrong. You didn't let anything cloud your judgment—you acted with courage and quick thinking that saved lives."

Jim was momentarily speechless, the chief's words catching him off guard. "Thank you, sir," he finally managed.

Chief Baker nodded, his expression softening slightly. "There's one more thing. That detective position we discussed? It's yours if you want it. You've more than earned it."

A complex mixture of emotions swept through Jim—pride, vindication, and gratitude. But there was something else too, a certainty that hadn't been there before. He glanced at Brock, drawing strength from the unwavering support in his eyes.

"Congratulations, Detective Williamson. The promotion is yours, effective immediately—once you are back to active duty/" The chief grinned.

A gentle knock on the door captured everyone's attention as a nurse stepped in, her face a blend of kindness and authority. Her voice was soft yet assertive. "Visiting hours are almost up. Just a few more minutes, everyone."

As his parents and friends began to trickle out, each offering heartfelt words of encouragement and playful promises to return soon, a serene silence enveloped the room, leaving Jim and Brock to share an intimate moment, just the two of them.

Brock tenderly caressed Jim's hand, his touch light and comforting. "I don't know how I ever got lucky enough to find you," he whispered, his voice filled with wonder.

Jim's smile spread warmly across his face, his eyes softening with affection. "I don't think it was luck, Brock. I think we were meant to find each other. Besides, you kept me waiting long enough," he replied, a teasing lilt in his voice.

Brock chuckled, a deep, resonant sound that filled the room and chased away the lingering shadows of the past few days. "I'm not letting you go, Jim. Not now, not ever," he vowed, his voice unwavering.

As they shared a tender kiss, Jim felt the last of his defenses crumble, leaving him exposed, vulnerable, and utterly content. There was no more hiding, no more running. This was his life, his love, and he intended to embrace it fully, savoring every precious moment.

# Chapter 24
# Second Chances

After spending several days in the hospital, Jim was finally back at Brock's house, a place that was gradually becoming synonymous with home for him. The soft, comforting glow of the bedside lamp bathed the room in a warm, golden hue, casting gentle shadows that danced across the walls and floor, creating a serene atmosphere. It was a stark contrast to the chaos that had unfolded over the past week, now settling into a peaceful calm.

The air was thick with unspoken emotions, each breath heavy with the weight of recent events and the lingering echoes of their terrifying ordeal. Jim's shoulder, still tender and sore from the gunshot wound, leaned against Brock's solid chest, a silent testament to the harrowing night they had barely survived. Brock shifted closer, his towering frame enveloping Jim in a protective embrace.

The scent of Brock's sandalwood cologne mingled with the sterile, antiseptic aroma of the hospital that still clung to their clothes, creating a strangely comforting blend that spoke of safety and unwavering support.

Jim gazed up into Brock's expressive blue eyes, finding there a profound depth of emotion that words could never fully capture, a silent promise of solace and understanding.

"Jim," Brock whispered, his voice husky with emotion, "I keep thinking about how close I came to losing you."

Jim reached up with his good arm, his fingers tracing the line of Brock's jaw. "But you didn't. I'm right here."

Brock leaned into the touch, his eyes closing briefly. When he opened them again, there was a new resolve shining through. "I want to ask you something, and I need you to be completely honest with me."

Jim nodded, shifting slightly to face Brock more directly, wincing as the movement pulled at his healing wound. "Always."

"Your apartment..." Brock began, hesitating for a moment. "The repairs are probably done by now, or they will be soon."

Jim felt his heart skip a beat, suddenly understanding where this conversation was heading. "Probably."

"I don't want you to go back there," Brock said, his voice steady but vulnerable. "I want you to stay here. With me. Not as a temporary roommate, not as a guest, and not in the guest room, but... as us. Together."

Jim's breath caught in his throat. Though they'd grown closer, though they'd confessed their love for each other, this felt like another threshold—a more permanent commitment, a clearer statement to the world about who they were to each other.

"Are you asking me to move in with you?" Jim asked softly, his eyes searching Brock's face.

Brock nodded, his expression a mix of hope and nervousness. "I know it might seem fast, but after everything that's happened... life's too short, Jim. When I thought I might lose you in that cabin, I realized I don't want to waste another day pretending we're anything less than what we are."

Jim's heart swelled with emotion as he reached for Brock's hand, intertwining their fingers.

"Brock, I..." he paused, gathering his thoughts. "Ever since I first saw you, something inside me changed. I didn't understand it at first, and I fought against it. But now, looking back, I think I've been falling for you since that very first moment."

Brock's eyes softened, his thumb gently stroking across Jim's knuckles.

"These past weeks with you have been the most honest I've ever been with myself," Jim continued. "And you're right—life is too short. After staring down the barrel of that gun, I know what matters." He squeezed Brock's hand. "Yes. Yes, I want to move in with you. I want to build a life with you."

Jim lifted his head, his eyes locking with Brock's in a gaze that laid bare a vulnerability reflecting his own. "I've wanted this for so long, Brock.

To feel your arms around me, to know that we're in this together, no matter what," he confessed, his voice trembling with sincerity.

Brock's heart swelled, brimming with a potent mixture of love and determination. With a gentle touch, he guided Jim to sit on the edge of the bed, the mattress letting out a soft creak under their combined weight. The room was enveloped in a serene silence, disturbed only by the distant, rhythmic hum of crickets—a soothing backdrop to the intense emotions swirling like a storm between them.

Brock watched Jim slip away, the soft click of the guest room door sounding louder than it should have.

"I just need a few minutes to myself," Jim had said, voice tight with emotion, eyes glistening like he was standing on the edge of something he wasn't sure he could survive.

Brock exhaled slowly, his chest tight with longing. *Take all the time you need, Jim.* Because Brock needed a few minutes, too. A few minutes to pull himself together. To make everything perfect.

He moved quickly through the master bedroom, energy thrumming under his skin, a mix of nerves and excitement he hadn't felt in years. Tonight wasn't about just sex. It was about showing Jim—with every touch, every kiss—that he was loved. Wanted. Treasured.

Brock lit a few candles, the room filling with a warm, golden glow that softened the edges of everything. He set the Bluetooth speaker on a playlist he'd made for nights just like this—slow, sensual beats that made your blood hum in your veins. He placed a small bottle of lube and a stack of clean towels on the nightstand, arranging them carefully, thoughtfully. *Prepared. Ready.*

Then, without hesitation, he slipped into his closet.

He peeled off his clothes quickly, his hands clumsy in his rush, and dug through the bottom drawer of his dresser. His fingers brushed against the familiar fabric—black spandex and mesh. The assless boxer briefs he'd picked up at Cannonball Bear Bash last year, half-joking with the guys, never actually thinking he'd have a reason to wear them for someone who *mattered.*

He tugged them on, adjusting himself in the snug pouch, the mesh doing little to hide his thickening cock or the way his body responded just thinking about Jim seeing him like this.

*God, what if he thinks it's too much?* Brock's stomach twisted, but he forced the thought away.

*No. Jim deserves to be worshiped. To feel wanted.* He quickly slipped his jeans back on and pulled his shirt back on so that the underwear would be a surprise.

He stepped out of the closet and toward the bed just as he heard the soft click of the bedroom door opening.

His breath caught.

There stood Jim, toweling his hair, still damp from his shower, curling a little at the ends, water droplets tracing lazy paths down his chest and stomach, dampening the waistband of his sweatpants. His erection was evident beneath the soft fabric.

Their eyes locked. The room seemed to tilt.

Jim's gaze slid over him, slow and hungry, and Brock felt the air between them thicken with need.

*He wants me,* Brock realized, a fierce wave of emotion crashing into him. Not just for tonight. Not just for release. But because being together was the safest, most honest thing either of them had found in a long time.

He took a step toward Jim, heart hammering against his ribs. The music swelled softly behind them, candles flickering like they knew something sacred was about to happen.

"You're beautiful," Brock rasped, voice rough, broken open with feeling. "Come here."

"Jim," Brock began, his voice unwavering but laced with raw emotion, "I love you. I can't imagine my life without you in it, not for a single moment."

Jim reached out, his fingers weaving into Brock's with a tender intimacy, their connection igniting a warmth that spread through both of them like a gentle, flickering flame.

"I love you, too, Brock. More than anything in this world. And tonight, I want us to truly be together. To take another step forward, to have you make love to me and seal our commitment to each other," he whispered, his words carrying the weight of a promise.

Brock's breath caught in his throat as he gazed at Jim, his eyes darkening with desire. Without a word, he leaned forward, capturing Jim's lips in a kiss that started gentle but quickly deepened with hunger. His hands moved to frame Jim's face, careful to avoid jostling his injured shoulder as he guided him back against the pillows.

"Are you sure?" Brock whispered against Jim's lips, his voice husky with restraint. "I don't want to hurt you."

"I've never been more sure of anything," Jim replied, his good hand sliding up Brock's chest to tangle in his hair. "I need you, Brock. All of you."

Brock's breath caught, his chest heaving as Jim's words, dripping with sincerity, stirred a primal, hungry desire within him. His mind was a whirlwind of thoughts, his heart pounding in his ears. Jim's only experiences with another man had been with him, and now, Jim wanted more. Was Jim truly ready to cross this boundary?

Brock had long accepted that he'd be content with their sex life as it was, he'd be happy to be the one taken, the one fucked, when it came to it. Before Jim, he'd had his share of experiences, both giving and receiving. But he knew his cock, thick and nine inches long, could be intimidating. He was well-endowed, much more than the average man, and he knew this would be Jim's first time experiencing something much larger and more invasive than a tongue or a few fingers.

He reached up, cupping Jim's face with a tender touch, his thumbs gently caressing the sides of Jim's cheeks. His voice was a low, husky whisper, "I've been wanting you to say that, Jim. I've been craving this. But listen to me," he paused, his eyes locked onto Jim's, "I'm absolutely content if we never switch roles. I love feeling you inside me, Jim. I love being fucked by you." His words were raw, laced with a hunger that sent a shiver down Jim's spine.

Jim nodded, his heart racing. "I want to experience everything with you, Brock. I trust you completely."

Brock's eyes darkened as he slowly rose from the bed, a seductive smile playing on his lips. "Then let me show you just how much I want you."

He stepped back, putting a few feet between them, and reached for the hem of his shirt. Instead of simply removing it, he began to move with deliberate slowness, his powerful body swaying slightly as his fingers toyed with the fabric. He lifted the shirt just enough to reveal a tantalizing strip of his hairy abdomen, then let it fall back down, his movements teasing and purposeful.

Jim's mouth went dry as he watched, transfixed. Brock's eyes never left his as he finally pulled the shirt up and over his head, flexing his broad chest and massive arms in a display that was both sensual and playful. The shirt dropped to the floor, and Brock's hands moved to his belt, unbuckling it with tantalizing slowness. His thumbs hooked into the waistband of his jeans, and he gave Jim a sultry smile as he began to sway his hips in a subtle, hypnotic motion.

"You like what you see?" Brock asked, his voice deep and rich.

Jim couldn't tear his eyes away, his pulse quickening as Brock gradually lowered his jeans, revealing powerful thighs dusted with reddish-brown hair. The fabric pooled at his feet, and he stepped out of it with grace that belied his size. Standing there in just the boxer briefs, Brock was magnificent—all hard muscle and masculine curves, his arousal evident beneath the thin fabric.

I've never wanted anyone the way I want you right now," Jim admitted, his voice thick with desire.

Brock's movements became more deliberate as he turned slowly, giving Jim a perfect view of his muscular back and the curve of his bareed ass not hidden by the mesh fabric. He hooked his thumbs into the waistband of his boxer briefs and began to ease them down with excruciating slowness, his hands playfully cupping inch by tantalizing inch of his firm buttocks. The fabric caught briefly on his erection before he freed himself completely, his cock springing forth, thick and hard.

Jim's breath hitched, his own arousal straining painfully against his sweatpants. Brock turned to face him fully, magnificently naked and unabashed, his massive erection jutting proudly from the nest of reddish-brown hair at his groin. He approached the bed with deliberate steps, his eyes dark with hunger and love. He stood at the edge of the bed, his body on full display for Jim's appreciative gaze.

"Your turn," Brock murmured, his voice a deep rumble that Jim could almost feel vibrating through his own chest.

With careful movements, mindful of Jim's injured shoulder, Brock leaned down and began to kiss him—first his lips, then along his jawline, working his way down the column of his throat to his chest where he uses his teeth to nip and tug at each of the pert nipples, hard with arousal.

"Let me take care of you," Brock whispered against Jim's navel, his breath hot against the sensitive skin.

Jim nodded, allowing Brock to guide him into a sitting position. With gentle precision, Brock slipped the shirt over Jim's head, careful not to disturb the bandage on his injured shoulder. As each new expanse of skin was revealed, Brock's lips followed, pressing soft, reverent kisses across Jim's chest. His beard tickled pleasantly against Jim's skin as Brock moved lower, his tongue tracing the definition of Jim's abdominal muscles, dipping into his navel.

"You're so beautiful," Brock murmured against Jim's skin, his large hands sliding down to the waistband of Jim's sweatpants. He hooked his fingers beneath the elastic and began to ease them down, his lips never leaving Jim's body.

Jim lifted his hips slightly, helping Brock as he slowly pulled the sweatpants down his legs. Brock's mouth followed the path of the fabric, kissing Jim's thighs, his knees, even his ankles as he removed the pants completely.

When Jim was fully naked beneath him, Brock's eyes darkened with desire as he took in Jim's naked form beneath him, appreciating every curve and plane of his lover's body. His hands caressed Jim's sides with a reverent touch, trailing downward until he reached Jim's hardening cock. He wrapped his fingers around it, stroking slowly as he leaned down to capture Jim's lips in a deep, passionate kiss.

"I want to make this perfect for you," Brock whispered, his voice husky with need. "Tell me if anything hurts your shoulder, okay?"

Jim nodded, his breath already coming in short gasps from Brock's ministrations. "I will," he promised, his good hand reaching up to tangle in Brock's hair, pulling him down for another kiss.

Brock reached for the nightstand, retrieving the bottle of lube he'd left there only minutes before. He knelt between Jim's legs, spreading them gently. With a tenderness that made Jim's heart swell, Brock leaned down and pressed soft kisses to the inside of Jim's thighs, working his way up slowly. His beard tickled against the sensitive skin, sending shivers of pleasure up Jim's spine.

"I'm going to take my time with you," Brock murmured, his breath hot against Jim's skin. "Make you feel so good you forget your own name."

Jim let out a shaky laugh that quickly turned into a moan as Brock's tongue flicked against his entrance. The warm, wet sensation was both familiar and thrilling, stoking the fire of desire building inside him. Brock's hands gripped Jim's thighs, holding him open as his tongue worked magic, circling and teasing the sensitive ring of muscle.

Brock then made his way up to Jim's perfect cock. The tip bulged a dark crimson and leaked a clear, thick stream of precum. Brock lapped at the tip, sending shivers up and down Jim's spine. His body was on fire for Brock.

When Jim gasped at the sensation, Brock smiled then lowered his mouth onto the throbbing shaft, sucking with intention. Jim writhed underneath his attention. Brock slid one hand up to rub Jim's firm pecs and pinch each nipple, rubbing his thumb over the hard nub repeatedly.

When Jim arched up into Brock's mouth, he caught each of Jim's muscular thighs and shifted them onto his shoulders, lifting his ass off the bed. Brock slid a couple of fingers into his mouth as he continued sucking Jim's dick, slicking them with his spit. Then he pulled them out of his mouth and started circling Jim's pucker with the wet digits. Jim moaned loudly. The sensation overwhelmed him. His nipple squeezed, his cock engulfed in Brock's warm wet suction, and his hole gently stimulated. "I'm so close," Jim's husky voice, a whisper of ecstasy.

"Not yet. I want you to feel even more," Brock whispered, releasing Jim's cock with a wet pop and reaching for the bottle of lube. He warmed the slick liquid between his fingers before returning to Jim's entrance, circling it gently before pressing one thick digit inside.

Jim gasped, his head falling back against the pillows as Brock's finger breached him. The slight burn quickly gave way to pleasure as Brock found that spot inside him that made stars dance behind his eyelids.

"God, Brock," Jim moaned, his hips moving of their own accord, seeking more.

"That's it, baby," Brock encouraged, his voice thick with desire. "Just relax for me." He worked a second finger in alongside the first, stretching Jim with meticulous care, watching his lover's face for any sign of discomfort.

Jim's body arched into the touch, his mind overwhelmed by sensations he'd never experienced before. Brock's fingers moved with expert precision, scissoring gently, preparing him for what was to come.

When Brock added a third finger, Jim felt a momentary flash of discomfort that quickly melted into pleasure as those skilled digits found his prostate again.

"Still okay?" Brock whispered, his eyes never leaving Jim's face.

"God, yes," Jim breathed, his chest rising and falling rapidly. "Please, Brock, I need you inside me."

Brock withdrew his fingers slowly, causing Jim to whimper at the sudden emptiness. He reached for the lube again, pouring a generous amount into his palm before stroking his impressive length, coating it thoroughly.

Jim watched, mesmerized by the sight of Brock touching himself, his massive cock glistening under the dim light. Brock positioned himself between Jim's spread thighs, the blunt head of his cock pressing gently against Jim's prepared entrance.

"Look at me," Brock whispered, and Jim's eyes locked with his. "I love you, Jim. Let me know if you need me to stop."

Jim reached up with his good arm, pulling Brock down for a tender kiss. "I love you, too. I'm ready."

With exquisite care, Brock began to push forward, the pressure mounting as the thick head of his cock breached Jim's entrance. Jim gasped, his body tensing momentarily at the intrusion.

"Breathe, baby," Brock murmured, his voice strained with the effort of holding back. "Just breathe through it."

Jim focused on his breathing, willing his body to relax as Brock pressed forward with infinite patience, allowing Jim's body to adjust to each inch of his considerable length. The initial discomfort gradually gave way to a profound fullness, a connection so deep and intimate that Jim felt tears spring to his eyes.

"You okay?" Brock whispered, his face hovering above Jim's, concern mingling with desire in his gaze.

"Yes," Jim breathed, his hands gripping Brock's broad shoulders. "Don't stop."

Brock began to move, slowly at first, shallow thrusts that gradually deepened as Jim's body yielded to him. The room filled with the sound of their mingled breaths and soft moans, the bed creaking gently beneath them. Jim's world narrowed to the exquisite sensation of Brock moving inside him, filling him completely, touching places within him that sent waves of pleasure cascading through his body.

"Jim," Brock breathed, his voice thick with emotion as he established a steady rhythm, "you feel incredible."

Jim's good arm wrapped around Brock's neck, pulling him closer as their bodies moved together in perfect harmony. The initial discomfort had completely dissolved into waves of pleasure that radiated through his entire being. Each thrust sent electric currents up his spine, his body arching to meet Brock's movements.

"Deeper," Jim urged, his voice barely above a whisper. "I want all of you."

Brock obliged, adjusting his angle slightly as he drove deeper into Jim's welcoming heat. When he brushed against Jim's prostate, Jim cried out, his body tensing with unexpected pleasure.

"There," Jim gasped, his eyes wide with wonder. "God, right there."

A smile of satisfaction spread across Brock's face as he maintained the angle, hitting that sweet spot with each deliberate thrust. His hand slid between their bodies to wrap around Jim's neglected cock, stroking in time with his movements. The dual sensation was overwhelming, and Jim felt himself hurtling toward the edge of oblivion.

"I'm close," Jim warned, his voice breaking as pleasure built to an almost unbearable crescendo.

"Let go for me," Brock urged, his rhythm faltering slightly as his own release approached. "I want to feel you come around me."

Those words were all it took to push Jim over the edge. His body tensed, back arching off the bed as waves of pleasure crashed through him. His cock pulsed in Brock's grip, painting both their stomachs with hot streaks of white as he cried out Brock's name, the sound echoing through the quiet room.

The sight of Jim coming undone beneath him, the feeling of Jim's body clenching around him in rhythmic pulses, pushed Brock past his own point of no return. With a deep, guttural groan, he buried himself to the hilt and surrendered to his release, his large body shuddering as he filled Jim with his warmth.

For several moments, they remained locked together, their bodies slick with sweat, their breathing ragged and synchronized. Brock braced himself on his forearms, careful not to put weight on Jim's injured shoulder, their foreheads touching as they shared the same air.

"That was..." Jim whispered, unable to find words adequate enough to describe the experience.

"Yeah," Brock agreed, pressing a tender kiss to Jim's lips. "It was."

With reluctance, Brock eventually withdrew, causing Jim to wince slightly at the sudden emptiness. Brock immediately gathered him close, mindful of his injured shoulder, and pressed tender kisses to his forehead, his cheeks, the corner of his mouth.

As they lay entwined, the world outside ceased to exist, leaving only the two of them in a bubble of warmth and tenderness. Brock traced patterns on Jim's back, his touch both protective and affectionate, while Jim's fingers played lightly over Brock's chest, feeling the solidity and strength that had become the foundation of their relationship.

"I never want to let you go," Brock murmured, his voice thick with emotion as he gazed into Jim's eyes. "You're my everything."

Jim smiled, a soft, genuine expression that lit up his entire face. "And you're mine, Brock. Always."

Their hearts beat in unison, a testament to the journey they had endured and the love that had only grown stronger through adversity. In that moment, surrounded by the lingering warmth of their embrace, Brock and Jim knew that they were ready to face whatever the world threw their way—together, hand in hand, heart to heart.

The night wrapped around them like a comforting blanket, the silent promise of forever echoing in the quiet room as they drifted into a peaceful, shared slumber, their souls entwined in a bond that nothing could ever break.

# Epilogue

*Five Months Later*

A warm, golden light poured over the bustling courtyard of Brookstone Point, the name of Brock's ambitious warehouse renovation project, now transformed into a vibrant heart of town life.

Jim strolled leisurely through the cobblestone paths, Brock keeping pace beside him, both observing the friendly chaos as shoppers meandered between quaint boutiques, pausing to chat animatedly under the blooming cherry trees.

The years' arduous labor and unwavering dedication had breathed new life into the decaying and forgotten warehouses, turning them into a space that was both alive and timeless, where modern elegance blended seamlessly with small-town charm.

The transformation was nothing short of remarkable. The luxury apartments, with their elegant brick facades and black iron balconies, stood proudly, overlooking the lively courtyard below. New businesses were making their mark on the ground floors of the refurbished warehouses, their presence a testament to the project's success.

The shops of Brookstone Point had become a magnet for travelers en route to the nearby beach or the major cities connected by the interstate and state highways, a mere thirty-minute drive away. Strategic marketing efforts had drawn in tourist crowds, adding to the bustling energy.

While downtown and most residences were a good fifteen minutes away, they remained free from heavy traffic yet reaped the benefits of increased revenue. Brock, along with many of the businesses, had started turning a profit almost immediately.

An art gallery, showcasing local talent, spilled bold colors from its windows, inviting each passerby to linger and admire the vibrant creations.

The sleek boutiques, filled with carefully curated fashion displays, had become a beacon for visitors from the surrounding areas, injecting a new hum of excitement into the town. Even a dog groomer had opened her doors, offering weekend doggie daycare that brought laughter and life to the courtyard.

Meanwhile, Ms. Claudean's Cupcake Shop had gained a devoted following. Her famous lavender-honey cupcakes had become an irresistible indulgence, drawing crowds eager to sample her sweet creations.

Brock nudged Jim's shoulder, a proud smile lighting up his face as he spotted Ms. Claudean, her warm brown skin glowing under her graying afro as she set up a tray of her latest creations outside. "I knew she'd be a hit," Brock said, with admiration in his voice, "but I don't think even she saw this level of success coming."

Jim chuckled, his eyes twinkling with fond memories. "She told me just last week that she's got people lining up for orders," he recounted with delight. "Said she might even need to hire help. Can you imagine that?"

Brock laughed heartily, the sound blending with the cheerful chatter around them. "I think we've done something special here, Jim," he said, his eyes scanning the lively scene before them. "Something really special."

Jim nodded, feeling a deep sense of fulfillment and warmth. "We sure have, Brock," he agreed, his voice filled with emotion. "We sure have."

They ambled leisurely toward a small wooden table nestled beneath the canopy of cherry blossoms, their pale pink petals fluttering gently in the spring breeze. Jim reclined comfortably, his eyes sweeping over the lively courtyard.

Since its renovation, the space has transformed into a bustling hub, hosting a myriad of events—weddings, anniversary parties, and vibrant farmers' markets. Each week infused the area with renewed energy and joy.

Jim marveled at the metamorphosis of once desolate and abandoned warehouses into a lively haven, brimming with laughter and conversation, the air filled with the playful shouts of children and the cheerful barking of dogs from the daycare area nearby.

Brock, meanwhile, pulled out his phone, his fingers dancing across the screen as he tapped through a slew of messages. He paused, leaning back with a satisfied sigh to survey the animated scene with palpable pride.

"Another inquiry?" Jim inquired, raising an inquisitive eyebrow as he took a leisurely sip of his steaming coffee.

"Two, actually," Brock replied, his voice tinged with excitement that reflected the realization of his long-held vision. "A hair salon wants to open next to the art gallery, and I just got a message about a local artisan interested in setting up a furniture store. Everything handcrafted, custom work."

Jim's face broke into a broad grin. "Seems like this town is finally on the map," he said, beaming. "And it's all thanks to you."

Brock shook his head modestly. "I couldn't have done it without the town embracing the changes. I just got it started." He reached over, intertwining his fingers with Jim's in a gesture of comfortable intimacy. Over the past year, their bond had solidified, and the quiet moments they shared now felt like home.

As they sat enjoying the peaceful ambiance, a familiar figure approached—a woman clad in a crisp new uniform, exuding a quiet confidence.

"Chief Martin," Jim greeted warmly, rising to his feet to shake her hand. Amanda rolled her eyes in a playful manner.

"Just Amanda is fine, Jim. The promotion doesn't change who I am," she grinned, offering Brock a friendly nod before turning her attention back to Jim. "Though I'm glad you're on the team. Couldn't think of a better lead detective to take the reins."

Jim's smile broadened, a mix of pride and responsibility settling on his shoulders. "Feels good, actually—like it was meant to be," he confessed, a sense of fulfillment washing over him.

"Well, after the past couple of years, I'd say we've earned it," Amanda replied with a satisfied sigh, her gaze sweeping over the bustling activity unfolding at the far end of the lot. She gestured to the farmer's market stalls being meticulously arranged, colorful banners fluttering in the gentle breeze. "I swear, I barely recognize this place. It's like a whole new world."

Jim nodded, following her gaze as familiar faces bustled about, setting up displays brimming with everything from golden jars of honey and intricately carved candles to vibrant fruits, vegetables, and wheels of artisan cheeses.

Each stall offered a kaleidoscope of colors and scents. "Change can be good," he mused thoughtfully, casting a glance at Brock, a subtle smile tugging at the corners of his mouth, as if sharing a private joke.

Amanda gave them both a knowing nod, her eyes twinkling with warmth. "Well, keep up the good work, gentlemen. If this is what retirement looks like for the chief, maybe I'll have to start planning early myself. Who knew it could be so rewarding?"

They shared a hearty laugh, the sound mingling with the lively morning atmosphere as Amanda continued on her way, her stride confident and relaxed.

Jim and Brock lingered, savoring the easy camaraderie and the crisp morning air. Jim's gaze wandered until it landed on Jennifer, who was sprinting towards them with KoKo hot on her heels, their laughter ringing out like music as they paused by Ms. Claudean's colorful display to eye the fresh cupcakes, each one a sugary masterpiece.

"Uncle Jim, Uncle Brock!" Jennifer called out, her face alight with excitement as she approached. "Ms. Claudean said we could pick out a cupcake. Can we, please?"

Brock put on an exaggerated look of deep deliberation, tapping his chin theatrically. "Oh, I don't know... do you two think you've been good enough for a cupcake?" he teased, his eyes twinkling with mischief.

Jennifer gasped in playful outrage, grabbing KoKo's hand as if for support against this grave injustice. "We've been amazing! Right, KoKo?"

KoKo nodded eagerly, her bright red curls bouncing with enthusiasm. "We helped Ms. Claudean carry her boxes inside!" she declared proudly, her voice a high-pitched testament to their good deeds.

Jim chuckled, reaching into his pocket to hand them each a crisp dollar bill. "Then I'd say you definitely deserve a cupcake. Just make sure you don't spoil your lunch, alright?"

The girls cheered, their faces lighting up with joy as they dashed off toward the cupcakes, their laughter trailing behind them. Brock watched them go with a contented sigh, his heart swelling with a quiet joy. He turned to Jim, his eyes reflecting a deep gratitude that seemed to encompass not just the moment, but the whole of his new life in Brookstone.

"Hard to believe how everything's come together," he murmured, almost to himself. "The town, our lives... all of it. It's like a dream I never knew I had coming true."

Jim's expression softened as he nodded. "It's like it was waiting for you to make it happen. Sometimes I think we were all just waiting for a little push."

As the girls came skipping back with their chosen treats, the courtyard continued to fill, friends and neighbors greeting each other, the sound of easy laughter filling the air. Jim took Brock's hand again, the unspoken promise between them. Brock had built all this. And they'd built something lasting here, something that could grow and flourish, just like the town itself.

And as the morning slipped into afternoon, they found themselves surrounded by the people and the place they'd come to love— Brookstone, the town they called home.

A few weeks later, a light breeze rustled through the courtyard of Brookstone Point on a sunny Sunday morning, bringing with it the fresh scents of baked goods and blossoming flowers. Jim walked alongside Brock, casting curious glances at the empty courtyard. "Odd, isn't it? Usually, the farmer's market has started by now," Jim murmured, his brow furrowing slightly.

"Maybe everyone decided to sleep in," Brock replied, keeping his tone light as he carried an enormous picnic basket with deliberate care.

They found a cozy corner beneath a blossoming magnolia tree, its petals drifting down like nature's confetti. Brock unfolded a plush plaid blanket over the cobblestone, arranging their picnic with meticulous detail—fluffy croissants, a bowl of strawberries, and a small charcuterie board complete with olives, roasted figs, wedges of cheese and slices of ham. Jim's eyes twinkled when he spotted the champagne bottle nestled in baggies of ice.

"Well, well, champagne on a Sunday morning. I can't say I'm complaining," Jim said, his grin softening as he looked at Brock. "What's the special Occasion?"

Brock smiled, an affectionate warmth in his gaze. "Today's special. I thought we could celebrate how far we've come. Exactly one year ago today, I was standing right over there looking at blueprints with Chandler, and the man of my dreams came strolling into my life."

Jim took a seat beside him, feeling a contentment he hadn't known before he moved to Brookstone. He reached for a strawberry, savoring the sweet juiciness. His gaze drifted over the courtyard, taking in the carefully planned greenery and the wrought-iron benches. Just a year ago, he never would have imagined living in a place like this—a town where life was slower, richer in ways he hadn't realized he'd been craving.

"It's hard to believe all this," Jim murmured. "A year ago, none of this was here. Just a dream on a blueprint."

Brock leaned closer, brushing a stray petal from Jim's shoulder. "Sometimes the dreams that seem impossible become the ones that change your life the most."

Brock reached into his back pocket and pulled out a Star Wars-themed envelope and waved it in front of Jim. Jim's eyes lit up, and a kid-like grin spread across his face as he took the envelope. He opened it to find two passes to Evergreen Retreat, the luxury spa and hot springs resort nestled in the mountains a few hours north of town. His eyes widened as he read the details of the package—a full day of couples treatments, private hot spring access, massages, and a gourmet lunch.

"Brock," Jim breathed, "this is incredible."

"I figured after everything we've been through this year, we deserve some pampering," Brock said, stepping closer to wrap his arms around Jim's waist. "Besides, I want to properly celebrate the best thing that's ever happened to me."

Jim leaned forward for a passionate kiss. "And the best thing that's ever happened to me," Jim replied after they finally pulled apart.

With a gentle smile, Brock took Jim's hand and led him toward the car. "Come on, let's get going. I packed our bags this morning while you were in the shower."

Jim shook his head in amazement. "You had this planned all along, didn't you?"

"Maybe," Brock admitted with a playful wink. "I've been looking forward to having you all to myself for a while now."

The drive to Evergreen Retreat was peaceful, winding through scenic countryside that gradually gave way to the foothills of the mountains. Jim watched as Brock drove, admiring his profile against the backdrop of towering pines and clear blue sky. It still amazed him sometimes how dramatically his life had changed in just one year.

Jim reached over and rested his hand on Brock's thick thigh. Immediately, Brock interlaced his fingers with Jim's. "I love you, Jim Williamson."

"I love you more, Brock Curry."

And the universe smiled on them as Erykah Badu began to sing *You Got Me*. Brock turned up the volume, and Jim leaned over, resting his head on Brock's shoulder as they headed into their happily ever after.